# A Lady's Guide to Witchcraft

## The Society of Witches
## Book 1

# By Alyxandra Harvey

## ARE YOU SIGNED UP FOR DRAGONBLADE'S BLOG?

You'll get the latest news and information on exclusive giveaways, exclusive excerpts, coming releases, sales, free books, cover reveals and more.

Check out our complete list of authors, too!

No spam, no junk. That's a promise!

### Sign Up Here

www.dragonbladepublishing.com

⌒

*Dearest Reader;*

*Thank you for your support of a small press. At Dragonblade Publishing, we strive to bring you the highest quality Historical Romance from some of the best authors in the business. Without your support, there is no 'us', so we sincerely hope you adore these stories and find some new favorite authors along the way.*

*Happy Reading!*

*CEO, Dragonblade Publishing*

# Additional Dragonblade books by Author Alyxandra Harvey

**The Society of Witches Series**
A Lady's Guide to Witchcraft (Book 1)

**The Spinster Society Series**
The Scandalous Spinster (Book 1)
A Deal With the Devil (Book 2)
Seduced by a Scoundrel (Book 3)

**The Dainty Devils Series**
The Duchess Games (Book 1)
The Countess Caper (Book 2)
The Husband Heist (Book 3)

**The Cinderella Society Series**
How to Marry an Earl (Book 1)
How to Marry a Duke (Book 2)
How to Marry a Viscount (Book 3)

# Chapter One

S OCIETY'S MOST NOTORIOUS witch lived in a pink cottage.

It made it surprisingly difficult for Ethan Swansea, also known as the Dragon, not to feel like a great sodding git for coming for a woman who lived in a pink sodding house.

Never mind her reputation.

Or the power in the amulet she had stolen.

Word had gotten out that a certain moon charm was no longer in the possession of London's Museum of Magic, sitting pretty in a display case as it had for decades. Surrounded by layers of defensive shields set by obsessed curators as well as Keepers from the Order of the Iron Nail. Not to mention tagged by every Iron Crow who had ever sauntered through the museum dreaming of the most perfect, most celebrated heist. Keepers patrolled; Crows stole. Curators obsessed.

And it was suddenly not enough.

Needless to say, the moon charm had been missing for little over an hour and every Iron Crow was already hunting for it.

Including Ethan.

Especially Ethan.

He was a little faster than most.

Mostly, it had to be said, because he'd been on the witch-island of Lyonesse on another job, already itching to take to the seas. The docks outside the village of Haven were clean, painted white, and teeming with witchlights scented with lavender. *Scented.* There wasn't a mermaid to be seen, nor even a fishing boat. Both would have been too messy for this bedeviled village. The docks were for pleasure cruises, stealing kisses under spectacular sunsets, gathering beach glass.

Definitely not for the likes of him.

And if the ridiculously named Miss Foxglove did not want to end up in iron chains in the custody of the Order, or else her magic drained by a warlock, she'd give up the amulet at the first opportunity. Give, sell, physically eject from her presence. *Anything.*

Especially before the curators came from her. The Sea Hags save him from curators and librarians.

And, of course, her name was Petal.

What could you expect from a woman who lived in a pink house in the magical spa town of Haven? Her familiar was likely to be a butterfly. She probably ate cake for breakfast.

Kraken's balls, but he hated Haven with its sweetshops, salt bathing machines, and frilly parasols for sale on every corner. Ladies, apparently, feared freckles the way sensible folk feared famine.

He'd be long gone if he could.

*If* he could.

There was no earthly reason why his ship was still docked, the waves refusing to answer his summons. The waves always answered his summons. What was the bloody point of being a water-whisperer if they didn't? Water listened to him, raindrop to ocean drop. That was fact, not boast.

Until tonight.

And since there was no earthly reason for the waves to be silent, that left only a magical reason.

Fucking Iron Crows.

Just because he was one himself, didn't mean he had to like the lot. They worked alone for a reason.

Never trust a Crow.

He could have told Miss Foxglove that, even before everything went thoroughly and spectacularly to hell.

# Chapter Two

N EVER TAP YOUR spoon on the edge of your teacup.

Sound advice for a debutante navigating the perils of her first London Season but less helpful for a witch living on the island of Lyonesse.

For one thing, teacups were a very useful magical item: stir three times sunwise to bring good fortune and three times moonwise to banish ill luck such as potato blight, nosy neighbors, and unwanted matchmaking advice. And as the owner of the Rose and Petal Teashop, Miss Briar Foxglove knew everything there was to know about teacups.

And the Social Season, however different it might be on Britain's magical secret island, still had its own set of rules. Etiquette was etiquette, after all.

Irritating, pervasive, and likely to give one a nasty rash.

Lyonesse's debutantes still traveled to London to make their curtsy to the queen, still wore white, were still expected to know which kind of lace was currently in fashion. They were also expected, however, not to let their animal familiars roam into private homes, to curb their instinct for theft if they were magpie girls, and, if a werewolf, not to chase random rabbits because a rabbit might also be someone's favorite aunt.

Rules notwithstanding, visitors were treated to every delicacy and courtesy and, above all, entertainment. Familiars could roam relatively free, glowing with that particular glittering light as they enjoyed a freedom not known anywhere else in England, even when invisible to mundane Society. Blending in was what kept you safe from witch hunters and warlocks and Iron Crows.

But on Haven, those fears could be put aside.

The main beach was carefully curated for every kind of luxury, from the lantern-lit pavilion to terraces created from gold-hued stones and waters so clear they rivaled those found in France and Italy. Shops lined the boardwalk, selling marzipan mermaids, pearls, lemon ices, healing lotions, charms to make one's skin brighter, or help one dance more gracefully.

Tonics were brewed to cure magical afflictions, not only bellies too full of sweets but also for spells gone awry or magic blocked in some random part of the body. Briar had once brewed a tea for a young boy whose first spell had caused violent hiccups that five weeks of patience had not cured. And a nettle and lavender tea for a woman whose voice had turned into the sound of broken glass, and worse, cut her lips when she dared speak.

The spell to find the culprit—a vicar whose marriage proposal she had declined—was enthusiastically free.

Mostly Briar steeped rose petals in honey for a good marriage, for thicker hair, whiter teeth. In the village of Holdfast, the spells were darker, slightly feral. They had teeth to keep everyone safe. In Hallow they came in illuminated grimoires, steeped in rhyme. They offered knowledge, history.

In Haven, it was all spun sugar.

With a spoonful of chaos, to be sure. The population of Haven, however small it might be, had tripled in the last two days alone. The Midsummer Festival was in less than a week and greenery hung from every lamppost, flowers from every doorway. They had been preparing for weeks. Briar had made more flower crowns than she could count, and her friend Sorcha had baked roughly a thousand of the traditional lemon cakes complete with marigold petal rays. Barrels of elderflower and strawberry wines were at the ready. Bonfires burned until dawn, tall enough to be seen from the mainland, if they weren't so well cloaked to mundane eyes.

And there would be more formal dancing every night. Like the rest of Haven, the assembly room glowed from the white-washed walls to the parquet floors inlaid with iridescent abalone shell. And it was paramount, according to Haven's mayor, that the odors of roasted meats from the light supper provided—or, God forbid, sweat—never overpower the perfume of lilies and lavender. She was especially insistent on the addition of lilacs, as they were out of season already and it would set Haven apart to have a green witch who could provide them—only in white, naturally.

Briar, despite the fact that she did not dance much, and certainly not with the lords and ladies down from London, was that lucky green witch.

As she needed the money, she did not complain.

The same could not be said for her companion. George had been summoned to provide the charms that filled the room with the strains of a pianoforte even when the orchestra stopped for a rest, as well as the illusion of pale butterflies billowing between the chandeliers. He was exceptionally talented. He was also much more interested in being down at the beach at the bonfires. His familiar, a glowing hedgehog, was just as unimpressed with the trays of crystal goblets, the chandeliers dripping pearls, and the swaths of white lilac bewitched with iridescent opal flames.

Aster Apothecary supplied the rest of the glamours, the ones that were offered in little tins of sweet mints, or sugar cubes for tea, strawberries for champagne flutes. Discreet when required. And very popular. George did an equally brisk business selling charmed mints that dispelled glamours. He was *not* popular with the Asters.

Briar would have welcomed that particular problem.

Her own mother had been a customer before she died, particularly interested in glamours that would cover Briar's limp. They always made her itch and break out into a rash. She would much rather limp. She was used to it and it never bothered her the way it had bothered her mother.

Briar reached into one of the many pockets of her apron where she kept the tools of a green witch: her silver boline knife with the crescent-moon blade, rowanberries, packets of seeds, pressed flowers. She whispered a charm to the ropes of white roses she'd wrapped around the window frames, so they would not wilt when the room grew stuffy with dancers.

"Briar?" George asked.

Briar knew exactly where this was going.

Because it was the only thing George ever said to her.

"Where is your sister?" He thought he sounded nonchalant, just inquiring politely over her family.

But Petal was staggeringly beautiful, with long red curls and gray eyes, and no one ever asked about her with any real nonchalance. And though she and Briar shared the same color eyes, that was where the resemblance ended. They might be twins, but they were definitely not *identical* twins. Briar's hair was dark brown, her hip was dodgy, and she had a swan for a familiar who was even now floating in the water fountain snapping at tourists who got too close. He was as cross as Briar was practical. Meaning: very.

Petal's familiar was a hare, and she had a magical talent for finding things. Briar grew roses. Well, anything green, really, from hemlock to hazel trees. Better, she grew every kind of herb and flower for teas and tisanes and infusions as well as the rare red roses her mother had preferred for love spells.

The other witches dealing with the preparations had already sniffed at her brown dress striped with pink. Even the eight-year-old boot boy had shaken his head at her with the sartorial disappointment better suited to an octogenarian duchess. The witches of Haven wore white. Full stop.

"Briar?" George pressed.

"What? Oh. I don't know where Petal is at the moment." She had not seen her sister much in the past few days. She tended to make herself scarce during the festivals. She was probably with Bramble, the rabbit witch she loved. Not that it ever stopped George. Or anyone, really.

"Will she dance tonight, do you think? I can add a charm for hares, just like her familiar," he added hopefully.

"I don't think so," Briar said gently. Petal was not fond of the assembly room.

George sighed dramatically, staring out the window. In the square below, the ornate carriages, painted white and gold like cupcakes, circled, pulled by witchcraft instead of horses. Horses were not allowed in the square or on the lower street with the shops facing the sea. Horses made messes. Instead, one of George's illusions pulled them: doves with gold beaks, using gold chains that glinted and glimmered.

It was lavish and extravagant.

Ridiculous.

So perfectly Haven.

Because George might have designed the glamour, but it took a minimum of nine witches to power it, day and night.

Haven was nothing if not dedicated to its image.

Briar added peonies and more lilies to the urns standing on Corinthian pillar pedestals. She was nearly done and would like to get home before the fashionable set descended and someone reminded them she was Petal's sister. George was not the only one who asked after her. There were several gentlemen who traveled to Haven annually for just that purpose.

Petal was definitely in hiding and would not come out again until after the solstice.

The only gentleman who asked after Briar was Charles.

Or Charles *Bloody* Aster, as he was known to the Foxglove sisters.

The senior Mr. Aster had been as kind as his family was…not. Which was saying rather a lot. He had visited the tearoom for a pot of oolong tea and anise candies to cure his fictional stomach upsets starting the day after Briar's mother died and every day following until he died. He knew how they sometimes struggled to pay the bills. His wife and son knew it as well. They counted on it.

Charles was nothing like his kind, red-cheeked father.

He was taller, leaner, with sandy-brown hair and a haughtiness that exceeded the royal family's. Of several countries. Together. He was wretchedly entitled and his mother fed the worst parts of his character.

And Briar's mother had died owing a considerable debt to them both.

One they were eager to claim.

Briar bit back every scalding remark that bubbled behind her teeth. "Mr. Aster," she said blandly. So blandly one of the lilies shivered, dusting his sleeve with yellow pollen. He jerked back. When she went to the window to adjust a garland, he followed.

"There's a spider on that leaf," he said.

"So there is." An orb spider, the kind that draped webs between the larkspurs and the hollyhocks.

Charles took out his handkerchief with a snap. "I shall get rid of him before the guests arrive."

Briar frowned and stepped in front of him. "No need." Spending as much time in gardens as she did, Briar had occasion to come across countless spiders, bees, wasps, beetles, earthworms. And once a very small mouse napping inside a tulip. "He doesn't want to be here any more than you want him here." *Or me.*

She urged the spider onto a twist of paper from a seed packet in her apron pocket and then pushed the window open to relocate him. "There."

Charles sniffed. "These flowers are looking a little wan, Miss Foxglove. Haven has standards."

"Then I must have more work to do," Briar replied. "If you'll excuse me."

She hurried away, feeling his eyes on her. His mother was stationed at the refreshment table, complaining that the cups for the punch were not fine enough to show off the glamour she had added to the ratafia-and-orange water mixture. There was a shimmer to it.

When Charles answered her summons, Briar took advantage

of the moment to slip away entirely.

BRIAR CROSSED THE village square with its giant oak tree and gurgling mermaid fountain. Pale marble statues stood sentinel at each corner, with more lining the streets leading out into the rest of the village. Delicate nymphs poured out water from a variety of bowls and amphora, even dripping off carved lilies. Not ordinary water but instead charmed to various purposes most suitable to Haven. The nymph with the bowl offered magic to encourage glowing skin. The maiden with the chalice gave one a bright singing voice. There was water for understanding any language spoken, for stealing kisses unseen by chaperones, for the ability to swim gracefully.

They wore flower crowns for the summer solstice, and they always gathered a crowd. Younger witches approached with blushing cheeks, daring each other to drink of a draught that would send them dreams of their true love. Locals were more cavalier, stopping on the way home from errands to the butcher for a sip that promised fewer wrinkles, shapely calves. More customers.

Briar chose the longer way home through the fields. Was it any wonder that she occasionally craved the company of gulls and foxes who did not care how straight their teeth were—or how crooked her leg was? The sea whispered to her, every shade of blue and green and purple, gilded as the sun set.

But even with the ache thrumming in her right hip, the walk was worth it. She found a patch of pink thrift flowers and bat's-wool moss. She loved village street and lonely cliffside equally. She considered herself lucky she had unfettered access to both.

The village, it had to be said, did not always feel the same.

She leaned a little heavier on her driftwood cane as the air shifted, cooling and heavy with salt from the ocean that sur-rounded them on all sides. A circle of salt was a witch's best protection—a circle of salty seawater worked just as well.

Usually.

Something skittered over her spine.

But as there was nothing but the stars peeking out and the sound of music drifting up from the main pavilion on the beach, Briar put it down to fatigue. The Midsummer Festival required a great deal of work. Besides the assembly rooms, she had been charming gardens for weeks so that they might show at their best. Not to mention making sure the tearoom was well stocked with tea blends and tinctures, especially willow bark tea for headaches and hangovers, rose salve for lips, peppermint and fennel for fresher breath.

When she reached the back garden gate, she noticed Bramble, waiting patiently. She faded into the shadows in her soft gray dress and the preternatural stillness of a girl who often turned into a rabbit. Bramble and her kin left the island even more seldom than Briar and Petal: that was, not at all. Society to a rabbit girl was fields and garden patches and the wind through blackberry hedges.

Petal wanted that society, and Bramble in particular, desperately. "I haven't seen her today," Briar said. "Do you want to come inside for…"

Bramble froze for a moment, before melting back into the shadows.

"…a cup of tea?" Briar finished, unsurprised that she was now standing quite alone. "Guess not."

She followed the stone path up to the tearoom, with the upstairs reserved for family. The cottage had a thatched roof with the traditional gargoyles perched at the corners for protection against baneful magics. And it was painted pink as a peony.

Briar loved every ridiculous inch of it.

Haven witches painted every single thing they could reach in a crisp, bright white, from walls to carriages to lampposts. It was meant to evoke a sense of elegance and calm, of healing. It hid nothing. It was trustworthy. As were the local witches who could heal your gout, your ennui, and that bothersome spot on your chin.

It was also deeply, *deeply* tiresome after a while.

Sometimes it felt like living inside a sugar cake.

Briar's mother was desperate to fit in, and so every inch of the shop, including the cramped closet in the family quarters that no one else ever saw, was painted white. The table, the chairs, the teapots. The floor. Every dress, and every ribbon.

Briar missed her mother, but the very first thing she had done once they'd come out of mourning was paint the cottage pink. The neighbors still whispered about it. To be fair, they whispered about everything the Foxglove family did. When your mother's magic revolved mostly around love potions, everyone was respectful but nobody cared to get too close.

They did make an exception for Petal, of course.

But the Foxgloves didn't deal in love spells anymore. Briar preferred mint tea with honey from her beehives. Petal preferred to run wild. It was a simple, pleasant life.

Which was how Briar knew the moment she stepped through the back door that something was amiss.

Her swan, whom she had named Snapdragon when she was seven, shot past like a falling star, a warning flurry of feathers and agitated hissing, but it was too late.

Briar had already stepped inside.

She knew she wasn't alone, even before she saw the teapot smashed into pieces on the floor. She'd *liked* that teapot. She froze for a moment while her mind screamed at her to *run, run, run.*

Too late.

The roses pressed at the windows, thorns scratching the glass as they pushed to reach her. The oak tree shivered, branches clawing and scraping. Given enough time she could have convinced the ivy to snake through the cracked windows and strangle the intruder. But she was more accustomed to coaxing slow and steady growth. Her swan bared its vicious teeth, small but shining like knives.

"Come here, you," a man barked at her.

Not just a man, an Iron Crow. He wore a leather cross-belt

bristling with knives as well as amulets and charms and tiny pouches filled with herbs and powdered crystals or ashes from sacred fires. A magical apothecary at the ready. Also, stocked with items illegal for a witch. Magic was simple, but not always kind. Iron Crows were neither.

Worse, he held a dagger.

And it was not particularly clean.

Was that dried blood on the hilt? Briar swallowed.

"Where is it?" he demanded. He smelled like lemon balm, like the dark magic of warlocks. It was soothing, meant to lull you into complacency.

She wanted very much to spin on her heel and run.

*Why* wasn't she spinning on her heel and running, dodgy hip notwithstanding? Her walking boots were glued to the floor.

"Answer me, gel."

She frowned at him. She might be scared, but she was also annoyed. Very, *very* annoyed. "Do you *know* how much that teapot cost me?"

"I'll break your face next if you don't tell me where it is."

"Where what is?" Her knees were soft. Even her eyelids were droopy.

This was not the time for a nap. What was wrong with—

The truth hit her like cold water, but it still wasn't enough to rouse her body.

Sleeping spell.

She tried to call up her magic, felt it burning through the witch's knot that marked every witch's palm.

It did not reply.

The witch knot was a circle with four interwoven petals, and hers lay like a dead coin in her hand. The yellow larkspurs in a vase on a nearby table glowed briefly, searching for her, but it wasn't enough. The spell had already taken hold. Her swan jumped into her chest for safety, sparking light, eyes glinting malevolently.

"Never mind," the Iron Crow said. "You'll answer me now or

you'll answer me screaming later."

A crash sounded at the back door, but she was disappointingly certain it was not the oak tree come to save her. At least Petal wasn't at home.

"Step away from her."

The Iron Crow looked past her and cursed. He was trying not to appear frightened, but even through her blurry vision, Briar could tell that he was. Sweat broke out along his dirty hairline. "Wot you doing here?"

Briar was slipping away. She had just enough energy to turn her head.

The man looming in the doorway looked like nothing so much as a pirate, though he also wore the cross-belt of an Iron Crow across his chest. A pale woman stood behind him, wearing violence the way a lady might wear a bonnet. Instinctively, easily, habitually. There was another man next to her, roughly the size of a bear, with tattoos on his chin.

"I was here first," the first Iron Crow spat, fingers flexing around his knife hilt.

"And now *I'm* here." The accent was Irish, the tone forbidding.

Her attacker cursed again and then fled through the side door.

Briar was still falling. She tried to smile her relief, to say thank you, *anything*. The not-quite-a-pirate came into focus, everything around him bleeding colors like a wet painting. He had dark hair, a sharp jaw. He was handsome in that hard, confident way. As if he knew perfectly well that he could handle anything the world threw at him. Fainting girls in pink houses were nothing to him.

"Thank you," she mumbled.

He raised an eyebrow, mildly amused even as he caught her before her head hit the floor. There were creases at the corners of his eyes from squinting into the wind.

"Oh, sweetheart, what makes you think I'm here to save you?"

## Chapter Three

**B**RIAR WOKE UP in the garden.

Naturally, it was raining.

Her hip ached and her eyes were sandy as she struggled to keep them open. Part of her wanted to lay her head in the nearest puddle and sink back into sleep. The swan inside her chest made a sound of pure fury. Witchcraft prickled through her, just out of reach. It was urgent, uncomfortable. The garden trembled but did not answer with a helpful spike of nettle or roots strong as iron chains.

And if that wasn't bad enough, the lady who wore violence like a bonnet was pointing a pistol at her. Briar would have been a lot more terrified if everything wasn't so hazy and syrupy. She tried to move without casting up her accounts. Although it would serve them all right if she ruined their boots. "That teapot was expensive," she said, once more.

It was ridiculous to focus on that triviality when she was quite literally stuck between a pistol and a lightning storm. Although, at second glance, the rain fell oddly. It was slow, barely touching her while pouring into the rosebushes as though from a pitcher. The sleep spell had packed more of a punch than she'd thought.

"What?" the lady asked, confused. She was tiny, delicate, but clearly strong as a whip. There was a beauty mark near the corner of her lip. Her hair moved ever so slightly, swaying as though underwater.

"You broke my teapot," Briar repeated, just this side of sulking. "Why are you stealing from a tearoom?" That was odd, even for an Iron Crow. Even during the crowded chaos of Midsummer. Pickpockets could make a year's worth of bounty on Midsummer night alone, so she could only imagine what an Iron Crow could do, especially ones like these, who did not work alone. They sought out magic and charms others might be hesitant to touch. Or wield.

Luckily, she kept her poisonous plants locked in a chest in the cleaning cupboard. If that was what they were after, she'd swallow the key before giving it to them.

"We're not here for the teapot," the not-quite-a-pirate said mildly. His voice was a contradiction, calm and also full of storms. His dark hair was salted with silver and his eyes were black and hard to read. He leaned against the garden wall as though he were bored.

Infuriating.

She was being robbed and he was *bored*.

He finally looked her way. The rain ran in rivulets under his boots, but all that thick, dark hair was dry. "Tell us where it is, Petal. There's only one way this ends."

The haziness crystallized at the sound of her sister's name.

It was such a sudden shock to her drowsy system that she flinched. The lady Crow may as well have shot her. She tried to cover the reaction, to blend it into the natural anxiety of waking up surrounded by magic thieves and housebreakers.

She was not entirely successful.

The Iron Crow pushed away from the wall, suddenly interested.

She inched back but there was nowhere to go.

He thought she was Petal.

As long as she did not disabuse him of the notion, her sister was safe. Briar might still be in a bit of a pickle, but Petal was safe. That was what mattered. She'd make that trade any day.

He crouched in front of her as the storm descended in earnest. His shoulders blocked out the garden. He was rather large.

Why did his muscles need muscles? "Tell me."

Briar shivered. "No."

Never mind that she had no idea what he was talking about—she needed to get them all away from the cottage before Petal returned.

He blinked, genuinely surprised. "*No?*"

Clearly, he did not hear the word very often. And just as clearly, someone ought to say it to him on a more regular basis. Getting your way all the time was bad for the digestion. There wasn't enough mint tea in all the gardens of the world.

The woman flashed a grin, and Briar wasn't sure if it was for her or for him. "Oh, I like this one, Dragon."

Briar froze. She knew that name. It woke a shiver inside her, as it was meant to. Witches everywhere knew that name.

The Dragon.

Ethan Swansea.

Not just any Iron Crow, but the leader of the notorious Sea Dragons. More of a pirate than she'd realized.

*Oh, Petal, what have you done?*

"I won't talk," Briar said.

Lightning flashed over them. Ethan's eyes gleamed silver in response, like water. Her mother would have ensnared him by now, convinced him he was desperately in love. Her sister might have done the same without saying a single word, she was that beautiful. In fact, this was not the first abduction attempt. Petal's beauty came with a heavy price to pay. One that was unjust and uncompromising. She'd said it more than once—being a rabbit girl would be better. One could hide, disappear.

And Briar might not be a rabbit girl, but she knew about blending in. And she was resourceful, with more than her share of the Foxglove stubbornness. She would save her sister.

Even if she had to kidnap herself to do it.

"We're likely to drown out here," she added, crisply. "So you may as well take me away."

"Take you away?" Ethan repeated.

She lifted her wrists, pressing them together.

He stared at her blankly.

"I imagine this is how one ties someone's hands?" she asked. "I've never had occasion to try it before."

"Sweetheart," he said softly, sternly, "do you have any idea what you're asking me?"

She swallowed, refusing to take the bait. She might be sprawled on the ground in a damp dress in a most suggestive way, but she was Miss Briar Foxglove. She could be naked and no one would notice.

Although someone might want to inform Ethan Swansea of that little fact.

Because he looked interested. Which was absurd. Moreover, he didn't look interested in a way that raised her hackles or made her want to kick him solidly in the kneecaps.

That was some trick.

She cleared her throat. "You're not very good at this, are you?"

His eyes narrowed. His accent thickened. "Beg pardon?"

"Kidnapping a woman." She reached out to pat his arm. Mistake. He was warm and strong under her fingers. "It's all right—that speaks to your character, I suppose."

She wasn't entirely certain the woman with the pistol wasn't going to make herself sick choking on all that laughter.

Ethan scowled. "Just get her on the horse, Anais."

"Aye, Captain," she chortled.

In the end, it was the giant with the tattooed face who helped her into the saddle. He was very gentle and polite. "Thank you, sir," Briar said. He had an angel's smile, utterly at odds with his cache of weapons and scars. His teeth were very white against his light-brown skin. He didn't tie her wrists together either.

She was barely seated when Ethan swung up behind her. Tension thrummed through her. "Stop flirting with Maleko," Ethan said drily. "He won't help you."

As if flirting was a weapon that she was likely to use with any degree of success. She might be a Foxglove, but she wasn't Petal. She wasn't her mother, Rose. Even her name said it all: Briar. A sharp, nettlesome thorn in the garden.

She lifted her chin. She could feel him watching her, his cheek grazing her ear, his breath touching her hair. He was warm and solid and sinewy for all of his bulk. The rain was cold and she barely resisted the urge to snuggle back into his warmth.

Snuggling your captor was probably frowned upon.

What the hell was wrong with her?

Meanwhile, every moment they wasted here in the shadow of the cottage put Petal in danger. "Have you ever abducted *anyone* before?" she asked.

He half smiled. "Yes."

"Oh." Well, this *was* the Dragon, after all. She ought to have known better.

"Why? Are you faltering, little flower?"

"No, you just seem to be taking an awful lot of time," she pointed out, trying to ignore the very interesting things his voice in her ear did to her thighs. If she had to needle him into action, she would. So she nudged the horse with her heels, quick and demanding. She'd never really ridden a horse before.

The horse took off, nearly unseating Ethan in the process.

His arms tightened around her, his breath rasping in her ear. "What the bloody hell?"

She had flummoxed the infamous Captain Ethan Swansea, Dragon of Dragons.

That was something, at least.

Even if it might well be the very last thing she ever did.

# Chapter Four

BRIAR HAD MISCALCULATED.

Of course, she had.

For all her cheeky comments and false courage, being abducted by the Dragon was not a good idea. Even when it was the only idea she had. Maybe *especially* then.

She knew it when Ethan dismounted and reached up to close his big, scarred hands around her waist, helping her slide to the ground.

She knew it when he released the horses, slapping their rumps to set them running back down the road into town. It only made sense that they were stolen—what did Iron Crows with the scent of the sea on them need with horses?

She knew it when they reached the end of the dock, painted white and hung with lanterns but far from the boardwalk and pleasure boats preferred by tourists. So far away that they may as well have been in Cornwall. There was no one to see them, to save her.

She knew it most of all when confronted with a ship painted maroon and sky-blue, hung with glittering glass witch globes for protection and with a figurehead carved into the likeness of a dragon. It was fully rigged, with three towering masts and cannons not often seen on the shores of Lyonesse. Especially during the Midsummer Festival. She'd wager that even Holdfast, with its darker magics, home to All Hallows ceremonies and the guardians of the dead, had not seen their like.

Briar gulped. There was nothing but sand and sea and wooden planks to respond to her magic. If she tried very, very hard, she might manage to get seaweed to stir. She wasn't sure what good that would do her, with Ethan at her back and the black sea before her. She was as likely to get eaten by a mermaid as rescued by one. The kelpies would absolutely murder her.

It had seemed like such a clever idea at the time.

Ethan paused at the end of the gangplank, angling a sidelong glance in her direction. She forced her chin up again. It was still a good idea. She was here and Petal was safe, wasn't she? That was the point. No way out but through.

She stepped on the gangplank, teetering slightly. Her hip ached deep in the joint after her falling to the ground and then being jostled about on a horse. Ethan reached out a big hand to steady her. "Easy."

Wind tugged at her dress. The rest of his crew paused to watch them. "That her, Dragon?" someone called out.

"Aye."

"We'll make ready."

She did not like the sound of *that*.

She scowled up at Ethan. "Ready for what, exactly?"

"Hmm. Time enough for that."

Fear twined with the exhilaration of successfully keeping her sister safe, edged with the annoying, primal curiosity she felt for this large, dangerous man. There was so much to see and take note of; from whether or not she could jump the distance between the ship and the dock and if her hip would let her swim the cold, dark waters to shore. Instead, she could not stop looking at him. He was both a threat and an escape, the wind and the anchor. Briar knew it in her blood.

She worked to remember what else she knew about him, now that the last of the sleep-spell murkiness was clearing from her head, washed away by the salt wind and her body's utterly inconvenient and embarrassing response to Ethan. The Dragon, Iron Crow and scoundrel, thief and ship's captain.

Iron Crows were known for skirting the line between the magic of witches and warlocks, between asking and taking. The Order of the Iron Nail spent as much time tracking them as it did needing their help in taking down warlocks who would drain a witch of her magic. So might an Iron Crow, for the right price. Witch society wasn't sure what to do with an Iron Crow.

Neither was Briar.

Ethan Swansea spent most of his time on his ship, purported to have power over the sea itself. There were stories of love affairs with mermaids, some dodgy business with a stolen heirloom, and killing a man in Scotland on behalf of a selkie woman who may or may not have been his stepsister. He was banned from the Goblin Market in London and so was known to pull his ship right up to the bridge to buy and sell his magical wares, from werewolf teeth to the ashes of a witch's funeral bonfire. He was ruthless, dangerous, determined.

And he was trying to feed her a strawberry scone.

He had led her into his cabin, which sent another frisson through her. Fear or more curiosity? Fear, definitely fear.

*Bollocks.*

He hadn't touched her except to brush against her, his breath against her cheek when he dipped his head too near, the warmth of him stirring the very air around her. The captain's cabin was neat and tidy, with very little ornamentation except for a shelf of wood whittled into the shapes of mermaids and kelpies and krakens. Candles flickered in tin lanterns swinging from the ceiling, more witch glass at the windows, swirling with glittering colors.

He offered her a chair with a red embroidered cushion. And a plate of scones, fresh strawberries, clotted cream. It only sharpened her disorientation. "You're trying to feed me?" she asked, confused. "Why?"

"I need you strong, don't I?"

"Why?" It was sheer madness to wonder what he needed her strong for, and if a great deal less clothing might be involved.

Blame the anxiety of being kidnapped. Kidnapping herself. The last vestiges of the sleep spell. His imperfectly perfect face.

"I need answers, sweetheart."

She nearly wrinkled her nose at him. At herself. He was courting answers, not bare skin under the moon. It was curious, though, that she wasn't more scared. She didn't trust him, of course. He was ruthless and looked more than capable of sacrificing maidens to the sea.

And yet…

She felt nervous, strange, wary. But she was far more frightened of Charles Aster and his devious mother and their conviction that she was going to marry him. He was weak and self-congratulatory. Ethan was none of those things.

She preferred a weapon she could see.

Still, she wasn't about to eat a scone. Or an apricot, or those gold-dusted hazelnuts, no matter how hungry she suddenly found herself. Being walloped by a spell did that sometimes. She folded her hands stubbornly in her lap.

She did eye the cutlery, though. It was gold and heavy with scrollwork, at odds with the rest of the plain dishes. Definitely stolen.

Still, sharp enough.

Ethan sat in a chair, sprawled comfortably, taking up all of the air and the attention, as though he were king. She supposed, on his own ship, he *was* a kind of king. *Petal,* she thought again, *what have you done?*

Ethan pushed the platter closer to her, smirking that not-quite-a-smirk. "It's not poisoned."

She raised her eyebrows. "As if you would say so if it were." Who was *this* Briar? She was accustomed to quiet hours in the garden with no one but the bees to talk to. Accustomed to polite murmurs and agreeable smiles, and here, where they might actually do her some good, she could find nary a one. Only the bite of mint, the tartness of rosehips.

It felt good.

Not *wise*.

But good.

Charles bloody Aster would have clicked his tongue at her, would have flared his nostrils with contempt for her manners. Ethan just smiled, slow and easy.

She felt that smile all the way to her toes.

"Why would I wait for you to wake up and bring you all the way out here, if I were just going to murder you? Not very efficient."

"Are you saying I'm not worth murdering?" Now what, exactly, did she think she was doing? She should eat a scone just to shut herself up.

Ethan blinked, as if she'd surprised him. Again. And he wasn't accustomed to it. She felt a little like Scheherazade keeping the mad king entertained so that he forgot to murder her. Still, she liked the tiny gleam of interest in his dark eyes.

She had clearly lost her mind.

Indignation was not the appropriate response to a reassurance that one wasn't about to be poisoned to death.

And she was always appropriate.

"This will go easier on you if you eat."

Eat a scone, save her sister.

The day was not precisely unfolding as she'd assumed.

# Chapter Five

E THAN WAS IN hell.

And it turned out that hell was ruled by a tiny woman with more guts than brains and pink flowers in her hair.

Ethan had not been surprised in a very long time. He'd done too much, seen too much.

But he had never seen anyone like Miss Foxglove, with her pert nose and her stubborn but shaky courage. She ought to have been plain, just another gentlewoman on an island filled with gentlewomen, but instead she was the most alarmingly intriguing creature he had ever met. Her voice was soft and throaty. She was a little teacake, sweet and surprisingly tart. He wanted to take a large bite.

Hell.

He wanted to devour her.

Almost as much as he wanted off this damned island.

The etiquette and the rules made him itchy—you never knew what anyone actually meant when they said anything, and they always, *always* said too much.

Except for Miss Foxglove, apparently.

She was incongruous in his gleaming, simple quarters. She wore a striped dress that should have made her look silly, but again only put him in mind of teacakes and pretty frosting. Of presents begging to be unwrapped.

Kraken's balls, this damned island was already getting to him.

He wasn't sure what he had been expecting from a witch bold

enough and clever enough to nick a fabled moon charm from the museum, but it wasn't this small, slightly bewildering woman who smelled like mint leaves and honey. She didn't wear gloves, and he'd forgotten how much he liked that. It was one of the only good things about Haven and its never-ending frills. No one wore gloves; no one hid their witch knot from each other. Her knuckles were faintly laced with scars, the kind gathered from thorns and prickly blackberry bushes. Her nails were clipped short, and he knew just how they'd feel raking down his back.

He narrowed his eyes at her. Was this part of her magic? To befuddle and confuse? The faint trembling in her fingers didn't sit well with him, though. Even though that was what he did. That was how he got what he wanted, every time. He scared people.

He didn't just want to devour her—he wanted to comfort her.

The Dragon hunted, he stole, he pushed men into the sea. He didn't *comfort*.

And yet he found himself reaching for a strawberry and popping it in his mouth, holding her gaze the entire time. "See?" he said. "No poison."

She nibbled on the edge of a scone, her tongue darting out to catch a crumb, and he nearly groaned out loud. She added a hunk of cheese to her plate. Some spells left you drained, some thirsty, some starving.

"Try the conserve of roses," he suggested. Boiled roses preserved in sugar and jelly never made much sense to him. It was like eating perfume. Someone tell that to his cook, Matthias.

She glanced at the pretty pink conserve. "No, thank you."

He didn't know exactly what was going on behind those gray eyes, but he'd poked some inner wound. He wanted to know every detail. Who had put that glimmer of bleakness, or wry weariness, in her face?

He wanted a name.

Vengeance.

Instead, he offered her something saltier, something with

backbone. Something hearty, as far from eating flowers as he could get without offering her salt cod and a dry sailor's biscuit. "How about a scotch egg?"

There were bowls of roasted quail, pigeon pies, salmon cakes with lemon. Sugar-dusted grapes, plum cakes, and gods knew what else. They didn't eat like sailors. Especially not since they'd made landfall in order to replenish stock and sell some bones to the Iron Witches of Holdfast. They'd come to Haven for other supplies—Holdfast might be more comfortable for someone like him, but they already had enough hard tack and salt cod and whiskey to supply a small kingdom. And Matthias wanted fiddleheads. Or was it rampion?

Matthias made a wonderful galley cook but a terrible Iron Crow. Ethan wasn't sure why he kept him on, except that at this point he might well be eaten alive anywhere else. The world didn't forget a Crow, even if he stopped being a Crow. Besides, he'd made promises. Matthias would be looked after.

Petal reached for an egg even as she glared at him. It was adorable.

It couldn't stand.

He couldn't be Ethan to get the job done. He had to be the Dragon.

His voice changed, without conscious thought, deepening, darkening.

"Get up, little flower."

# Chapter Six

WHATEVER SMALL AND strange intimate moment had snuck between them shattered.

The feeling that something invisible bound them remained—but now it thrummed darkly in the spaces between their bodies, with a hint of menace. There was a hardness in his face, and to the shift in the energy in the cabin. Even the sound of the waves at the hull was more forceful, as if it too wanted mysteries solved, secrets shared.

But whatever Ethan wanted, she would not be able to provide.

Because what he wanted was her sister.

This situation was not new. Oh, the trappings of it were different: an Iron Crow, a ship, a secret. But in the end, she was not her sister.

She was not beautiful like a siren, and she did not sing like an angel. More often than not she had dirt on her hands. And she liked it that way.

And she loved her sister. She had made peace with living in the shadows a long time ago and, in fact, preferred it. It was soft and cool and quiet. She knew Petal envied that the way other people envied her beauty.

But this time, oh, this time, Briar wished, just a little, to be unforgettable. To lodge herself under Ethan's skin. Like a thorn, if nothing else.

He loomed behind her, voice rough as it touched her ear.

"Did you just sigh?"

"N…no?"

"Am I boring you?" he asked, hard as flint. One spark and the whole ship would burn. A dare. A promise.

It wasn't that she wasn't scared. Of course she was. But she'd never tell him that. He already held all the advantages. And she'd never tell him she wished she was more than she was, sometimes. Just sometimes.

Nor would she mention the gold fork she had managed to slide into her stays, lodged carefully between her breasts.

"Move."

She moved. What other choice did she have? Better to be out in the open than trapped in a cabin. And the thought of fighting him and winning was laughable. He was twice her size, and if her hip decided to give out, she'd be sprawled on the ground at his feet. No, thank you.

He marched her back out into the windy darkness of the deck, sailors turning to watch them as they passed. There were dozens of them, from countries all over the world. She saw tattoos, charms of holed stones such as visitors hunted the beaches for, rowanberries strung around the rails. White sigils were painted on barrels and the wooden boards under her feet. Feathers strung with crystals dangled from hooks. Magic thrummed next to muskets and cannons and the promise of a bloody death. It was lovely, in its own way. She wondered what that said about her.

And then it didn't matter anymore. Whatever story she'd been weaving inside her own head to convince herself that she wasn't in mortal peril unraveled.

The threads loosened, the loom snapped.

It made no difference if she was struggling between acting scared and acting brave and not knowing which was more likely to save her sister. It was too late for that. She knew it in her bones. Her trembling, anxious bones.

The warning twisted through every sailor on deck, the way

they looked at her, but more in the way they watched the Dragon. With deference, respect, fear. There would be no help from any of them, not even Anais, who claimed to like her. And she still didn't know why she was here, what taking Petal to this ship would have accomplished, were it really Petal here keeping her balance on the rolling deck and not Briar. Was it just because she was beautiful? Was that why they wanted to steal her sister away?

Like hell.

"Where is the moon charm?" Ethan asked.

A moon charm? Had Petal stolen a piece of magic? To what purpose? And from whom? The Dragon? That seemed mad, even for Briar's impulsive sister. "I...don't have it."

Ethan turned with the kind of lethal grace only gained by knowing you could keep your feet even as the waves pitched you about. He crowded her, walking her backward until she hit the mast. "Don't you?"

"N-no." She swallowed, inching to the side.

"Ah, ah." He blocked her with his body, slowly, inexorably. He reached around, pressing himself against her until her hands were wrapped around the mast, rope tightening around her wrists. Her breath stuttered in her chest. She pulled but already knew it was useless. "Am I going to have to search you, Miss Foxglove?"

Briar did not know what to say to that. *No? Yes, please? Somebody help me?*

Her swan stayed firmly behind her ribcage, waiting. It would be safer there than out where it might be captured. Did Iron Crows steal a witch's familiar the way the Order of the Iron Nail did as punishment for the practice of baneful magics?

And despite those fears, her body strained toward him. Unacceptable. Her body was not in charge—she also had a brain in her head.

But it *also* was inappropriately curious.

*Blast.*

She did not acquiesce. But she could imagine it all too easily. The way he would crowd even closer, closing that tiny fraction of space between them. His palms closing around her shoulders, running down her bare arms, thumbs stroking under her breasts. Moving up her leg, between her thighs. That twitch at the corner of his mouth, as if he might smile. For her. While touching *her*. All while she was bound, with no choice but to let her body react and react and…

She bit her bottom lip when she was afraid she might gasp out loud.

Ethan's eyes flared, before narrowing on her with deadly focus.

It did not dissuade her imagination. Or body. Her brain.

Not one bit.

Someone should remind her that she was kidnapped and tied to a bloody ship's mast.

Clearly that sleeping spell had muddled her—possibly even caused irrevocable damage. She would have to seek out a doctor as soon as she was able to.

"You are a surprise," Ethan murmured, low and deep. Still watching her, he motioned to Anais. "Check her."

Anais was brisk and efficient and surprisingly respectful for an Iron Crow. More respectful than the very respectable Charles Bloody Aster, for one. She checked all of the pockets of Briar's apron, as well as the heavy knot of her hair coming loose at her nape. Her shoes. Her petticoats.

She did not find the gold fork. It was lodged too firmly along the padded boning of Briar's stays and clearly had no magical aura to give it away. They weren't worried that someone like her carried a weapon or that she might best them with it. She wouldn't have worried about it either, were she them. Plus, they were looking for a charm. A weapon did very little when you were tied to a mast.

"What's this?" Anais demanded, pulling a small glass vial from Briar's pocket.

"Dandelion fluff."

"It stinks of magic."

"They're for wishing."

"Wishing," Anais stated, shaking her head. After a few minutes of searching, she stepped back. "Nothing," she confirmed. "Flowers and seeds. No moon charm."

Ethan shook his head. "I can't sense it either. Fucking hell." The whip of his voice was soft and quiet, and it had every member of his crew standing at attention. Someone's mouse familiar scurried into a nest of coiled ropes.

"Where is it?" Ethan asked Briar. He still did not raise his voice. His very presence was threat enough. "Eyes on me," he demanded, gaze hardening when Snapdragon fluttered his wings, suddenly sharp as knives. "No spells."

She didn't need eye contact for her magic. But she did need plants, flowers. A seed. Moss. She did not think the felled and polished wood of the mast behind her would respond. She pushed a little power into it, searching for a hint of acorn or ash leaf or pine needle. She closed her eyes, trying to picture a tree that could hear her. They weren't as chatty as flowers or herbs, but they usually responded, if in their own time.

Ethan gripped her chin, forcing her head up. "I *said*, eyes on me."

She felt his gaze all the way down her thighs.

The mast had been uninterested in having a conversation with her anyway. The wood had too long ago been cut, soaked in salt water and whatever else sailors used to seal the deck.

She struggled uselessly and only succeeded in chafing her skin. The rope was sturdy and scratchy and unlikely to give way. She already knew that. She pulled again anyway.

She was well and truly trapped.

"We want to go home and you're going to help us," Ethan said. "One way or another."

She paused. "I don't understand any of this."

He studied her face. He was close enough that she could see

the faint scar along his jaw, at the side of his throat, as though someone had tried to cut it. Moonlight and torchlight gleamed over the knives strapped to his chest. "You might even be telling the truth," he said finally, quietly, so only she could hear him.

"I am."

"More's the pity." He released her. "It doesn't matter if you understand it or not—magic is magic."

"I have *green* magic," she said as his crew began to move around them. She didn't know what they were doing exactly, but ropes were loosened, shouts were traded. Were they casting off? "I grow things," she explained frantically. Even Petal did not have magic to power a ship, moon charm or no moon charm. "Herbs, flowers. Berries. I can't get you home!"

"But you can," he said. "When you came back here with your little stolen trinket—which on any other day I would congratulate you for, by the by—you triggered the shields on the island. No one goes in or out. Not by portal, not by sea." And those were the only two ways on or off Lyonesse. There was no bridge, and no magical dirigible or even hot air balloon that would not be caught by the shield's power.

Was that what she had felt on her cliff walk? That odd shudder passing through her?

That was…not good. It was spectacularly *bad*, in fact. The last time the shields of Lyonesse had locked in such a way was when her grandmother was a girl. They had taken weeks to open and three witches had drowned; another had burned inside the portal when he decided he was strong enough to get through. They had nearly hanged a woman on the suspicion that she was involved.

"I'm sure you're mistaken," she said, not because she thought he was, but mostly because she *wanted* him to be.

"Set sail." Everyone scrambled to obey. "Prove me wrong," he added to Briar in that lilt of his.

"How am I supposed to do that?" she nearly wailed.

"Easy," Ethan said, even though there was nothing easy about him. "You dropped the shields; you should be able to lift them."

"How?" Shield magic was beyond her ken. It was the providence of the Iron Witches in Holdfast. The mast was hard at her back, but at least it held her up. Her hip ached. "Am I to throw rose petals at them? Grow them strawberries?" She'd had no idea until that moment that sarcasm was a perfectly reasonable reaction to panic.

"The shields will react to your presence," he told her. "It should be enough. Moon charm or no."

Which might well have been true, were she Petal.

"And then what? I swim to shore?"

"If you like."

Her hip would never take her that far. She'd worry about that later if she wasn't dead.

Right now, sparks of pale-blue light shimmered above the waves, hanging like a curtain. A warning. The power of it lifted the goosebumps on the back of her neck. Sailors shifted from foot to foot. A witch ball shattered.

The ship pressed on.

The sparks intensified. The smell of water was tinged with fennel seeds and salt, a mark of strong magic. Her witch knot burned in her palm, as if she were holding a hot coal. She wasn't the only one, judging by the way the others rubbed their hands and cursed.

The waves moved against the hull and the wood creaked, straining, like some great beast on an invisible leash.

But the ship did not advance.

The prow was bathed in that eerie blue light, hoarfrost clinging to the rails and the floorboards and the anchor. The dragon figurehead wavered like a mirage and then snarled. The sound shivered around them, rattled their bones.

But the shields held.

Of course they did. She was Briar Foxglove. She made flower crowns and nettle tea and rosehip tonics for broken hearts.

Something snapped. Loudly, violently. Briar couldn't see what it was, rope or board or sail.

"Fall back!"

The shields had formed a kind of bubble around the island, one made of magic and ice and a power that could not be reckoned with. It would take more than Briar's presence to break them. More than Petal's as well, she imagined.

There was a collective silence for a moment, wrapping around them like the Order's iron chains, the ones that trapped a witch's magic.

"Bleed her dry, cap'n," one of the sailors shouted suddenly. "Feed the shields until they break!"

Briar went cold.

But not as cold as Ethan.

His entire body might well be a sword. He turned slowly, all sharpness and threat and blood on the floorboards. The sailor was already advancing, dagger in his hand. He didn't make it more than three feet. Ethan laid him out with a single, savage punch to the throat. He landed on his arse, gagging. "You'll treat her with respect, Erasmus, or I'll feed you the kraken. In pieces. Balls first."

The man gulped, even as he tried to posture from his sprawl. Blood dripped from his crooked nose. "Yes, Captain. Beg your pardon."

Anais was disgusted. "Up into the crow's nest and shut your gob unless you want to be demoted back to swabbing," she snapped at him.

Briar barely heard her.

They would try to bleed her sister dry when they found her. If not the Sea Dragons, then the fine lords from London who could not get home.

The entire island of Lyonesse would be after Petal. Including hundreds of Midsummer visitors. If the shields rusted shut, they were likely to try any manner of spell to open them, including pushing Petal right off a cliff or offering her to the mermaids if they thought it would do any good. They'd use her blood, her bones, anything at all when they got desperate. A new kind of fear bloomed in Briar's belly.

She wouldn't let that happen.

Even if Petal had stolen the bloody moon and damned them all.

"Let me send my swan out," Briar said. Snapdragon was made of magic. And Petal was her twin, so their magic was linked. Always had been. It was worth a try. As many tries as necessary.

Ethan eyed her for a short, silent moment before nodding. Ice cracked and exploded behind him, sending shrapnel into the water. He didn't flinch, only kept his focus on her. "Go on."

She lifted her chin, pretending she was a woman who drank whiskey instead of mint tea. Her swan pushed from her chest, crackling with energy and hissing with spite. Now *it* would have drunk a barrel of whiskey and knocked the sailors overboard with a wing tip given half a chance. Light streamed from each feather, filling the air with the same kind of cold light that made up the stars. The crew stepped back, feeling the shiver of witchcraft, the bite of lightning. The shields of Lyonesse.

Ethan tipped his head back, tracking her familiar. Snapdragon snapped its beak in his direction and then flew toward the prow. Powerful wings beat and beat, but still it only hovered at the edge of the shields, blue light singeing its feathers. The taste of mint was strong on her tongue, the way it sometimes was when she reached too deeply into her well of magic. Pain prickled through her. Sweat gathered under her hair the harder her swan pushed.

All to no avail.

Finally, Snapdragon landed on the deck, screeching, light flickering. Briar slumped. She jerked once, violently, when the swan slammed home, shoving into her chest.

"Guess not," Anais said.

Ethan's jaw clenched. "Cut her down. We're not out of options yet."

Like hell.

Briar waited until Anais undid the knots, the rope dropping to the deck. Her shoulders protested when she rolled them forward, stiff and sore. She had mere moments to act. She took the gold fork from between her breasts.

And then she stabbed Ethan Swansea in the back.

# Chapter Seven

BRIAR WAITED FOR horror to choke her.

Regret, shame, nausea. Something.

Not a giggle.

But there it was, sticking in her throat like honey.

A *giggle*.

Surely she ought to be weeping. Swooning. Ladies did not stab people in the back. Ladies from *Haven* did not stab people, ever. For any reason. It was simply too déclassé. A pointed remark, a discreet hex, a cut direct—these were acceptable reactions. *Civilized* reactions.

Briar did not feel particularly civilized.

It was kind of nice.

The strange out-of-real-life feeling intensified when Ethan froze and then glanced calmly over his shoulder as though being skewered like crudité for a fancy nuncheon was perfectly reasonable. "I can't say I didn't deserve that." He raised an eyebrow. "But in the back, sweetheart? I didn't know you had it in you."

Why did he sound mildly affectionate? It slid over her like sweetened cream, like those whiskey rose custards her mother had said were too risqué to sell at the shop counter. Fear and something much sweeter coursed through her. He was touching her everywhere and he had not moved from where he stood, except to pluck the gold fork from his shoulder.

She felt a tiny bit bad when blood seeped into his shirt.

Just a bit.

"It's a clean fork," she offered. She'd made too many comfrey and honey tonics for cuts that had festered. Needless to say, festering wounds were not quite the tone Haven wished to convey. Even farmers and fishermen could not escape expectations. Vinegar rinses were handed out, ointments donated by earl's daughters and duchesses. The smell of lavender hung over the fish docks, and fishing boats were often garlanded with flowers when they came close to the village.

Why was she thinking about flower garlands?

Oh, right. Because she had just stabbed a man and she had no idea what the next step was.

It hadn't brought her any closer to freedom. In fact, she was fairly certain there was a musket trained on her. Maybe three. "Stand down, Anais," Ethan said wearily, confirming her speculation.

She couldn't run, even if there was somewhere to run to. Her hip had had quite enough excitement for one day, thank you very much. If she tried to jump overboard, she was trading drowning for whatever other fate awaited her on board.

She eyed the waves anyway.

"Don't even think about it," Ethan growled, suddenly right there beside her. "You've caused quite enough trouble already."

"*I* have?" she shot back incredulously. "*You* abducted me."

He smiled slowly. "You practically begged me to." His smile died and he leaned down closer, invading her space. He smelled like salt and wood smoke. "Why is that, I wonder?"

"I have no idea what you mean." As a statement, it would have sounded so much more convincing if she hadn't squeaked it.

His eyes kept her pressed to the mast just as effectively as the ropes had. "Hmm."

She didn't know how to interpret that sound. Not a growl, not a grunt, but somewhere between the two. Did it mean he believed her? Why would he, when she'd just stabbed him? With a fork.

"You do look proud of yourself," he said, wryly.

She tried not to. It probably wouldn't help matters.

"Come on," he added. He paused when she did not immediately move, then pressed a hand to his wound. A shot of darkness ran through his voice. "Don't make me ask you again."

She followed him because there was an entire ship's crew between her and the sea, between her and the docks. Between her and home.

Her hip snagged, freezing the way it sometimes did. She should have asked to be abducted with her driftwood cane. She limped, gritting her teeth. *Please let me stay upright.* For some reason the idea of falling into a heap was worse than everything else. She knew the looks she'd get in Haven; she could only imagine how much worse it would be on a ship packed with Iron Crows who already did not think particularly well of her. They'd see it as a weakness, and she could not afford that.

Ethan narrowed his eyes in her direction when she faltered.

"I don't have my sea legs," she lied.

"Hmm." That sound again.

He pressed his palm to her lower back, and she knew it must look as though he was shoving her forward, but in reality it felt very much as though he was steadying her. The silence of the captain's cabin welcomed them, the water whispering below. Ethan peeled his bloody shirt away from the punctures. She tried not to care.

Instead, she muttered, "I need water and comfrey. And honey if you have it."

He looked amused. "It's barely a wound."

Affronted, she made her own sound in the back of her throat. Let him decipher it this time.

His grin, while fleeting, suggested he had no trouble whatsoever. "The apothecary chest is in that corner."

It was a heavy wooden chest inlaid with mother-of-pearl and abalone-studded handles. It was beautiful and very well stocked. He rose slightly higher in her estimation. She nearly said as much.

And then she turned around.

He'd pulled his lawn shirt over his head, revealing a sculpted chest, thick with muscles. Two swallows were tattooed on his pectorals, with dark hair curling between them. He was sun-kissed, suggesting that shirts were not generally required. His pants hung low, exposing more muscles, more sun-browned skin.

She almost forgot she was trapped. *Almost.* Just for a *moment.*

She struggled not to blush. She had no business blushing. Doctors did not blush. Nor did women who found themselves taken by pirates and then stabbed them. As they deserved. His smile was slow, knowing. *She* deserved it, really. Who let themselves be distracted by a bare chest, by corded arm muscles, by—

*Briar Foxglove, get yourself sorted.*

"Turn around," she ordered him briskly. Not at all breathily.

He turned, still smirking. The fork had left three deep holes, bleeding sluggishly. She pressed her lips together.

"Don't apologize," Ethan said. How was it he saw her so clearly when he did not even know her? "You'll ruin the effect."

"Well, I *am* from Haven," she allowed. "And we do like an effect."

He smiled faintly and it was different, softer. More *real,* somehow. She slapped a wet cloth over his punctures with more force than was strictly necessary. It took no time to wash them clean. She added the comfrey and then a layer of honey. "You'll need a bandage," she said. "Or your shirt will stick."

"Then I suppose I won't wear one."

Of course not. There was another tattoo, just below where she'd stabbed him. A nautical star, carefully shaded. She resisted the urge to brush her fingertips over it. Tattoos were not uncommon among witches, however rare they might be among mundane society. They held magic, sometimes in the ink itself, sometimes in the symbolism. "What does the star mean?" she asked, before she could stop herself.

"The star guides a sailor home no matter where they might

be," he explained, facing her again. "Although not through Lyonesse's bleeding shields, apparently."

She smiled weakly. "And the swallows?"

"Every swallow marks five thousand miles traveled."

She couldn't help a wistful little sigh. "This is as far from Lyonesse as I've ever been." She'd never made her curtsy to the queen—she was a shopgirl, after all, not a lord's daughter.

He raised an eyebrow. "How do you like it so far?"

She raised her eyebrow right back. "It needs work."

His laugh was quick and rusty. "I'll bet it does, at that."

She wiped her hands on her skirt to rub away the honey. "Now what will you do with me?"

"I was just wondering the same thing." He scrubbed a hand over his face. "I suppose it was too much to hope there would be an easy solution. I forgot how this island can pack a punch." His dark eyes pierced her. "We'll need that charm after all."

"I don't know where it is." That was mostly the truth. She didn't know where Petal was. Had she made it back to the cottage? Had Bramble found her? Were they even now hiding somewhere? There was no one better suited to hiding than a rabbit witch. That was a comfort, at the very least.

And really, at this point, why bother keeping up the subterfuge? It had worked for the moment in which it needed to work, but now she knew more. She couldn't break the shields and it would take two minutes in Haven for someone to tell Ethan that she was not Petal. She was the other sister.

"I'm not Petal," she mumbled. "I'm Briar."

"Ah." Why did he seem oddly vindicated? Pleased, even? "That's better."

She blinked. "It is?"

"It suits."

She sighed. "Of course it does."

So her mother had thought when Petal was born perfect and pink and glowing like a rose, followed immediately by Briar, whose right leg had stuck out at an odd angle. *Like a little thorn,* their mother had said. *Petal, Rose, and Thorn—we shall be a little garden.*

"What's that expression?" Ethan asked softly.

"Nothing." She tried to make her face calm, cheerful. Anything but whatever it was doing that made him arrow in on her that way. Like he would pluck the secrets from her as easily as treasures from a ship run aground. "Petal is my twin sister," she said finally.

A pause. "Ah."

"But I don't know where she is," she rushed to add.

"And you would tell me, if you did?"

"Absolutely not."

"That's my girl."

Everything about that was deeply inappropriate, up to and including the heat that it kindled in her belly.

"But we're still going to need her, little thorn," he said. "Though I suppose it can wait until morning." He stepped aside, bowing with a flourish like a gentleman in a London ballroom. With that hint of mockery, of course. The bite of a certain kind of darkness.

"You're letting me go?"

"Do you want to stay?"

Absolutely not.

Maybe.

*Briar Foxglove, stop being such a goose.*

She had no business feeling safe with him. He'd tied her to a mast. She'd *stabbed* him.

"Go home, little thorn." His voice was a promise and a threat. He really was very good at that. "It's not like any of us are going anywhere."

# Chapter Eight

S HE HAD STABBED the infamous Dragon with a fork.

In the *back*.

Had Briar been the sort to imagine ever meeting an Iron Crow, much less an infamous one, she might have imagined him to be less amused with her in general, as though she was entertaining. Possibly there would also have been less stabbing involved.

And fewer strawberry scones.

Ostensibly to keep her strong for questioning? Maybe torture. But none of that felt right. Why had he really fed her a strawberry scone? And why did it feel like it mattered?

The weeds poking through the dirt road bloomed under her boots, nettles and thistles stretching tall, dandelions releasing wishes. The rain fell hard into the sea behind her and over the hills, like silver coins tossed by an angry hand, but it was soft in her hair. Gentle. A contradiction, just like Ethan Swansea.

But thinking about the width of the shoulders of the man who had abducted her because he thought she was her sister was not helpful. It did not make the mud less slick underfoot or the ache settling deep into her hip easier as she limped home. She had walked too far, sat on a horse, been tied to a mast. Her hip bone had every right to be vexed.

*She* was vexed.

A great many other emotions struggled to take root, but she could not afford to accommodate them all at the moment. She had bigger worries.

Her sister might really be missing.

And she had thrown herself, as well as the entire island, into some sort of danger. The shields of Lyonesse did not lock without dire need.

If no one knew where her sister was, that might lend Petal some security. If they could not find her, they could not harm her. But that *Briar* also did not know was unacceptable. How was she supposed to protect Petal? What if she was hurt? Stranded?

There were spells, maps, pendulums. Briar would read the tea leaves. Nettle and lavender, her sister's favorite brew. That and the blood that connected them would lend her power accuracy.

Hopefully.

Maybe.

Haven, shining bright as the moon and thrumming with music from the revels of visitors for the Midsummer Festival, glowed below her, welcoming. For now. Had they realized that the shields had locked? And that the portal had also closed, making travel back to London and Edinburgh and Dublin impossible? How long before the news traveled through the shops and inns and restaurants? How long before they came looking for her sister?

Not long enough.

Briar forced her hip to keep moving, stopping only long enough to drag a thick branch out of the scrub to use as a staff. It helped. So did the rain, turning to mist as she approached her cottage where no one waited for her with torches and pitchforks.

Finally, a little luck.

She had to prop up the broken back door to keep out the worst of the rain until she found a way to fix it in the morning. Muddy water puddled under her shoes, running in rivulets around the mounds of shattered crockery. A chair lay on its side, one leg splintered.

All in all, it was not an encouraging welcome.

Leaves touched the windowpanes as the oak tree closest to

the cottage tried to offer its own kind of comfort. Snapdragon was sulking inside her chest, sparking magic like tiny firecrackers. Her hip was screaming. But she was home, at last.

Bedraggled, befuddled, and bewildered. But home.

And not alone.

The drop in her stomach told her that her body registered the presence of another person before her brain did and that her eyeballs were the very last to be informed.

A girl in a gray dress.

Standing just inside the cottage, eyes wide, still as a rabbit.

"Bramble," Briar gasped, her skin still prickling painfully with fear. No one could hide like a rabbit girl. Briar would be impressed, just as soon as her heart started back up again. She thumped her chest, just in case. She was not made for this kind of night. She was used to the slow patience of unfurling pea vines, roses, and mugwort drying from the rafters, hot water in a kettle boiling for tea.

"Come," Bramble whispered. It wasn't soft or patient. It was a command. She was muddy all over, just like Briar. Clearly frightened, just like Briar.

Briar's heart began to race again. "Show me."

*Don't be Petal. Don't be Petal. Please, don't be Petal.*

It was Petal.

The tree branches immediately pressed closer, rosebushes and raspberry canes and blackberry hedge growing in a thick tangle no one could spy through. Petal lay on the edge of the garden, pale as rose petals. Her hare familiar also slept, curled in on itself on top of her chest, glowing only faintly, long, soft ears limp.

Briar did not like that.

Petal's familiar was usually bright as a sword, all teeth and light.

But it was rainwater, not blood, soaking her sister's red hair. Mud, not bruises. Relief was just like swan wings in her chest. "What happened?" Briar whispered.

"I found her like this," Bramble replied. "On the other side of the garden fence."

"Did anyone see you?"

Bramble shot her a disgusted look.

"You might have rabbit magic," Briar muttered, "but my unconscious sister does not."

"We were not seen."

"Let's get her inside before she catches her death."

Just then, because clearly a bad day could always get so much worse, there came a single knock on the front door. Mint tingled on Briar's tongue, along with a hint of lilac from the tree by the front step. A warning.

The Order of the Iron Nail.

Briar knew it, even from the other side of the cottage. The pink gargoyle set on the edge of the roof spread its stone wings. All witch houses had a gargoyle meant to gobble up errant or baneful magic. The Order of the Iron Nail was the force tasked with policing witches all over the country. It sent Keepers to track warlocks, break curses, find thieves.

And her sister.

They carried so many charms and stank so of magic that gargoyles might not attack them, but they certainly perked up in their presence. Watchful. Suspicious. And gargoyles on Lyonesse were not like the ones in London. Here, they were used to so much more magic thrumming through the air. Haven alone had spells to make sure the gutters sparkled clean, the fish at market never sent its smells toward the village square. Charms to clear the rain clouds over the beach of an afternoon, to keep the ants from the picnics, the jellyfish from the swimming areas. And that was on an ordinary day, never mind Midsummer.

But even here, the Order had near-absolute authority.

If they had come for Petal, there was very little Briar could do to stop them. Sending a solicitor to the Council would take weeks. And that was only once the shields were lifted. In the meantime, they would take Petal to Holdfast, where the dungeons were made of stone lined with jet to counter spellwork. Where the Iron Witches guarded the bones of dead witches and used them to feed the shields.

The only way to save Petal was to make sure they never found her.

Bramble was already on her feet, snarling slightly as she stood over Petal's prone body. Never mind wolf shifters and serpent clans—never cross a rabbit girl. That made Briar feel a bit better. "I'll get rid of them," she murmured.

How, she had no idea. One unmitigated disaster at a time.

The rain fell harder, sharp as thorns. She used it to feed the rosebushes, along with a generous push of her magic. Thicket and tangle to keep her sister safe.

Her hip protested the climb out of the greenery, the whole evening in general. If she made it to the cottage without her leg giving out completely, it would be a start. At least the cocoon of leaves and branches had woven tightly enough around Petal to protect her from the worst of the weather. And from prying eyes. The Order had so many ways to see into the shadow of things.

But not here. This was her house. Her sister.

She had sworn to keep her sister safe the day Petal saved Briar from a riptide by their favorite cove. They were thirteen years old and Briar had spotted a mermaid, had heard her soft, bright singing. She was no match for the pull and push of the sea, the laugh of a mermaid.

Petal was the one to drag her back to the shore, cutting herself on the rocks. The wound had festered, bringing on a dangerous fever. Neither the doctor nor the healers had been able to help. Mermaid magic locked its teeth wherever it could. And Petal had ventured too near for someone whose beauty rivaled even that of a mermaid.

All to save Briar.

Briar had gathered comfrey and honey and spiders' webs. She had made a crown of seaweed for Petal's red brow and drawn sigils with salt under her bed. And then sat with her, clutching her hand for three days and three nights until the fever broke.

In the end, a traveling peddler had offered a magical cure in exchange for one kiss from the beautiful Petal.

Their mother, desperate, had agreed.

Instead, Briar had offered him a cup of tea laced with vervain, and when he slumped in the hall, snoring loudly, she had stolen the charm from his pocket. She had replaced it with jack-in-the-pulpit flowers, with a whisper that they remember their witching name: fillet of fenny snake. The peddler had woken with his pockets full of garden snakes and run from the cottage. Petal, finally awake, had watched him from her bedroom window.

He never returned to Haven after that.

The thorns on all of the rosebushes sharpened as the memory made Briar's fists clench. The smell of wet flowers hung thick as veils. The rain added another layer of sound, of distraction to the eye. The little pink cottage sat gently in a moat of blossoms, harmless as a teacake.

She could do this.

She *had* to do this.

She hurried through the back door, snagging a cane from an umbrella basket. Another knock sounded, loud, imperious. A summons. There was no time to dry her hair or change her muddy dress. She would use as much of the truth as possible.

And she would go on the offense before they could.

They would not expect it from her, a witch who ran a tea-room that used to specialize in love spells. Another weapon in her arsenal, however small. Small charms, small magics. Sometimes they were more effective than the flashier, more powerful ones, the witch bottles the Order used to steal and trap a witch's familiar, the binding spells of jet and bone. The iron collar soaked in seawater.

Sometimes.

# Chapter Nine

U NSURPRISINGLY, ETHAN'S FAMILIAR was a dragon.

More surprisingly, when he curled around the crow's nest, glowing darkly, he appeared to be sulking. It was embarrassing.

And all because Briar was walking away from the ship.

Limping.

Ethan wasn't sure if he was growling or if it was his dragon, flicking his tail like a giant whip made of knives. "Get yourself together," he muttered.

The dragon's glare was baleful and vengeful in response.

Erasmus took a healthy step away from the mast, frowning at the dragon. The witch glass clinked together, as much part of the song of the sea as the steady waves and the creaking wood. Spells had a way of waking up when you least wanted them to. There were a dozen on his cross-belt alone, never mind the rest of the crew. Or the many hexes and curses and evil eyes flung their way courtesy of Keepers, warlocks, other Iron Crows. Pirates, highwaymen, spellsingers, cursebreakers, Fae kings, shifters. Once, notably, a vampire.

Iron Crows might be necessary, but no one much liked that fact.

They liked the Sea Dragons even less.

Ethan didn't care if he was liked. He cared that Briar Foxglove was limping home alone.

He sighed and flicked a glance at his dragon, who immediately unfurled his scaled wings and flew off after the green witch. Ethan was protecting his investment, that was all. His way off this damned island. He had cargo waiting in the hull, filled with spell ingredients for a warlock. There was a new bounty on his head that he had to go discourage. Violently. And a hundred more reasons to want to be anywhere but here.

"Do you trust her?" Anais asked, climbing the steps to the quarterdeck. Her familiar, a white ferret, sat on her shoulder.

"Hell no." Except that he did, which made no sense at all. Briar Foxglove was a green witch who was clearly keeping secrets, not to mention the twin sister to the bloody witch who had trapped them here.

And she had stabbed him.

After needling him so very gently to abduct her.

She was a mystery. With pockets full of flowers.

*Fucking Haven.*

He hadn't met a single person in his life who wore flowers like daggers. Not his mother before she died, his father before he left. And Granny Gallows was as gentle as her name suggested. He'd been all of ten years old, working as a cabin boy on a ship whose captain had even fewer scruples than the average Iron Crow. He had grabbed a weather witch out of Padstow, right off the beach where she sold the winds knotted into cords to sailors. One knot for a breeze, two for a storm, three for a gale. There were only a few people still alive to tell tales about the fourth knot.

The captain had decided he was tired of buying knot charms and it would be much easier to steal an old woman along with heirlooms and gold from the locals.

No one came for Granny Gallows. She had one eye, a hagstone around her neck, and a single iron fingernail on her left hand no one dared ask about. When she wasn't giving people the evil eye, she was knitting and drinking tea dark as bracken.

But she'd taken a shine to young Ethan, the only one brave enough to bring her salt cod and black tea where she hunched on the deck, spitting at the other sailors. He could only imagine what she would have made of Briar, soft-hipped, with flowers in her hair, thorn-tangle scars on her fingers, and a fierce stubbornness under the sugar frosting of her. Granny Gallows would have adored her recalcitrant swan, if nothing else. Her own familiar was a gull who perched on the railing behind her and screeched until the captain downed a bottle of rum, his ears spotted with blood, and promised to return her to the next port.

But then Granny Gallows decided to stay.

She kept a sharp eye on Ethan and an even sharper eye on anyone who might give him trouble. When the captain whipped Ethan for an infraction he could not even recall, she had called up a gale so fierce the ship tilted on its side and Ethan scooped salt water into his palms to cool the searing pain of his witch knot. The captain had used an iron-tipped cat-o'-nine-tails smeared with rowanberry juice. Granny Gallows threatened to capsize them all and drown every person on board (except for Ethan and the chickens the cook kept, because they amused her and it was hardly their fault they were on board) if the captain so much as touched Ethan again.

No one even looked at Ethan crossly after that.

A captain was never gainsaid on his own ship. But you angered a weather witch at your peril. They could drown you with a mouthful of water. Ethan learned that fear, wielded properly, did most of the work for you. As did rumors, and half-whispered horror stories.

If he had killed even half of the men he'd been accused of murdering, he would have been a monster.

Well, more of a monster. He had no illusions.

Even if Briar Foxglove made him wish he had.

"So what now?" Anais asked.

"Same as always. We take no quarter." No matter how delicious that soft-looking flower witches might be. "Hunt the amulet," he ordered her. Anais was best at hunting out magic. She would not get distracted by Briar licking the crumbs of a strawberry scone off her thumb like a bloody green lad.

"Aye, captain."

"And Anais?"

She paused. "Captain?"

"Next time, find the sodding fork."

"Oh, I knew it was there. I wanted to get her measure. To see what she was capable of."

Ethan knew she was exactly as apologetic as she sounded: that was, not at all. He slanted her a glare.

She shrugged. "Now we know."


BRIAR SWUNG THE door open to two Keepers wearing the jet-and-iron-nail wheel pendants of their station. Also: daggers, a pistol, a sword. And beaver-crowned hats, proper frock coats, and Hessian boots. The Keepers from Haven were fashionable, but the ones from the villages of Hallow and Holdfast tended more toward the thick sweaters and sturdy boots of fishermen. But these men were clearly from London; she could tell by the quality of the gold threads around their buttons. They had no doubt come for the festival before the shields dropped, and now they were as stuck as everyone else.

"About time," Briar said, before they could say anything. The one on the left blinked at her, the sky shaking with thunder over his head. He was probably in his fifties, with dark skin and laugh lines at the corners of his mouth. His red-haired companion was the exact opposite, exuding the pompous authority of the Order, pale as a fish belly.

"I hope you've come about that Iron Crow," Briar added.

"Beg your pardon, miss?"

"He broke into the shop. And he shattered my favorite teapot."

"Your teapot."

"Yes, the one with the violets. It took me a long time to paint them, you know. The trick is in the right consistency for the paint." She tilted her head. Water dripped from their hair and under their collars. "Speaking of violets, they are very good for calming the blood, and you do seem agitated," she added to the younger Keeper. "I have a syrup. I admit, it does taste a bit like soap, but it is very effective."

"We were not speaking of violets," he snapped in an agitated manner.

"I was," Briar said mildly, hoping they did not see the way her knuckles whitened as she gripped her cane. "Can you track him or not?"

"*Who?*"

It might not be wise to irritate a self-important Keeper quite so thoroughly, but it *was* fun.

"The Iron Crow!" She turned to the older Keeper. "Is he new at his post?"

The sound of grinding teeth could be heard even over the rain. It was rather gratifying.

The older Keeper smiled. "No, miss. I'm Bear."

His familiar was indeed a bear, glowing as though it were made of candlelight, ambling toward the garden. Briar tried not to react. It would not find Petal—her familiar was sleeping too soundly, which was a different, equally urgent concern, but it would keep her from being spotted. And as a shifter, Bramble did not have a familiar. Her entire self shifted into rabbit form at will. There was nothing to sniff out, nothing to hunt. Just a wild tangle of branches and thick mud.

"This here is Mr. Oliver Dawson," Bear continued.

"A pleasure," Briar said. Oliver's familiar was a nearly perfectly round bluebird, cheerful and rotund. It was lovely and Briar was quite certain the man did not deserve it. "I suppose you'd better come inside."

She let them in despite the fact that every nerve in her body was shouting for her to slam the door shut and lock it. And add a circle of salt. Stinging nettles. Flying daggers. Anything to keep them far, far away from her sister.

She carried the oil lamp, casting light on the whitewashed

walls, the woven rag rugs, the tin sconces patterned with roses. The kitchen was on the left, opening to the small, private family parlor that had once been her mother's bedroom. On the right were the two parlor rooms turned into the teashop. There was a wooden counter carved with roses, with shelves of jarred teas behind it, and iron tables, all painted white, of course. Several chairs still lay on their sides.

"There," Briar said, pointing. "My favorite teapot. And as you can see, quite unsalvageable." She scowled. "It was rather expensive, I don't mind telling you. Do you think the Order will compensate me? I thought the control of Iron Crows was under your purview." She had no idea if that were true. None at all. Lyonesse was the witching answer to Brighton, and it had very different objectives than London. Pleasure gardens, rest, the sea cure for ailments. Diversion for witches without having to hide what they were.

"Are you Miss Petal Foxglove?" Oliver demanded, exasperated and suspicious. He marched around the shop, glaring into the shadows. Bear merely stood, all politeness. Briar knew without being told that he would be the one to watch. Oliver would cause her no end of trouble, but Bear might actually see what she did not wish him to.

She raised her eyebrows at Oliver. "Am I to understand that you show up unannounced at my door and do not know who I am?"

"We are here for Miss Petal Foxglove."

"Ah. Well, I am not she. I am *Briar* Foxglove. Proprietress. I have never had any Council infractions." Which was saying something when your mother used to deal in love spells. The Council of Witches and the Council Arcanum, who oversaw all magical beings, were not particularly fond of the trouble a love spell could cause. Obsession, secrets shared, magical etiquette abandoned, oaths broken. It was a messy, unpredictable business. With some success, certainly. But it required more care and respect than most people cared to give it.

"I demand you tell me where your sister is."

Briar leaned on her cane. There was no pretense in the fatigue in the motion. This had already been the longest night of her life, and it promised to go on for some time more. "Why?"

"Because I am a *Keeper*!"

Briar knew she did not look impressed, because she was *not* impressed. "St. John is the Keeper assigned to Haven. He's been in charge for the last twenty-five years." He mostly dealt with tourists and security around the portal. But the shields were every witch's responsibility, from the Iron Witches to the scullery maids of the fine vacation houses on the lower streets of Haven.

"We are from the London chapter," Bear said, mildly.

"I see."

Oliver was getting rather red in the face. She nearly offered him that syrup of violets again. "Your sister," he spat.

"What about her?"

"*Where is she?*"

"She is not here."

"But w*here* is she?"

She shrugged. "I imagine she is at the assembly rooms for the dancing. Or on the beach for the bonfires."

"She is *not*."

"Ah."

"Is that all you have to say?"

She frowned. "My sister is a woman grown, Oliver."

"Mr. Dawson," he corrected her stiffly.

"Mr. Dawson, then," she amended. "It is Midsummer. We do not ask questions that could prove to be awkward. Even in Haven. Surely you have been to a Midsummer Festival before?"

"*You* are not asking the questions—I am. And you will answer."

"I thought I just had?" She shot Bear a questioning glance. Oliver's bluebird familiar was flying in increasingly frantic circles overhead. "Poor dear," she said. "Are you anxious? Familiars can sense your emotions, you know. You should have a care."

Her own swan was shivering inside her chest, frantic to be released so it could do some damage.

"I have a tea of chamomile and rose petals that ought to do the trick," she added. "If you are not fond of violets."

"As amusing as this is," Bear said quietly, "I am afraid we really do need you to answer our questions."

"Or we shall take you in chains to the jail!" Oliver added, with some relish, it had to be said.

"You say an Iron Crow broke in?" Bear asked. She nodded. "How do you know he was a Crow?"

"I interrupted him."

"What was he looking for?"

"He did not say." She shrugged. "Money, I assume, though we mostly have teas and flowers here." It was becoming a bit of a problem that there were more flowers than coins, truth be told. Midsummer was meant to keep them in flour and sugar and meat until the next festival. "Threshold Days always bring in more business, so I suppose I should only be surprised this has not happened before. He was tall, brown hair. *Not* very amiable."

"What did he take?"

"I'm not sure. He dropped me with a sleep spell and it's all been a bit muddled since."

"That's convenient," Oliver snapped.

"I did not find it so."

"I say we take her in. Question her properly!"

Briar's pulse was too loud in her ears. Keepers had spells and charms she could not hope to fight against, not with ivy vines and rose petals. Not even with a helpful blackberry bush or a giant oak tree. Or poison berry.

Bear only asked her, "Where were you that you came upon him? Did you not hear him break in? The state of your door implies he was not subtle."

"I was out for a walk," she replied.

"At night?" Oliver asked.

She laughed. It only sounded a little strangled. Surely allowances could be made for a shopgirl who had faced down an Iron Crow. Not to mention the Sea Dragons. Not that she had any intention of telling *them* about Ethan. Nor his crew, or his ship. And not that she was entirely sure why she was determined not to. "It is the Midsummer Festival, Mr. Dawson. You will struggle to find anyone at home."

The actual solstice was not for several days, but Haven was already bustling. The bakeries were filled with pastries and pies, the bathing machines lined up on the beach for rental. Bunting draped from the white houses with fluttering ribbons. There were bonfires in the sand, fireworks, stalls that stayed open late to sell strawberry wine and pasties filled with potatoes and green peas.

And by now, she imagined Haven was fair bursting with whispers of the shields slamming shut.

"What is this about?" she asked. "Why are you looking for my sister?"

"We have it on good authority that she has stolen something of great import."

Briar sucked in an offended breath. "How *dare* you, sir. My sister is not a thief." Except for when she absolutely was.

"If we could talk to her, we could be on our way," Bear said.

"I wish you would, as I am quite sure she could clear up this ridiculous misunderstanding." She tilted her head. "Surely you have charms and the like? For tracking? As *Keepers*."

"We do," Oliver replied stiffly.

She was going to hazard a guess that that meant they had tried but not been successful in tracking her sister. Some of the trepidation tightening her chest loosened. Bramble must be the reason behind it. Rabbit-girl magic was the best for hiding. Even the Order was no match for them.

As to that, Briar ought to take advantage of it while she could.

"You are welcome to check her room upstairs," she offered. "If it will put your mind at ease." Better to search her room now than later. It might buy them a few days. A few hours. Even a few minutes would help at the moment. "If you'll follow me?"

Briar stopped to take a lemon sweet from a glass jar on the long counter. Fatigue was nibbling at her, and even the fear was not enough to stop it fuzzing her thoughts. And she could not afford that.

"What's that you've got there?" Oliver demanded suspiciously.

Briar showed him the candied lemon drop before popping it in her mouth. "It was made with water and honey gathered under the noon sun last Midsummer. People use them on solstice night to stay awake for the dawn watch of the sunrise. It should help counteract the last of the sleep spell. I am not feeling at all well." She wondered if being ill all over his shiny London Hessian boots would hurry him along. It was not outside the realm of possibility. She really did feel awful.

The white stairs were painted with red roses, pots of wild mint and violets on each step. There was a crack in the plaster they had not had a chance to mend. The traditional blue evil eye was painted over doorways and windows. Just the very ordinary cottage of two witches on a summer island. Nothing of import to see.

No stolen moon charm.

No Dragon.

"What did you say Petal was accused of hiding?" That was something she ought to ask, wasn't it? "And who accused her? I should like to give them a piece of my mind."

"A moon charm has gone missing from the Museum of Magic," Bear said.

Briar frowned. "The museum in London?"

"The very one."

"Well, that solves that," she said with a shrug. "Petal has never been to London."

"And yet she used the portal twice today to that very purpose before the shields locked it down."

"She…did?" Briar halted on the stairs. She had forgotten the portal tracked who used it and to what purpose, as she had never had occasion to use it herself. *Blast*. Petal was really in it this time. A house tour of crocheted blankets and seashell wind chimes was unlikely to halt the tide of this investigation for very long.

"You did not know?"

She shook her head and forced herself to keep climbing. "She must have gone for provisions. We are perilously low on water from Saint Dympna's well in Meath. Outside of Ireland, it's only available at the Goblin Market and makes the best tea for the nerves." She eyed Oliver again, full of false sympathy. "You might want to try it."

The Goblin Market was hidden on London Bridge, filled end to end with shops that sold grimoires and rare gold teeth from giants, scales from sea serpents. It was frequented by witches from the oldest families, but also Iron Crows and goblins and ghosts and animal shifters. She had heard the stories of siren songs trapped in glass bottles, of goblin men with bewitched fruits. Fairy women who could drive you mad with a single kiss.

"Here we are." Briar set the lamp down inside Petal's bedroom, on a table cluttered with ribbons and pencils and shells gathered from the beach. There was a brass rabbit on the windowsill, sketches of hares framed on the wall. Muddy boots, a gray cloak. The coverlet was crocheted in a rose pattern, with yet more hares painted on the floorboards.

"Her familiar is a hare," Briar explained before they could get the idea to question the rabbit witches or link the moon charm to those same witches who were obsessed with the moon. "As you can see, she is not here. You may check under the bed, if you like." She rubbed her arms, feeling chilled from the weight of the day. Had it really only been an hour since she had stabbed a man with a fork?

Not just a man. The Dragon. She did not know why she needed to keep reminding herself of that fact.

"I hope you find Petal soon," she said quietly. "If the portal locked, as you said, might she be trapped in between?"

"It's possible."

"Then find her," she begged, and her desperation was not feigned. "Please."

BRIAR WAITED HALF an hour before going back out into the gardens. She sent her swan out to patrol in case the Keepers had left behind their own familiars. Or in case Oliver was lurking. If he was hiding in a tree, she would make sure the branch broke beneath him. But the Keepers had moved on to the next house and the next, and now it was only the storm growing wilder and wetter. The lights from the village square and down on the beach flickered, bonfires struggling to burn.

Not at all a favorable omen.

As if Briar needed reminding.

The evening festivities would have been interrupted by the news of the shields and the locked portal by now. Villagers and tourists alike would be starting back to their beds at the various inns and boardinghouses.

"How is she?" Briar asked, crouching next to her sister, too pale and too still. "Has she woken at all?"

Bramble shook her head. Lightning flashed, sending fingers of sharp light between the leaves.

"We need to get her inside. I know it's too obvious to hide her in her own bedroom, but we don't have any other options at the moment. I had them search her room before they left."

"Clever," Bramble approved. It was the most she had ever said to Briar at one time. "Hiding in plain sight is underestimated, but it's effective. And it will do for one night. I'll stay with her."

"Thank you. They as good as admitted they could not track her." Briar knew she had Bramble to thank for that.

"As if a Keeper could track a rabbit," Bramble said with her own particular brand of feral haughtiness. Briar found it rather comforting. Especially as they struggled to lift Petal off the ground. Bramble was stronger than she looked, but Briar had already pushed her hip too far.

It was very slow going, with the thunder shaking the sky and the branches and vines receding just enough to let them pass. Thorns snagged at Briar's dress, in warning, in comfort. Sometimes it was hard to tell with thorns. Blood bloomed over her knuckles, on her wrists.

They managed to get Petal inside and then set her down behind the tea counter so they could catch their breath. The witch knot on Briar's left palm stung as she pushed more magic through her exhausted body, pulling ivy and roses and nettles thickly around the broken doorway. It would not stop a Keeper or an Iron Crow, but it would give them a warning, if nothing else. A few extra minutes to pray to the Green Man for a miracle. Or to the Moon Mother, which might be more appropriate.

"Did you find the amulet?" Briar whispered. Her sister was wearing her best dress, edged with a blue ribbon. It had no pockets underneath, as it would have interfered with the fall of the skirts. She carried no reticule. "Do we even know what it looks like?"

Bramble shook her head grimly. "There's nothing."

They dragged Petal to her room, and it was an ungainly, awkward affair that would result in headaches and bruises for all involved. But finally she was in her own bed, Bramble squeezing water from Petal's hair with a shawl she found in a heap on the chair. Fear scratched at Briar's throat. "We should fetch a doctor. Or a curse-breaker? Do you know anyone discreet?"

Bramble shook her head again.

"Bloody hell, this is a mess." Briar scrubbed a hand over her face. "Do you need anything? Tea?"

Another shake of the head. Thank God. Briar did not think she had it in her to carry a tray up the stairs.

Bramble lay next to Petal, curling protectively around her. The shadows of the room grew deeper, everything else grew blurrier. Rabbit-girl magic.

Briar found her own bed and collapsed into it, exhausted down to her teeth but wide awake until the dawn birds began to sing in the hedgerows. She gave up and limped back down to the kitchen to boil water for tea. A pot of strong black tea made with moonwater left out under a summer full moon might help.

She let the tea steep until it was dark and rich, and then she added a slice of lemon for yet more clarity. She stirred three times sunwise with a spoon made of carved willow wood. She drank it until there were wet dregs left, then added rose petals for her sister and powdered moonstone for the moon. She turned the cup upside down on the saucer, spinning it three more times.

And then she searched for patterns and shapes that might tell her more than she knew. She was rubbish with tarot cards, passable with a pendulum. Village girls might not go to Mayfair to attend the Rowanstone Academy for Young Ladies, but they learned all the same. They gathered their spells from family grimoires and recipes, from the visitors that came to Lyonesse. From the sea. And tea leaf reading had always been in her blood. Not for nothing had her mother run a tearoom from blends mostly grown by Briar's magic.

The leaves clumped together and she searched for patterns, symbols. Anything that might help her navigate the current situation.

A hare and a crescent moon. A dragon. But also a rose, a tower, a scatter of stars.

As far as the truth went, it was…unclear.

And she had a feeling there weren't lemon trees enough from Dover to Orkney to make a thousand lemon drops to clear things up. And she could not exactly take it to Ollamh, the village soothsayer, for an explanation. He saw more than he ought to and blurted it out for all to hear. She would avoid him at all costs. As he tended to sing his premonitions—loudly—while he went about his day, it would not be a difficult feat.

When Briar caught a flash of movement through the window, she shot to her feet. She was not sure what she was expecting: more Keepers, the French army, redcap goblins on the hunt for human blood to wash their caps.

Not a rabbit.

She was used to rabbits, even without Bramble. If you had a garden, you had rabbits. And if you had cabbages, you had rabbits and no cabbages. Briar had gotten creative with wire cages over her vegetables, strung with crystals. Because if you lived on Lyonesse, rabbits were protected by magical law. They might be a witch, after all.

But this rabbit was not after the cabbages.

For one thing, it was entirely white.

Moon-white.

And outside the other windows, more white rabbits gathered until they sat in a perfect circle around the cottage, staring in.

A shiver worked its way up her spine.

"Shoo," she whispered through the crack in the glass. "You can eat all of the cabbages if you just go away."

They did not move for a very long time.

# Chapter Ten

"Y OU LOOK GHASTLY," her friend Sorcha said as she walked into the tearoom two hours later, raising an eyebrow at the back door, which was still only barely propped open, and then that same eyebrow at Briar.

"Well, cheers for that," Briar said, though she was quite sure it was the truth. Her eyes were gritty and she didn't need a looking glass to know there were smudges beneath them. She had tied on an apron patterned with violets to match them.

"Your swan's being beastly, even for a swan," Sorcha added, dropping the covered basket she carried onto the counter. She had two more slung on her other arm and a wagon waiting outside with more. "She tried to bite me when I came up the path."

"I am sure she is very sorry."

"I am sure she is *not*." Sorcha snorted, not the least bit offended. She was too used to roaming the hills every day with all manner of creatures, both ordinary and magical. She lived alone in her family's abandoned manor house, baking for the shops in Haven and Hallow. It would have made much more sense for her to move into one of the villages, but she claimed she would only start biting people, which would be bad for business.

Instead, she sent the blacksmith's son with a cart full of breads and sweets, only popping down herself when the mood struck. But for the Midsummer Festival it was all hands on deck.

"I made what feels like another thousand sunwheel cookies.

Do you have any more marigolds? I'm running out of petals."

"I think I do." Briar encouraged the marigolds and sunflowers to grow for the festival. And some families hired her to visit their own gardens for a little extra green magic for the season, something to show off to visitors. It was bad luck to run out of them before the solstice.

"So, what happened here, then?" Sorcha added, watching Briar sweep up the last of the broken crockery dust and mud.

"Storm broke the door and made a mess."

Sorcha leaned against the counter. Her dark hair was in its usual side plait. Haven might strive to be as fashionable as Mayfair, but Sorcha would rather lick rust, and said so on a regular basis. "And here I thought it was having two Keepers on your doorstep last night that has given you that delightful pallor." She narrowed her hazel eyes in accusation.

Her crow familiar cawed from the threshold. Also accusingly.

As Sorcha had named him Elderberry, he had a great many things to be accusatory about.

"There were Keepers here," Briar admitted.

"Whatever for?"

*Because my sister stole a piece of magic.*

*Because she's in trouble.*

*Because I can't wake her up.*

She didn't say any of these things, of course. Not with two customers wandering in, talking in hushed, worried tones, followed by Mr. Allens, the busiest busybody that had ever busybodied. He wore his green cravat that he claimed had been blessed by the Toad Mother in the Goblin Market. He was bordering on ancient, and his many years had not made him any kinder.

"Surely you've heard the shields have dropped?" Briar asked her friend instead. It must be common knowledge by now. Though happily, neither Bear nor Oliver had returned. Yet. She knew it was only a matter of time.

In the meantime, Petal still slept. Bramble said she had not woken once during the night, not even when the thunder rattled the windows. Her breathing was easy, her color healthy. She did not appear to be suffering.

But she would not wake.

Not even when Briar had cracked a sunlight charm right over her. The acorn had split, revealing a burst of light strong as the sun at noon. She and Bramble had to cover their eyes. It had no effect whatsoever on Petal. Neither had a ring of peppercorns, or iron against the witch knot on her palm.

"There isn't a single vole left in the deepest den who hasn't heard about the shields," Sorcha said.

"It's just awful," one of the visitors interjected. "I didn't sleep a wink all night."

"My sister frets," the other said, rolling her eyes. "Magic is tricky, even in Lyonesse." She patted her sister's arm. Rather forcefully, it had to be said. "The Keepers will sort it out by the time we have to go home. In the meantime, it would be a shame to waste a perfectly good festival vacation."

"We saved up for ages to afford it," the fretful sister admitted. She had black hair to her sister's blonde. Her familiar was a tiny garden snake curled among the silk flowers pinned to the brim of her bonnet. It glowed fitfully, as if it had eaten fireflies.

Briar nodded with her best shopkeeper's smile. "I have just the tea for you. A little chamomile, a touch of passionflower. You'll sleep like a baby."

"Not valerian?"

"Heavens no—valerian is all well and good, but it tastes like an old sock. No matter how much honey you add."

The visitor chuckled. "You're not wrong about that."

"No sockwater tea at the Rose and Petal Teashop," Sorcha promised.

"And are you Rose or Petal?" the black-haired sister asked as Briar scooped herbs from glass jars into muslin bags.

"Neither," Briar replied. "I'm Briar Foxglove."

"No greater green witch on the island," Sorcha said loyally, all while keeping an eye on Mr. Allens and his cat familiar, who kept hissing in her direction. Animals loved her, even the magical ones. "I'm telling you there's something wrong with that cat," she muttered.

Briar added rose-petal honey without a comment when the blonde sister blushed over simply inquiring about it out loud. It was a popular love charm, just a little nudge, really, always in demand. There was barely any magic at all, truth be told. It was such a well-known custom that just offering the honey to someone or adding it to your tea was statement enough.

One of the musicians who played at the assembly came in to ask Briar if she would come down to his house to deal with the wild roses choking out the climbing peas. Someone else came in to inquire if there was a tea that might stop her father from reading her private letters. As Briar had met the father in question, the answer was, regrettably, no.

Once they had left, Sorcha frowned quizzically. "What on earth do the shields have to do with you?"

"Pardon?"

"Why would Keepers come *here*?"

"Oh. Nothing, of course." Everything. Briar glanced at Mr. Allens, who was examining one of the many flower crowns she had woven for the festival. He had only ever bought a single thing from her: a charm for baldness, at midnight at the back door, even though she sold them at the counter all the day long. "I think they must have started at the top of the hill before working their way down."

"Making a fuss over every little thing, as usual."

"You're not worried about the shields?" Briar asked.

Sorcha shrugged, pragmatic as ever. "I'm worried I'll run out of sunwheel cookies or strawberry jam. Or my oven chimney will clog. Like *I've* ever been through the portal."

"Still."

She nodded, relenting. "I suppose."

There was something odd and faintly itchy about the shields

being locked around the island. They might not be visible, but when you grew up on Lyonesse, you learned the feel of them, the way you learned what it felt like when the winds changed and a storm was brewing.

And it had felt utterly wrong and deeply uncomfortable when Briar was forced through the barrier. And not just because she had been tied to a mast. What was Ethan doing now? Had the Keepers found him? Would he tell them what he knew? That didn't seem likely. Iron Crows did not share. Especially not with Keepers.

"What's that look on your face for?" Sorcha asked.

"Oh, nothing." *Ethan.* She was fairly sure whatever her face was doing was the fault of one Ethan Swansea.

Mr. Allens, drifting closer, knocked over a bowl of rose petals. It was next to a jar of mustard seeds labelled *eye of newt* and poppy seeds labelled *blindworm's sting.* His neck mottled red when an eavesdropping charm fell out of his pocket.

Sorcha's crow swooped at the few strands of hair left on top of his head.

"Go on," Sorcha barked after him when he hurried away. "Or it's the last bakery delivery you'll see from me, you old fishguts."

Briar had to smile. "I do actually need my customers."

"That wasn't a customer—it was Mr. Allens. And he never paid for his last order of sticky buns." Sorcha poked her head out. "And take your mangy familiar with you!"

The cat slunk away, tail bristling with insult.

Fired with righteous indignation, Sorcha turned back to Briar, crossing her arms. "Well, now that that's over with, are you going to tell me why you are lying to my face?"

"I'm not…" Briar glanced around to be sure they were alone.

Sorcha poked her. Hard. "You are a lying liar, Briar Foxglove."

"Ouch." Briar poked her back. "Just hush a minute."

And because Mr. Allens was not the only gossip in Haven, she reached into a jar of tin charms, the kind every child had sewn to their clothes for good luck, every lover hoping for a kiss, every old man cursing his painful joints. They came in all types: eyes to blind the evil eye, roses for love, shells for secrets whispered between friends, horses for leaping over obstacles. Also, every body part from eyeball to baby toe, mostly used for healing spells.

Briar pulled out a tiny ear and placed it down on the counter. She turned a teacup over it, around which she also drew a circle of salt. She could not risk anyone overhearing. Not a single syllable.

"Who do you suppose is trying to eavesdrop on us?" Sorcha asked. Her crow hopped up onto the windowsill to keep a close watch.

"The Keepers were looking for Petal," Briar whispered.

"What? Whatever for?"

"They say she stole a moon charm from the London Museum of Magic."

"Get away."

"They're blaming her for the shields and the locked portal."

"*Petal?* Did she flirt the museum guards into puddles of useless goo? That's not even her magic, but your sister does have a talent."

Petal barely even bothered to flirt. It was only that people took one look at her face and became instantly stupid.

"You don't believe them, do you?" Sorcha asked.

"Well, as it happens—" Briar broke off, groaning. Charles bloody Aster and his horrid mother were coming up the path.

Sorcha followed Briar's gaze and groaned even louder. "Bloody hell, not those two. I wish you'd knock his teeth out, just once."

"I can't."

"You absolutely can. No one would blame you." When Briar only shook her head, Sorcha added, "*I* could knock his teeth out. It would be my pleasure."

And it would be a pleasure to behold. Briar did not care if that made her bloodthirsty. But instead she could only dredge up her best shopkeeper's smile and the very last of her patience. "Mrs. Aster, Mr. Aster. Good morning to you."

*Go away, go away, go away.*

Charles, in his new hat directly from Piccadilly, and his mother, with her capelet fringed with silver tassels, even though it was far too hot for a capelet of any sort, and her perpetually pursed mouth. Her familiar stalked beside her, an elegant egret. Charles's familiar was a toad and rarely made an appearance. It was far too common, not nearly smart enough for fashionable company. Briar thought it rather sweet—the only sweet thing about him.

Briar could not afford to have them here with Petal as she was. They were too nosy, too meddlesome. But she also could not afford to antagonize them either. Not when she had yet to pay her mother's debts and time was running out.

"What can I get you?"

"You look tired, my dear," Mrs. Aster said with a glance at Briar's cane. "I do wish you'd let us help you. It's simply too much land for two girls to manage alone. You must see that now." Sometimes they were *girls*; sometimes they were *sad spinsters* in need of a soothing skin tonic to keep the wrinkles at bay. Pointed insults, barbed compliments. Mrs. Aster made a meal of them all.

Aster Apothecary was a favorite of the Mayfair set when they visited the island. And the Asters had an eye on the Foxglove cottage, had done for many years. They wanted Briar's garden. Charles's father had kept them at bay for a time, but now the only things standing in their way were the Foxglove sisters.

Who were struggling to pay their bills, truth be told.

The notoriety of the Keepers' late visit would not help matters, not to mention Petal's being involved. Once word was out about that, Briar might well lose her Midsummer customers, the very ones she depended on to see her through to Samhain. One never knew until it was far too late if notoriety would end in infamy or ostracism. Infamy would at least pay the bills.

And Mrs. Aster had been denied, and that she would not

have. When her attempts to foist her son onto Briar in order to claim the land that way was also thwarted, her ire grew. She meant to have her way.

Briar might have told her that she only had to wait for her rent to come due.

She didn't, of course.

But every month it was more and more difficult to pay what was owed. Tearooms and green witches were not rare, even on Lyonesse. Their mother's love spells had been the real draw, as they discovered.

Briar forced herself to breathe calmly through her nose when one of the elms slapped a branch against the window. Behind it, the sun shone placidly on her boisterous garden, humming with honeybees, birdbaths filled with sparrows. Charles watched her with the same expression he always wore: some combination of a leer and a sneer that always set her teeth on edge.

"We manage just fine, Mrs. Aster. Thank you for your concern. Tea? Honey scones?" There wasn't enough charmed honey in all of England to sweeten that woman's disposition. But Briar did try. "We have dandelion suns for Midsummer." They were made of hardened honey with yellow dandelion petals laid out flat like sunrays on willow wands.

"And so many left in the jar." Mrs. Aster clicked her tongue. "You really ought to try harder, dear, if you mean to make a go of it."

Briar kept her smile in place while shifting to the right in order to step on Sorcha's foot. Her friend was beginning to snarl.

"And now this terrible business with the shields," Mrs. Aster continued. "And Keepers at your door." She shook her head with patently false sympathy. "Just *dreadful*."

"What can I get for you, Mrs. Aster?" Briar asked mildly.

"Sweet custards for a sunnier disposition?" Sorcha suggested with an equally false smile, one that was all teeth. At least she wasn't biting anyone. Yet.

"Rose-chamomile tea," Mrs. Aster demanded. "And none of

those currant rolls of yours." She sniffed. "Far too common. I'll take three strawberry petit fours instead."

Briar wondered if the woman knew how close she came to Sorcha shoving one of those common currant rolls right up her left nostril.

"You may bring it to us outside, if you please. And sit with my Charles when you do—he's come all this way to see you. You ought to be grateful. He was so popular with all of the ladies at the assembly room last night."

Sorcha snorted. Loudly.

Mrs. Aster sailed away. "Come along, Charles. And do use sunwater for the tea. I shall know if you skimp."

Briar scooped the tea into her least favorite pot and went into the kitchen for the boiling water. Her worktable was scrubbed clean, herbs drying from the ceiling above. The cupboard shelves were packed with jars filled with dried rose petals, chamomile flowers, mints, and other herbs. There were bottles of water gathered under the full moon, under the noon sun, at midnight, from sacred wells, rivers, the ocean.

Sorcha had followed her, incensed. "Why do you let them talk to you like that?"

"You know why."

"If they call in your mother's debt, I shall lend you money."

"You have no money," Briar pointed out fondly.

"Blast. You're right. Well, you're not marrying that tosspot."

"Certainly not."

"Fine, then," Sorcha said, mollified. "Use dishwater for their tea. And add something to turn her stomach, I beg you."

Briar felt a little better as she carried the tray, willing her hip to stay steady. Was there any fortification better than a fierce friend at your back?

The garden glowed, the sun glinting off the last of the rain dripping from the trees and hanging heavy in the roses. Clay pots burst with marigolds and irises under the lemon tree Mrs. Aster envied so much. It did not grow naturally on the island, and it was one of the few that Briar did not encourage anywhere else but the cottage. She had to use every trick to keep customers coming back. Even smiling at Charles when he sat and waited to be served upon with that haughty, entitled expression.

Briar set the tray down on the wrought-iron table, still painted white. She had not yet had a chance to paint everything her mother had insisted on drowning in white. "That pink is not at all the thing for a house," Mrs. Aster said, somehow pursing her already pursed lips at the house. "You really ought to listen to me."

Briar would paint the tables the same pink to match before the day was done.

"Here's your tea," she said.

"Do sit with my Charles, after you pour."

"I really can't," Briar said. "I must get back to the counter."

"I insist!" Mrs. Aster snapped. "Your prospects are not so fine that you can afford to be so particular. Acting as though it is not a great honor. The *audacity*."

"We're going to marry eventually," Charles said, sounding bored. "Mother always gets what she wants, and your only other alternative is to live on the beach with the vagrants. So sit down and stop embarrassing me."

The roses grew silver thorns like daggers behind him. He did not notice.

"Well, now. Such romance will make a girl swoon."

Briar knew that voice: low and rough and perfect, touched with the wild green of Ireland.

Ethan Swansea.

# Chapter Eleven

ETHAN'S EYES SEARED through her. He looked the same as he had the night before, wind-worn and ready for a fight. It was there in the way he stood, in the alert sharpness of him. She had half convinced herself she had conjured him up. He was entirely too primal for a place like Lyonesse. Certainly for the garden of a tearoom.

Something inside her calmed even as her heart picked up its pace. He was a very confusing man.

Charles did not look confused. He looked suspicious and nervous. Mrs. Aster set her cup down with a snap. "Who is *this*?"

"A friend," Ethan replied before Briar could answer. What would she have said? Iron Crow? The notorious Dragon? Too handsome for his own good? For *her* own good? She would never have considered something as mild as *friend*.

After all, did a *friend* tie you to the mast of his ship?

*Never mind that now, Briar Foxglove,* she told herself sternly when her imagination presented her with several improper suggestions as to how and why a friend might tie one down. She had not realized she had such a good imagination, truth be told. But it had not stopped providing her with tantalizing images since Ethan had offered to search her for the moon charm.

Her cheeks flushed. Her stays were too tight. Sweaty. Was she sweating?

"Miss Foxglove is busy," Mrs. Aster said. "I require cream for my tea."

No one added cream to rose-chamomile tea. It bordered on criminal.

"I have cream right here," Sorcha announced cheerfully, sailing out of the cottage holding the hedgehog-shaped creamer aloft like a war banner. She plunked it down with the same care and courtesy as one might give to some muddy, trampled bloody war banner.

Then she stepped back and smiled at Ethan, who was too tall and too rugged and too sure of himself for the garden. The wisteria plant did not seem to think so. It was curling embarrassingly close to him. If he noticed, Briar would be mortified. It suddenly smelled like a hundred different flowers. The peonies were embarrassing themselves, drooping lazily as they grew too fat and ruffled for their stems in his shadow.

"You don't look the sort to drink tea," Sorcha told Ethan. "Rum, definitely. Gin, maybe. Brine? Mermaid tears?"

Ethan only looked amused. Sorcha usually provoked amusement or irritation and not much in between. "I drink tea."

"Oh good, Briar will make you some. She makes the best."

"Briar is taking tea with *Charles*," Mrs. Aster snapped.

"She is *not*," Sorcha retorted.

"They are affianced."

Sorcha only snorted. Elderberry cawed mockingly. She smiled pointedly at Briar. "Go on and make the tea, and I'll make sure the Asters have *everything* they need." It was most definitely a threat and could not be interpreted otherwise.

Briar returned to the back door, Ethan stalking silently behind her, the grass pressing against his boots. "You're not marrying that bloody tosspot." It was a statement, not a question.

"Of course not." But she said it with more confidence than she actually felt. Please the Moon Mother, let it not be the only option that saved her cottage and her sister.

"He's not good enough for you."

Something warm bloomed inside her chest. Her swan threatened to lift its feathers in a preen. *Don't you dare.* "You don't know him," Briar pointed out. "You don't know *me.*"

"I know enough."

"What are you doing here?" Briar asked, because she did not know what to say to that. Or why that heated awareness of him burned even brighter than it had last night. Or why she felt the urge to pat her hair to make sure it had not slipped from its pins. She was worried about her sister and the shields and the moon charm. Not about the state of her hair. That would be absurd.

"What did the Keepers have to say for themselves last night?" he asked in that hard, but somehow lazy way of his, as though nothing could ruffle him. As though shields and the threat of a Keeper's iron collar were just idle threats, flies to be swatted away.

She led him into the kitchen, where he leaned in the doorway with his arms crossed, watching her fill the kettle. "How did you know they were here?" she asked.

"Of course they were here. Meddling is what they do best."

"But when *you* stomp through my house, it's not meddling, I suppose?" she said archly.

He nearly smiled. Not quite, but it was close. "I go where I like."

When she rolled her eyes at him, he did smile, however briefly.

"You don't really want tea, do you?" she asked.

"I can want more than one thing at the same time."

She wasn't sure why that sounded like a threat. A promise. Complicated.

Did he know Petal was upstairs even now, vulnerable and helpless? Was that why he was here? It must be. Would he demand to look around? She did not know exactly how strong Bramble's rabbit-magic shields were. They wouldn't turn Petal entirely invisible, that much she knew.

Briar hung the kettle on its hook and swung it back over the fire, to stop herself from looking toward the stairs. She was not entirely sure how good she was at keeping secrets. She did not have much practice. She felt his gaze on her back. She was all nerves and exposed skin. She had never realized how vulnerable the back of one's neck could feel.

And how it might not always be an unpleasant thing.

She clearly needed a proper night's sleep. And a plate of cheese. Petal was convinced cheese solved most of life's problems.

The wind blew in through the window, heavy with salt water and roses and approaching rain. She heard Ethan take a step closer to her. Goosebumps lifted along her nape, shivered down her spine.

And then one of the bottles of moonwater cracked.

Abruptly. Loudly.

The sound made her jump. She turned toward it just as another bottle exploded, sending shards ricocheting through the warm kitchen.

Ethan pressed her against the wall, brows drawn low as he shielded her with his body, hard and hot against hers. Every single bottle of moonwater, every bowl holding moonstones, every jar of dried moonflowers burst, shooting glass every which way. It sounded like the peppering fire of musket shot. Ethan did not move an inch. He stayed exactly where he was, arms on either side of her, tucking her head under his chin.

She had stabbed him with a fork just last night and now he was protecting her.

Behind him his familiar unfurled giant, burning wings, his scaled neck extending in another kind of armor, woven with glittering light. Briar had never seen a dragon familiar, nor any familiar as grand and majestic and severe. It would have taken her breath away if she'd had any left in her lungs.

The kitchen went quiet again, but Ethan remained where he was, only inching back far enough to lift her chin toward him. It was intimate, his infamously lethal focus entirely on her. "Are you cut?"

She shook her head. Puddles of water gleamed on the stone

floor behind him, broken glass sparkling. "But *you* must have been cut," she said softly.

He ran his palm over the back of his neck, wiping away spots of blood. "Barely scratched. Nothing at all like being stabbed with a fork."

She winced. He only grinned, fleeting and rare. She might have only just met him, but anyone could see his grins were rare—the ones that reflected in his shadowed eyes, at least. They must be guarded more fiercely than pirate's gold.

"Mind telling me what the hell that was about?" he asked.

"I don't know."

"Don't you?" It was a quiet question, but no less powerful than a demand at sword point. His voice wrapped around her like a velvet ribbon, tightening. "Lying to an Iron Crow, little thorn? You *are* brave."

She swallowed, confused by the sensations running rampant throughout her body like a herd of wild horses. "Are you suggesting I exploded my own kitchen?"

"Did you?"

"No."

"All right."

She blinked. "All right? That's it?"

His gaze pierced her. "Did you want more?"

*Yes. No.*

"I could be lying."

"Are you?"

"No." She frowned. "This is a ridiculous conversation."

"Is it?" He still had her pressed to the wall. "I didn't realize we were having a conversation. I thought you were trying to throw me off the scent." He leaned a little closer, dragging his nose up her throat. "Won't work. I've caught it now."

She swallowed, nervous, tingling in places she had no time to address. Heat kindled in her ribcage. "I'm not doing anything."

His lips moved gently against her skin but his voice was hard again. "Aren't you?"

He stepped back, and it was a struggle to breathe normally when it suddenly felt as though she had run a race. She wanted to blame it on the lingering effects of the sleeping spell, the anxiety of a visit from two Keepers, the shields dropping. Her sister.

But she already knew that wasn't it.

Sometimes people were drawn to each other even when it made no sense.

It didn't mean anything.

And it was Midsummer. Everything burned a little brighter at the solstice. It was always the ones you'd least expect who had to be fished out of the mermaid fountain in the square. Naked.

"I should make sure Sorcha has not murdered my customers," Briar murmured.

He let her pass when she knew very well he could have kept her pinned to the wall. A jug of water on the counter had cracked into pieces. The moonstones embedded in the wooden window-sill had exploded, crushed to chalky dust on her floor, next to crescent-shaped sugar biscuits. Even the clock, painted with the phases of the moon, had fallen off the wall.

All of it related to moon magic in some way.

That could *not* be a coincidence.

Was it only here at the cottage? Was it because Petal was upstairs, even if the moon charm was not? Were more Keepers on the way even now? How was she supposed to protect her sister?

"Your hands are shaking," Ethan said.

She curled her fingers into her palm. "It's nothing."

"Hmm."

She hurried out to the garden, suddenly wanting to feel the sun on her face, to smell the comforting lushness of earth and lilies and wild mint. The statue of a woman in the center of the night-blooming moon garden had also been affected. One arm had been shorn clean off, and her moon crown lay in a clump of night-blooming jasmine.

The Asters were on their feet, eyes wide. Charles was clearly shaken, his mother furious. The contents of the teapot stained his complicated cravat and Mrs. Aster's silvery capelet. The Asters did not care to be disheveled.

"Is he still here?" Ethan asked evenly. Right before the sky cracked, full of rain and shaking thunder and the searing flash of lightning. Mrs. Aster squeaked, pulling her bonnet lower over her head. Charles instantly resembled nothing so much as a wet goat. His toad familiar was perched on his toe, looking hopeful. Poor thing.

Sorcha grinned, rain dripping off her nose. "Have a currant roll," she said to Ethan as the Asters hurried away. The rain followed them. "My treat."

Briar leaned against the nearest chair. Ethan's gaze sharpened on her and she straightened, aching hip be damned. A lamb did not limp in front of a wolf. "Mr. Swansea was just leaving."

"Was I now?" He was amused again, though his eyes suggested he was taking her apart to seek out her weaknesses, her secrets. As though there was more to her than met the eye. No one had ever looked at her like that. He inclined his head. "Careful," he said. "Weather is unpredictable today."

And then he walked away as if nothing at all untoward had happened. Briar watched him because she could not help herself. Sorcha turned to her, eyebrows raised so high she was likely to strain a forehead muscle. "What was *that*, then?"

"What was what?"

"Briar Foxglove, you are not going to stand there and pretend that the air did not nearly catch on fire between the two of you."

"I'm sure I don't know what you mean." Had it? Had it really? It wasn't her imagination after all? "Oh, all right," Briar relented before her friend launched herself bodily at her in frustration. "He has a…presence."

"I have seen actual giant dire wolves on the moor with less *presence*. And he could not take his eyes off you."

Well, that was simple enough to explain: he did not trust her. He was hunting her sister, like everyone else.

"And he scared Charles away, which I will cherish forever."

That was harder to explain. Why should he have bothered? For her? It must be part of his plans somehow. It was obvious he wanted to be anywhere but on the island. The Dragon sipping tea from porcelain cups painted with hedgehogs. Eating pink petit fours shaped like swans and almonds rubbed with gold leaf. Drinking champagne at the assembly rooms in polished boots. Absurd.

Briar scrubbed at her face, exhausted.

Sorcha slipped her arm through hers. "What can I do?"

"You *can* help, as it happens. I need to know that Petal is not in any physical, mortal danger before I figure out how to get her out of this mess." *Grow the plant, pick the plant, dry the plants, make the tea.* Everything could be broken down into manageable steps.

Even saving her sister.

# Chapter Twelve

B RIAR LEFT HER swan at the back door and two nails crossed on the floor to bar entry while she was upstairs. Bramble was waiting for them in Petal's room, standing in front of the bed and snarling. She held a brutal-looking pair of iron scissors in her hands. Her eyes were tired, her teeth sharp. There was salt and rowanberries on the windowsill.

"Sorcha is a friend," Briar reminded her quickly.

"I'm only here to help," Sorcha added. "I've known Petal since we were children."

Bramble did not look convinced. The air was heavy, blurry, as though filling with mist. It made Briar tired, fuzzy-headed. She was sure she had left something important downstairs. That she ought to leave this room and go check. Right now.

Rabbit magic.

"She can tell us if Petal is hurt," Briar said, still fighting the urge to wander away. Did she need to go to the well for more water? Had she picked enough raspberry leaf for summer teas?

Bramble lowered her scissors and the mists cleared.

Briar forgot about wells and summer teas and being anywhere else. Sorcha rubbed the bridge of her nose as the pressure in the small room lifted. "I did not enjoy that."

Bramble stepped aside but stayed tense, tracking Sorcha's every movement. Petal did not look worse than she had earlier, but she did not look better either. Her hare familiar was curled up in the same spot, its light dim but steady.

Sorcha exhaled. "What happened to her?"

"We don't know," Briar said. "Something to do with the shields? The moon charm?"

"We might need Pippa. If it's in a book, she can find it."

"I have a feeling any messages I send out of Haven will be intercepted."

Pippa Cavendish was a book witch who lived in Hallow, working at one of the libraries there. She could find something in a book the way Briar could grow roses. But Hallow was half a day's walk on foot or several hours in a carriage. Which Briar did not own. Finding one to rent during a festival would take some doing.

"You might be right." Sorcha approached the bed cautiously. "Don't bite me, Bramble. I bite back."

"Why don't you go to my room?" Briar suggested to Bramble softly. "You need to rest."

"I'm not leaving her."

Briar was relieved to hear it. Anything she might be able to do for Petal would only be done if she was safely watched over by someone Briar trusted. Bramble. Sorcha. Pippa. And that was the end of the list. "I'll bring you a tray," she said.

"Thank you. Someone was downstairs with sharp eyes." Bramble sat on Petal's chair, scissors still in hand. Her cheeks were pale. "I needed to use more magic than I thought."

Sorcha stood at the foot of the bed, watching Petal sleep. There was a faint frown between her brows. Her crow appeared on her shoulder, head tilted, eyes glittering.

She had perfected a spell she used on the lost and wounded creatures she had been finding since they were girls. Not one of the doctors and midwives, the healers and veterinarians, could replicate it half so well. From injured horse to sick dog, from spell sickness to the fairy-led, Sorcha's spell knew what it was searching for and would not be distracted.

She pulled out one of the many paper birds she kept tucked about her person. Some were covered in writing, the words unknown even to Briar. Sorcha stood the little bird on her witch knot and then blew it into the air. It dipped, plummeting briefly before soaring up toward the ceiling. It circled there, paper rustling. Once, twice, three times.

It finally returned to Sorcha's palm. She unfolded it, studying the crinkled paper, then nodded. "Petal's not in any pain, and there's nothing that leads me to believe she is not merely sleeping. The spell is far more concerned with your hip and Bramble's fatigue. And the state of your roof. Abysmal."

"Don't remind me," Briar muttered, lightheaded with the release of the tension radiating through her. Her sister was not dying. Anything else might be fixed. *Would* be fixed. "Magic sleep."

"Magic sleep, yes. She'll probably wake up feeling more refreshed than either of us ever have, knowing Petal."

"When?" Bramble demanded sharply, though her shoulders had lost some of their tension.

"I don't know," Sorcha replied. "But whatever this is, she's remarkably well. Honestly, I would ignore her if I stumbled across her in the moors."

Briar slumped against the doorjamb, relief stealing the last of her strength. "Thank the Mothers."

"If you give the moon charm back, maybe the spell will lift?" Sorcha said.

"If we only knew where it was."

"Bollocks."

"Precisely."

WHEN BRIAR MADE it back downstairs, Ethan was still in the garden.

Not only that, but he appeared to be mending her broken door.

Sorcha grinned. "I'll leave *that* in your capable hands."

"He's after the moon charm," Briar said.

"That's not all he's after."

"Don't be daft."

Sorcha snorted. "One of us is being daft, and it's not me."

"He tied me to the mast of his ship!"

"Oh, well now, things *are* getting interesting. Do tell."

Briar laughed. It was nice to know she had not forgotten how to in the last twenty-four hours. "Oh, go on."

Sorcha waggled her eyebrows suggestively before darting out the front door.

"Wait," Briar called after her. "Aren't you going to the oak tree? For solstice?"

"I've had more than enough of the village for one day. Send word if you need me!" Sorcha waved and vanished into the fields, her red hair bright as copper pennies.

Briar noticed more than a few neighbors gathering on the road and casting glances in her direction. She smiled her shopkeeper smile and locked the door. Firmly. She added a sigil for privacy for good measure. Her mother had created it for her customers who bought love spells for someone who they had not married, or should not be seen with. Briar would also wash the windows with salt water as soon as possible. But first, she needed to get Ethan away from the cottage.

Unfortunately.

Fortunately.

Snapdragon, normally peevish by nature, looked smitten. If a swan could look smitten. Not a good sign. Especially when she pecked at Briar's feet to hurry her along outside. "Not you too," she muttered.

Ethan had fixed the warped hinges. The sun glinted on his silver rings, his sun-browned forearms. His sleeves were rolled up, which made perfect sense on a ship, but was rarely seen in Haven. If it wasn't the thing in Mayfair, it wasn't the thing in Haven.

Mayfair was missing out.

"One of the hinge pins was bent," he said. There was a stamped tin ship's anchor votive pinned to his shirt, the same tattooed on his right forearm. "Easy enough to fix. Looked worse than it was."

She could only stare as he lifted the door off the ground and fit it into place, before working the screws through the doorjamb. He made it look easy, muscles flexing in the sun. The grass was warm as it tickled her ankles, growing a little faster than was natural. The hollyhocks swayed on their tall stalks, as though reaching for Ethan. He did not notice, thankfully. Snapdragon extended her long neck, magical light sparking like sun on water. Briar just shook her head. This was getting embarrassing. Wasn't it bad enough that her sister was a thief and now the whole island would be hunting for her? Did Briar also have to have some kind of magical physical manifestation every time Ethan glanced her way?

"Thank you," she said, softly, trying not to sound feather-brained. No one had ever done anything like this for her before. For some reason she had to clear her throat. "That was kind of you."

Ethan did not smile but his eyes were not unkind, only wry. "I'm not kind."

She wondered about that. He made it sound like a warning, and there was a definite flutter in her chest at his stern, uncompromising tone, but she was not entirely convinced. He was here for her sister, for the moon charm. She wasn't a fool. But there was something else to him, something beneath the surface. "Well, thank you all the same," she said.

"Keepers will be back," he said. "I don't fancy making things easy for them."

"Nor I." And now she could walk down to the village square. It was tradition to gather at the oak tree and tie ribbons and small flower wreaths for good luck. By the end of the week, there would also be ashes from the solstice bonfires in little glass vials for sale, as well as seawater gathered under the noon sun, Pegasus feathers, and hagstones from the beach. Painted gold, naturally.

If Briar did not attend, it would be noticed, and she could not afford to be noticed. It wouldn't be long now before Petal's name began to be whispered. Briar imagined it had only been quiet this long because the Keepers wanted the advantage. And the Iron Crows, like Ethan. And since Briar always tied ribbons to the oak tree at Midsummer and she always sold wreaths and circlets of flowers, she would do so today. Even if the idea of leaving Petal made her break out in hives. Her sister was as safe as she could be for the moment. And the moment was all Briar had, all she could focus on.

Oak tree, flowers.

Ethan.

She locked the door, grateful she had brought down her trunk of circlets the day before in the wagon. She would have had the devil's own luck managing it today.

"Where are you off to?" Ethan asked.

"The square. We tie the wish ribbons at noon on the first day of the festival."

"I'll go with you," he said, falling into step with her.

She tilted her head knowingly. "Keen on making wishes, are you?" He did not seem the type. Of course, he had not seemed the type to mend her broken door unbidden, either.

He snorted. "Haven traditions are not high on my list of entertainment, no."

She imagined not. What *did* he find entertaining? Fighting? Drinking rum down at the tavern? Bar fights? Mermaids? Seducing women by the bonfires, as so many did?

She'd bite her tongue off before asking.

"I'm not letting Keepers and Iron Crows snatch you away for the moon charm. Gods know what they'd do with it, and then I'd never get the hell off this island."

*Ah.*

Of course.

"We'll find it first," he added, and she was glad that whatever absurd twinge of disappointment she might have felt was not obvious in her expression. She was a green witch. He was a notorious sailor and Iron Crow. He stole magic and traded with warlocks. She grew daffodils.

In a village with its very own soothsayer.

Just thinking of Ollamh earlier during her tea leaf reading had apparently summoned him. He was walking toward them, pale eyes glinting in that kind, faraway, and slightly mad way.

And he was singing.

That was never a good thing.

He might have a beautiful voice, but he tended to sing about everyone's secrets without even meaning to. People tended to avoid him. Briar had never bothered before because there was never any need. But between her sister and the Crow at her side—and the song Ollamh sang as he caught her glance, quite by accident—she suddenly understood why George had once climbed right up the side of a house to avoid his attention.

*"My heart is pierced by Cupid; I disdain all glittering gold…"*

That wasn't so bad.

Maybe he had looked at her by accident. Nothing about her sister, or stolen charms.

But then he continued to sing.

*"There is nothing can console me, but my jolly sailor bold."*

Briar flatly refused to glance at Ethan even out of the corner of her eye.

*"His hair, it hangs in ringlets, his eyes as black as coal. My happiness attend him wherever he may go… My jolly sailor bold."*

She was entirely too tired to deal with soothsayers and murky predictions with just enough clarity to be potentially mortifying.

Absolutely not.

Next he would start singing about Ethan's muscular arms, his scarred jaw. His Irish lilt.

Briar leapt into a decorative yew without so much as a warning to the poor thing. A traveling acrobat had trimmed it into the likeness of a hare, after she saw Petal and her familiar for approximately three minutes. At least the yew was welcoming despite her rude intrusion. The starling near her head was not so forgiving. He exploded into a flurry of feathers and scolding squawks.

Ollamh's song drifted off as he lost his magical focus.

Briar breathed a sigh of relief. He could have started singing about Petal. That he might be singing about Briar was bad enough.

Even if Ethan was *not* her *jolly sailor bold*. There was nothing jolly about him.

"*My heart is pierced by Cupid; I disdain all glittering gold...*" Ollamh tried again, then wandered away, frowning.

Briar stayed where she was until Ethan's gaze found her through the green needles, piercing. Amused.

"I do not disdain all glittering gold," she announced. Like an absolute turnip.

She emerged from the hedge as though jumping into the bushes to avoid a sea shanty was a perfectly normal thing to do. As if she wasn't blushing to the roots of her hair for no reason at all. Ethan still had not said a word. She could not decide if that made it better or so much worse.

Groaning, she brushed needles off her sleeve and marched with renewed determination to the village square. White pennants were strung from window to window of the houses lining the cobbles, because Haven was Haven, no matter the festival. Even in the gloom of Samhain, when ghosts were known to join and red was the color of protection, the pennants were white. White as the houses, the carriages, the bathing machine. White as bone, white as salt. White as the moon.

At least some enterprising soul had added yellow ribbons between the pennants, and they fluttered cheerfully in the salt breeze. The locals who considered themselves anyone at all wore white as well. The tourists had on every color, heavy on yellow for the Summer Solstice. Briar wore her usual apron over her dress. It was sewn with dozens of pockets for seeds and cuttings and her silver boline. The curved knife blade was best for cutting sacred plants, such as St. John's wort, without draining the magic or harming the plant. There was mud on her, and stains of green. Not quite the pristine muslins and silk flowers of Haven ladies. She had not let that bother her in ages. She wouldn't now. Anyway, no one was looking at her. They were used to green witches and shopkeepers.

They were *not* used to the Dragon.

He could not have been more incongruous in his open-necked lawn shirt, no cravat to be seen, only chest hair and the edge of a swallow's-wing tattoo. Wild against the civilized and forced genteelness of Haven. There were scars on his hands, a dagger in his boot. Next to him, the embroidered handkerchief and jeweled shoe buckles were ridiculous. All spun sugar and no substance. Even the Asters' glamours could not compete.

And how that would infuriate them.

"What are you smiling at?" Ethan asked her.

Briar glanced away from Charles, petulant and jealous when the ladies caught sight of Ethan and stopped listening to Charles's sales pitches and compliments. Who could blame them?

"There's the devil in that smile," Ethan added.

She shrugged because he was very likely correct. And at least no one was singing about Cupid and jolly sailors. "Mr. Swansea," she said in lieu of a parting, "happy Midsummer."

His eyes snapped to her, flashing with what looked very much like insult. Outrage, even. "*Mr. Swansea?*" he repeated, and there was something dangerous in his voice.

She blinked. "It's your name, isn't it?" Was he trying to be anonymous? Because there was no pretending he wasn't an Iron Crow, never mind Dragon, the most infamous Iron Crow of them all.

He muttered something but she did not quite catch it.

Probably for the best.

She left him leaning against the stone wall and glowering, and went to her stall. It was in the corner, under a striped lavender awning. Her locked trunk waited under the table, and she made quick work of setting out her wares, little wreaths made of willow twigs and decorated with wheat stalks, yellow roses. Mint for healing, roses for love, St. John's wort and lavender for the customary solstice blessings.

The square had been scrubbed to shining brightness, freshly whitewashed, the fountain scoured free of moss and algae. Someone had glamoured the mermaid statues so that their eyes followed you. Stalls lined the edges, selling everything from strawberry wine and potato-leek pasties to witching supplies such as keys and evil-eye beads and crystals, and the ubiquitous rowanberries and iron nails. Ink made with crushed pearls. Mermaid scales that came in with the tide. Unicorn mane strands from the only stable in England. Water gathered from the footprint of a wolf. Fairy fruits only a fool would eat.

The great oak tree stood in the center, majestic branches heavy with leaves. The triple spiral of Lyonesse had been drawn on the trunk in white chalk. It was the oldest tree in the village, aside from the ancient yew in the churchyard. The atmosphere was cheerful and lively, even with the threat of the locked shields. A fiddler played a jaunty drinking song not usually heard in Haven but still welcome under the circumstances.

The smell of roses wafted toward Briar. There was a profusion growing from a row of urns outside the haberdashery, more climbing up the inn's stable roof. Something about them tickled at her witch knot.

"Have you tried the strawberry-honey mead?" Basil asked from the stall next to hers. He sold bells in brass, silver, and iron, used to summon fairy deer, or to banish pixies who had gotten into the wine cellar. Certain ghosts did not like the sound either. "Best batch yet!"

"John will be happy to hear that." He brewed the village mead, competing fiercely with his brother, Grant, who made the wine. It was a delicious rivalry for everyone else, if rather more bloodthirsty for the brothers. Three years ago the meadery had been cursed with boggarts. Boggarts caused chaos, enjoying destruction. And the odd spot of murder. They weren't as dangerous as Redcaps, but they were kissing cousins. Then the vineyards came down with a suspicious case of a mold that made everyone within a league sneeze uncontrollably. After the fire, they were forbidden from setting foot on each other's land by order of the mayor, the Order of the Iron Nail, and Haven's beautification council.

"Try some of mine." Basil tipped some from his bottle into a shell.

The mead was sweet but not heavy on her tongue, and bright with berries. "That *is* the best one yet."

"Don't tell Grant. His strawberry wine isn't moving as well this year."

"I wouldn't dare."

It was hard not to keep glancing back at Ethan, hard not to be aware of him even across the crowded square. He didn't look in her direction, which was as expected. But everyone certainly looked *his* way. Concern, fear, curiosity, interest, lust. It was all there, like honeybees spotting the hive. Even the mayor, in her gold chain of office hung with charms, could not hold attention so easily. And she wore glamours the way a May Queen wore a flower crown. From Aster Apothecary, naturally.

"Did you see what happened earlier?" Basil asked. "All of the moonwater in the apothecary exploded!"

"Did it?" Not just in Briar's cottage, then. It was somewhat of a relief.

That relief was very short lived.

The crowd parted briefly, affording Briar a glimpse of the far side of the square and the green hillock just beyond it. The portal stood there as it had for several centuries, a red door opened seemingly to nothing. But when activated, the empty space shimmered and one could step through into London proper, or Edinburgh or Dublin. It had been hung with garlands of flowers and leaves before it was locked. It was now surrounded by a circle of white stones and iron nails stabbed into the grass to ground the considerable magic of a portal gone unpredictable.

It was also surrounded with Keepers, serious of face, eyes searching for guilty witches. Or warlocks, though they were rare on the island. A cart waited nearby, equipped with the Order's iron chains and collars that trapped a witch's magic inside herself. Jet stones gleamed at the cross-points of the bars. Briar shivered and looked away.

Unfortunately right at Oliver, and worse, he noticed. He glared in her direction, the jet-and-iron pendant around his neck catching the sunlight. Briar's witch knot began to itch on her palm. The heavy, grim presence of the Keepers and the knowledge that some kind of unknown magic had locked the shields cast ripples of unease through the festivities. There was a determination to act as though everything was perfectly normal, but it was hard won.

"Mrs. Aster near threw a fit, I don't mind telling you," Basil continued. "She had shelves and shelves of moonwater. Charles nearly lost an eye from a shard."

Mrs. Aster would take it as a personal affront and dedicate herself to finding the culprit. There was no proof that it was Petal. At least, not directly. She had already been in her swoon, after all. Indirectly...

Mrs. Aster was currently overseeing the table set up just outside of her shop, brimming with tasteful bottles of scents with matching ribbons, all glamours of one kind of another. For beauty, power, whiter teeth, sweeter breath. They were *very* popular. All the year long. She did not have to rely on festivals. Haven's official Keeper, Mr. St. John, lingered nearby, an Aster glamour already in his pocket. Everyone knew he favored the ones that made the calves look thicker.

Basil glanced furtively from the corner of his eye. "Briar?"

"Yes?"

"Do you have any of those love charms?"

"I'm sorry, Basil, you know my mother made those."

"I know. I just thought..."

"I don't have the knack of it like she did." If she had, the debt would not be an issue pressing on her. Her most serious issue before Petal went and stole the moon for her beloved.

It might have been romantic if it wasn't such a mess.

Briar did a reasonably brisk business despite her unseemly ogling of an Iron Crow, selling wreaths to tourists and also to more familiar faces. Mr. Field, the butcher, the Weatherby sisters. Even Bear bought a circlet of dried sunflowers and said nothing more about her sister.

It was going well enough, considering.

At least until Mrs. Aster noticed.

She did not care for Briar to do well. She knew Briar relied on festivals like this one. Mrs. Aster nodded in her direction, while whispering to one of her customers. Mrs. Poplar stopped for her usual wreath of forget-me-nots in honor of her late beau some thirty years gone, until she noticed Mrs. Aster and then smiled weakly at Briar before walking away, coins still firmly in her hand. Even the tourists noticed the tension and began to avoid her stall. Basil drifted to the far side of his table, sweating.

Briar sighed, wishing she was more surprised, but the Asters were doubling their efforts to claim her cottage and her gardens. Scents and lotions required flowers and herbs, and a green witch's garden was an asset. Her mother had leveraged that desire poorly, unfortunately.

Never mind. Briar had a sister and a moon charm to worry about today. And the dancing was about to start. When the sun had reached its zenith, the fiddle player was joined by a bodhran player, a flautist, and two more fiddlers. As the music picked up, the crowd made three concentric circles around the oak tree. They began to dance, alternating circles going sunwise and widdershins.

Above them, familiars sparkled like shooting stars. Owls, hawks, sparrows, pigeons. And even further above them, three phoenixes circled, tails scattering sparks. Lyonesse was one of the only places where they still lived wild, safe in the hilltops and the caves.

There was laughter and shouts of excitement as the dancers went around, faster and faster. Even from the old ladies in their fine pearls and the men in the starchiest of cravats. The oak branches swayed, ribbons and flower wreaths twirling.

They were dancing too fast for Briar to keep up with her unpredictable hip. And anyway, she needed to slip away, and this was as good a time as any. No one would notice. Even the Asters had joined in the circle dancing. Bramble's magic was strong, but she couldn't protect Petal alone. Not forever.

Briar slipped away from the merry crowd, hurrying up the cobblestone road to home.

## Chapter Thirteen

M R. *SWANSEA*.
Ethan couldn't have said why it infuriated him to his bones to have Briar address him so politely. So formally. Never mind that no one had called him *Mr.* Swansea in years. He was Dragon.

He wanted to hear his name on her lips.

It was addlepated of him. But also true. No use denying it. She was all wrong for him and he couldn't keep his damned eyes off her regardless. Partly because he knew Crows and Keepers were also watching her and he'd have that moon charm first. He had that cargo on his ship that he needed to get to Lowestoft, and a mermaid who had promised him a song he could bottle. He had the work of an Iron Crow. The call of the sea.

Even if Briar was dangerously intriguing. Quiet and brave, saucy and polite. Surprisingly sensual, with that thick hair scattered with flowers and those delicious curves. Soft, sharp.

And just a little bit sad.

He saw it when the villagers turned awkward around her, fluttering about in their white dresses and pearls. In the way she smiled politely through it. It made him want to burn the square down.

Starting with Aster. *Useless git.* The way he smirked at her made it a fact that he was going to end with broken teeth before Ethan left the island. Before the end of the day, if it came to it. Aster and his mother were trying to wear her down like water wore through stone.

Ethan watched Briar nod off, just for a moment, the strain and exhaustion of the last two days taking its toll. Who was taking care of her? Who was making sure she ate and rested her hip, which clearly pained her? Had she had an accident to cause such a lasting wound? Was there someone still out there who needed to pay for it?

Why were those questions wrapping around his brain like a kraken around a ship?

It was none of his business. He needed Petal, not Briar.

Still. There was a connection there, a fascination. His entire body felt the need to turn toward her, to fill his lungs with her flowery scent, his hands with her warm curves. His mouth with her everything.

The interruption by one of his crew was timely. It saved him from doing something truly stupid. Like finding a Midsummer posy for the teashop girl.

Young Matthias had never looked happier, his feet on solid ground, his arms full of fresh greens, eggs, bread that wasn't hard as the ship's hull. It had been months since he'd come aboard as cook and exactly the same number of days that made it obvious he was not a sailor at heart. But he refused to give in. And he made the best damn jugged hare with red wine and juniper berries, which made more of a difference to morale than anyone could have guessed, so the crew coddled him. But he'd end up at the bottom of the sea as a mermaid's plaything if they weren't careful.

"Dragon, they have fresh thyme. Do you know how long it's been since we've had thyme? Fresh herbs of any kind?"

"Thrilling."

"You *will* be thrilled when you taste the omelets I can make with this. Maybe I'll make a mushroom tart to go with them." His blue eyes took on a dreamy, faraway look. Something else that would get him killed. The life of an Iron Crow was no kinder than the life of a sailor.

"First, I need to know about this bloody town we're stuck in," Ethan said.

Matthias straightened. "Of course. I thought you'd been here before."

"Too many times," Ethan muttered. Matthias was good at cookery and gossip. Even his familiar, an otter with glowing eyes and a chortle, was friendly. Ethan was neither. "I need to know about the Asters over there."

Matthias followed the direction of his nod, then frowned. "Gits."

Ethan snorted. "I knew that already. We need to sort the locals from the tourists. And I need to know who went wandering last night. And a list of the other bloody Crows hanging about."

"Aye, Dragon."

Ethan watched Briar slip away, darting back up the hill, flowers blooming in her wake.

And he needed to know about *her*.

But that was a task he would take great pleasure in seeing to himself.

THE LEFT SIDE of the cottage was being swallowed by roses.

Vines crawled up the wall, bristling with thorns and heavy with fat white damask roses. They perfumed the air until even the salt of the sea was overpowered. Salt white, bone white.

Moon-white.

And they would not respond to Briar's magic. They were *ignoring* her. Which was just rude, frankly. Snapdragon, often disgruntled, was positively insulted.

Briar let herself inside and everything was quiet and smelled of mint and tea and lilac flowers. And roses. But nothing seemed immediately out of place. "Bramble?" she called up the stairs. "Have you noticed the roses?"

Which were utterly forgotten when she caught movement on the other side of the glass.

Not Bramble. She would never be caught out like that. Her

magic turned her to mist and smoke, just another part of the scenery. Briar knew the back door was secure—and none of her house shields had alerted her of any intruders.

They didn't have the time.

Her front door burst open, slamming into the wall.

Ethan was crowned with the blazing light behind him, his face in shadows. There was something cold and vicious about the glitter of his eyes. The dagger in his hand. He had crossed the hall in the time it took for her to frown at him. She stumbled back into the teashop as the back door also crashed open. She didn't have a chance to reach for a weapon, even if she had one to reach for. Instead, there was only a jar of dried rosebuds, a locked box of Darjeeling tea, a potted violet. A tray of ivy cuttings. A metal tea leaf strainer in the shape of a dove.

She was truly a threat to all.

And then Ethan was on her, fingers digging into the hair at the nape of her neck. His grip was firm but not painful, but nor did it allow for any defiance on her part. "What are you—?"

Her words died in her throat, at the exact spot he pressed his dagger against.

She froze. Her heart beat loudly. Ethan was too strong, too fierce. She had begun to think of him as if not a friend, then at least an ally. She'd been working on nothing more than instinct. Hope.

*Fool.*

She shifted onto her good hip, wondering if she could kick back into his kneecap.

"Don't." His voice was barely a breath in her ear, a quiet warning only she could hear. It shivered down her spine.

A woman stalked into the shop, the leather strap between her breasts hung with charms and daggers. The mark of an Iron Crow. She was short, strong enough to take out an ox. She had muscles, graying hair in a thick braid, and a Black Shuck on an iron chain wrapped with nettles and Lady's Mantle. Its folk name was Nine Hooks for a reason.

Briar hissed out a breath. Black Shucks resembled giant, shaggy dogs, with too many teeth, fiery eyes, and the ability to make you mad with terror with only three barks. They were meant to be wild, roaming the moors and eating the wind. Not trapped. Ensnared in iron. If Sorcha were here, she would find a way to free the poor beast.

Briar wanted to do the same, but mostly she hoped it would not eat her.

Black Shucks were not tame or gentle, and this one had bloody welts from the iron chains pockmarking his fur. He snapped his jaws, saliva dripping in thick strings to the floor. Where they fell, the wooden boards smoked, burned through.

"Twyla," Ethan greeted the woman calmly, as if they were meeting in the square, under the oak tree. As if they were drinking tepid lemonade at a ball, which Briar could not imagine. There was nothing tepid about the undercurrents.

Or the blade still at her throat.

She was not entirely certain the sharpness of the very air would not cut her before the dagger. Ethan angled it slightly, tilting Briar's head back. She made a choked sound of protest and clutched at his arm, but it was useless. She may as well have been clutching at the mast of his ship for all the good it did her.

The Black Shuck growled, and every hair on Briar's body prickled as if they had turned to needles. "Call off your mutt," Ethan said. "And may he eat your liver for what you've done to him."

Twyla snorted. "I've seen what *you* can do, Dragon."

Everyone knew the stories, even green witches who lived in pink cottages: stolen grimoires, duels at dawn. Victims tossed over the side of his ship to be eaten by the kelpies, their water-horse teeth smeared with blood.

Ethan smiled. Briar felt it against the top of her head.

It was not comforting.

"Then you'll remember that you don't want to fight me, Twyla," he said evenly. "Leave while you still can."

"I want the moon charm."

"Don't we all."

"That one has it." Twyla nodded to Briar even as she released another foot of chain. The Black Shuck advanced, eyes red.

"You've got the wrong sister."

The right sister was upstairs, unconscious in her bed.

"And anything they have belongs to me, Twyla. Cut your losses and I might let you leave with both your arms."

"You won't kill her if she still knows something."

Ethan's retort was flat, chilling. "You know me well enough to know that I'll kill her before I let any of her secrets go to you or another fucking Crow."

Twyla paused. She clearly believed him.

Ethan turned his head, dragging his mouth along Briar's temple and into her hair. She shivered. "And this one especially is mine. She tastes like mint leaves."

Somehow he made it sound like a threat.

While their magic seared the air, spiky with the scents of salt and fennel seeds, vibrating with the snarls of the Black Shuck, Petal was vulnerable. Hiding her in plain sight was a fine idea when Keepers were watching and there had been no other options, but now?

Nowhere near good enough.

"I'm Pet—" Briar's declaration was cut short when Ethan tightened his grip.

The dagger nicked at her. Her feet left the ground entirely as he hauled her up against his chest. "Quiet," he ordered her, dark and menacing as the flash of a sea serpent under the waves. There was nothing of Mr. Swansea about him. Nor even Ethan. He was the Dragon, through and through. She could only gasp.

And then Twyla let go of the iron chain.

# Chapter Fourteen

THE BLACK SHUCK lunged.

He was even larger when he was coming directly at you, teeth gleaming, eyes flashing. The teacups rattled under the force of his growling. Panic crawled up Briar's throat, choking her.

Ethan twisted, spinning her out of his arms as if they were dancing. She skidded toward the counter, catching her bad hip. Ethan did not hesitate; even as he had spun her, he had taken another dagger—this one made of iron—from his belt. He slammed it into the floor.

Magic exploded, the familiar salt-and-fennel smell momentarily overpowering the acrid blister of the Black Shuck's breath, too close, too close.

But Ethan's shield held.

The Black Shuck hit a wall of witching energy and fell back, paws scrabbling. His saliva hit the corner of Briar's apron, sizzling through the thick cloth.

"Get behind the counter," Ethan snapped. A single iron dagger shield would not last long. They needed a coven of bog witches, swords forged on Samhain. A feather plucked from the tail of a gryphon. None of which Briar stocked next to the chamomile and the apple-mint tea.

Twyla cursed, throwing her own knives. Ethan slapped one away before it could pierce his eyeball.

When three Keepers thundered down the hall, it was not an improvement.

An oil painting of cliff grasses under a storm fell off a nail and crashed to the floor. Something else shattered in the kitchen.

"By order of the—Gah!" Oliver, because of course he was the one to lead the Keepers into her cottage, broke off with a choked yelp when the Black Shuck turned his head and barked. The teacups shivered more violently in their saucers. The violet flowers in the clay pot closed up on themselves.

"Fucking mayhem," Ethan muttered at Briar. "Are you sure you're not part demon?"

"This wasn't my idea! None of you were invited here!"

"Just stay the hell down."

As she had no intention of having her throat ripped out by a Black Shuck—*or* sliced by a knife, she thought pointedly in Ethan's direction—Briar stayed down.

She had never had occasion to witness a true magical battle. She battled slugs and root-rot and pixies who stole the foxglove flowers to drink out of because it intensified the effect of mead. Haven mostly dealt with complaints about the hotel beds, glamours, the cost of pearls. John and Grant fighting over their competing businesses. Once, the mayor and a duchess came to blows inside the fountain over a game of magical pall-mall. And her mother had dealings with irate spouses on a regular basis, but Petal's face usually softened much of their ire.

A proper magical battle was messy.

Even without a Black Shuck. He rippled with power and rancor. Briar could hardly blame him. Usually, salt and iron were used to stop most magic in its tracks. It worked for village witches and cunning men and charm-singers.

It was not quite enough to stop a Crow.

Or a Keeper, regrettably.

They worked with iron on a regular basis, using it against each other so often that while a scatter of iron nails on the floor was enough to make Briar's green magic hesitate, it was not nearly enough to make the others pause. They had so much more experience pushing through the pain and the prowl of power.

Briar gritted her teeth. She had her own skills pushing through the pain. Let them deal with a dodgy hip on a daily basis and see how well they fared.

But in the end, they did not fight with spells. Instead, it was daggers and fists and a great deal of trying to avoid the giant, angry magical dog. Snapdragon vanished inside her chest, tucking his feathers in.

The Keepers split their focus between Twyla and Ethan. The Black Shuck did not appear to care whom he mauled, as long as he got blood in his mouth. And throughout it all, Ethan was dark and calm, like a shadow in a garden on a hot day. A place to retreat to, a storm cloud that might drive you indoors but would also steal away the scorching heat. His dagger caught Twyla in the thigh when she tossed a charm in Briar's direction.

Oliver tried to stab Ethan and hit the wall instead, blood streaming from his nose. Two teapots crashed to the ground.

The Black Shuck snapped his jaws at one of the Keepers, knocking over a chair in the process.

Twyla threw a potted ficus.

The tearoom would not survive much more of this.

And even without the use of spells, the cacophony was attracting boggarts.

Briar saw the quick shadows, heard the telling, raspy giggling from the hydrangeas. The bells on the door handle and the wind chimes in the trees would not be enough to keep them out, not from this. They consumed wayward witchcraft as well as freshly baked loaves of bread left unattended, the last best bit of the stew in the pot, the freshest cream. But they loved mayhem best of all.

Haven worked hard to keep boggarts from the streets and the back gardens and the beaches. They were mischievous, hungry creatures who sowed chaos and dissent. They undid knots, tangled skeins, mixed up the potions and the poisons on the shelf. They were exceedingly dangerous in the kitchen of a green witch.

And one of them crouched on her threshold, short and wrinkled, and cackling. Behind it, an oak tree branch cracked, falling and cleaving a table in two.

Not in her house.

And not in her bloody garden.

She might not be able to take down the Order or an Iron Crow, but she could do *something*. Even if it was with rose-petal honey and a fistful of flowers. A few herbs, a silver boline. She needed everyone to get the hell out of her house.

Immediately.

She stayed on her hands and knees, reaching up for one of the ivy clippings and a teacup. She dropped the ivy in the cup, and added bits of amber, remembering a honeybee she had once seen trapped in an amber egg in a museum in Hallow. She needed something more, something with kick.

Ethan stabbed down, slicing through Oliver's sleeve. Blood spattered. His silver crow claw and hagstone tangled around his neck. His silver rings flashed. So did the amulets hanging from his cross-belt and the leather pouches at his hip. And the glass vial with a single strand of dark hair, the color of wet seaweed and glittering with magic.

One did not grow up on a magical island and not learn to recognize a strand of mermaid's hair.

She darted forward, then waited for him to smash his dagger down on the other Keeper's knife, sending it clattering to the floor. She pivoted and tugged the bottle free. When she popped the top off, she was immediately inundated with the sound of the sea on the sand, the taste of salt, a song she could not quite make out, but she knew someone was singing it just for her. Mermaid magic. She remembered it from that day on the beach with Petal.

It could fill a witch's mouth with seawater until they drowned.

But used in a binding spell, it could also strengthen every aspect of the work.

She wrapped it around the ivy and covered it all with honey. Thick, glistening honey that was too dear to waste. It stuck and held the ivy fast. She whispered over it, the way she whispered to her plants, "Bind them fast."

She crawled to the edge of the counter, peeking out. Magic and blood clogged the air. Three more teacups had broken. Her mother's statue of Aphrodite, made entirely of seashells, lay in shards.

"*Enough,*" Briar said.

It was as good an incantation as any spell written in any ancient grimoire.

Because she meant it. To the depths of her soul.

She threw the teacup. It shattered, yet more crockery she would have to replace. She would be serving tea in seashells if this kept up. Assuming she even had a tearoom left to run.

That desperation, more than anything, added fuel to the spell.

The ivy vines shot out of the cup, gleaming with honey. They reached the Black Shuck first, then the Keepers, Twyla, and, finally, Ethan. The green tendrils were not strong enough to hold anyone in place on their own—that was for the imbued honey to do, and the whisper of Briar's desperate magic, the strand of mermaid hair.

The sudden silence rang in her ears.

Oliver reached for his jet pendant, but he was moving too slowly. The honey and the ivy were already doing their work. The other Keeper struggled, the tendons of his neck swelling with effort, all to no avail. The last Keeper, who did not look like a Keeper at all, merely looked curious, as if he would have taken notes if he could have. Twyla ground out a curse, but there was no magic available to make it real.

Briar pulled herself to her feet. "You lot have no manners at all," she declared, thoroughly disgruntled.

While they remained stuck, she limped toward the Black Shuck. He was also straining against the honey spell. His teeth really did resemble knives from this close up, breath fetid like smoke and bog water. Briar reached for the chain around his neck, and he growled. She tensed. "I don't like this either, I assure you. So don't make such a fuss."

"Briar," Ethan warned softly. He was the only one not fighting the spell, the only one waiting patiently to spring into action. And he was still the only one who looked properly menacing.

It didn't stop her from replying, "Hush, I'm busy."

She would pay for that remark later, she had no doubt. She felt it in the narrowing of his eyes.

The iron chain was cold, the kind of unnatural cold that burned. The Black Shuck's growl faded to a whimper. "I know," she said. "We're going to get this horrid thing off you."

"Don't you dare!" Twyla struggled, sweat beading her brow. "It took me months to break him."

"Just count yourself lucky I don't let him eat you," Briar snapped. She hoped the same for herself, if she was honest. This was not her most clever plan, but it had to be done. Quickly. The spell would not last much longer. "It's no less than you deserve."

"He's mine."

"He belongs to the moors," Briar returned. She pulled the chain free of the Black Shuck, his fur matted and snarled with dried blood. "Don't eat me, if you please."

She pushed against him with her entire body weight, aiming him toward the door into the garden. With any luck, instinct would carry him in that direction and not toward the others. The chains she carried to Twyla, looping them around her shoulders. Her fingers felt frostbitten already. Twyla cursed at her.

"Briar, don't let her touch you. Back away from her," Ethan ordered her quietly. "*Now.*"

Briar, though current evidence might suggest otherwise, was not a fool. She backed away hastily.

"Behind me," Ethan said. "Quickly."

Oliver had managed to finally pull his jet pendant from his neck. It had already cracked, absorbing the wild magic lashing the air. He let a shard fall and ground it into the ivy with the heel of his boot.

Her makeshift spell severed.

The Black Shuck streaked through the open door and leapt over the potted geraniums, and the far stone wall, before the others could fully pull themselves free. The boggarts screeched and fled, leaving a trail of shredded leaves and flattened grasses.

Twyla staggered under the weight of her spelled chains, turning pale. She had no time to wriggle free, no magic left to help her. She went down to her knees. One of the Keepers followed, pressing a jet pendant to her chest. She choked.

"The entrapment of magical creatures without a license is quite illegal," the man in the buff trousers with a pocket watch said dispassionately. "You'll be kept until you can be tried for your crimes."

He was clearly not a Keeper, but they obeyed him as though he was. Oliver snapped an iron collar around Twyla's neck. Twyla shuddered, going even paler.

When Briar also shuddered, Ethan stepped in front of her. The tearoom was full of the sounds of witches trying to catch their breaths. There was blood on the floor. The acid breath of the Black Shuck lingered, as did the scorched smell of salt and fennel and the sticky sweetness of honey.

And a lady at the back door, squeaking in surprise. There were dahlias on her bonnet.

Briar sent her a shopkeeper's smile, weary at the edges. "I am afraid we are closed this morning."

# Chapter Fifteen

WHEN HER ONE customer had fled, no doubt to tell the rest of Haven that The Rose and Petal was in shambles and its proprietress was sprawled on the floor with Keepers and Iron Crows, Ethan helped Briar to her feet. He turned to the vaguely academic-looking man.

"What the hell are you doing here, Coventry?"

Briar frowned up at him. "You know him?"

"Aye."

"Aidan Hunt, London Museum of Magic," the man introduced himself.

*Bollocks.*

"Lord Coventry," Ethan elaborated without even a drop of respect for the title. Unsurprisingly.

Aidan stepped over Twyla as though she had ceased to be interesting. "I am in charge of rare antiquities for the museum."

*Bollocks again.*

Even if she wanted to run, she could not. Petal was upstairs. And her hip was currently shooting pain down her leg with a vengeance. She would be lucky to remain upright for the remainder of this conversation.

Aidan pulled a piece of parchment from inside his waistcoat and unfolded it. The sketch was detailed, but also artistic in a way she would not have expected from someone who wore such precise spectacles and whose cravat was still pristine when the rest of them were smudged with dirt and sweat. "Have you seen this?" he asked.

She could honestly say she had not. She had not even known what the moon charm looked like until now. It was an egg-shaped moonstone set inside a cage of silver filigree studded with pearls. It was much smaller than she had imagined. It loomed so large that she supposed she had expected it to be the size of an actual egg. Perhaps from a goose. Or a gryphon.

"I have not," she said. "Is this why you're here?"

"Yes. This is the moon egg charm. It was originally found in Suffolk. It dates back to the sixteenth century."

"And it dropped the shields? What else does it do?" That seemed like something she ought to know. The next time Petal went off on a wild tear, she had better leave detailed and copious notes.

"We don't know," Aidan admitted. That was surprising. And considerably unhelpful.

Ethan, however, did not look surprised.

"Likely not much, as it's been stored in salt and iron over the years when not on display," Aidan continued. "Just to be safe."

"Then how did it drop the shields?"

"The tracking spell from the museum was triggered when the charm was stolen by one Miss Petal Foxglove."

"I'm sure I don't know what you mean. My sister would *never*." Except when she would, of course.

He frowned. "The tracking spell led me here. And that spell is never wrong. I devised it myself." He did not sound particularly arrogant, only very sure. Like one of the professors who had seen too many decades in the academies of Hallow.

"If you cast the spell, can you not uncast it? If it is not working as it should be?"

"Apparently not."

"That is disappointing."

"Indeed. Can you tell me, Miss Foxglove, why your sister would steal this particular moon charm from the museum? It might help."

Briar tilted her chin up. "You claim that she stole it, but I am not convinced. My sister has never been to London before, and she has no need for a moon egg." She crossed her arms. "And if your spell is misfiring, how do you know this is not all *your* doing? A misunderstanding laid at my sister's feet as a convenient scapegoat."

Ethan grunted, a low rumble of amusement. She refused to look in his direction.

"I wish I could help you, Lord Coventry," she added. "But I'm afraid I don't know anything."

"She's lying," Oliver spat.

"You're very rude," she said calmly. And quite correct, unfortunately. She had every intention of continuing to lie her face off if it would help her sister.

"Then you'll submit to testing," he added.

She did not know what that might entail exactly, only that the Order was not known for being gentle. Sweat broke out at the nape of her neck.

"The hell she will," Ethan said with the kind of icy calm that could not be breached. He'd had his dagger to her throat minutes before, and now he seemed to want to protect her.

He really was a very confusing man.

"This is business of the Order, Crow."

Ethan smiled, and it was sharp and deadly, as sharp and deadly as the dagger in his hand. "That's Dragon to you."

Oliver gulped. He tried to hide it, but Briar noticed. And she did not care how petty it made her—she enjoyed the sight. He was a pain in her backside in a way that only a Keeper with something to prove could be. She hoped Bear would arrive soon to keep him in order. Or better yet, let them decide that Petal had made her way to Hallow or Holdfast. Or the actual moon. Anywhere but right here, in the room above their heads.

Aidan held up a hand. "The spell led me here. There's no need to test Miss Foxglove. A simple search of the cottage will do."

"We'll take another look in her bedroom." Oliver smiled, and it made Briar a little sick to her stomach.

She could only follow as they marched up the stairs, helplessness choking her.

Oliver kicked Petal's bedroom door open.

Briar waited for the shout of triumph, for an iron collar, the suffocation of her familiar trapped in a witch's bottle. For Bramble to attack with her scissors, her teeth. She didn't know how she could fight her way to her sister's side, or even what to do when she got there.

A tree branch knocked loudly on the roof. Warning or comfort? She could not say.

"Nice work," Ethan said, all sarcasm and boredom as he looked over their heads. "An empty bedroom. Nothing less than I'd expect from a Keeper."

Oliver sputtered, face reddening. Briar inched closer. Petal's bed lay empty, quilt rumpled. Bramble was also gone. The white roses pressed against the window, thorns dragging like claws. Oliver stomped around, knocking over books, pulling dresses out of Petal's armoire. But there was no Petal and no moon egg.

Briar sagged against the doorjamb. She had no idea what was happening, but at least her sister was not being carted away in iron chains soaked in salt water for her familiar to be bottled. That was something. Everything. And neither was Briar.

Yet.

"If you are quite done stomping through my house in your muddy boots," she said crisply to cover the unease still bubbling through her. "You can all see yourselves out."

Sometimes all you could do was snap orders like a disappointed governess and hope for the best.

Seeing as most Keepers had been raised by nannies and governesses of one type or another, it was surprisingly effective. Oliver's neck mottled even redder. Aidan looked embarrassed. Ethan just leaned against the back wall of the hall, one eyebrow lifted. If he had been raised by a governess, the lessons had not taken. But he was not the one she was trying to get rid of.

Briar looked down her nose at Oliver, which did take some doing, as he was much taller than she. "I will expect the Order to reimburse me for the mess you made. Teacups do not grow on trees."

He glowered around the room once more. "Are you *sure* it's not her?" he demanded of Aidan while pointing at Briar. "The Foxglove sisters are twins."

"We are not identical," Briar said drily. "Believe me, it is not hard to tell the difference."

"I saw Petal Foxglove with my own two eyes." Aidan was apologetic, clearly mortified to have been impolite in any way, but also not convinced that he was in the wrong. He was obviously very good at his work as a curator of magical artifacts. He knew something was amiss, but not *what*, exactly. It would have to be good enough for now.

Oliver shoved past them toward the stairs. "We'll be watching you, Miss Foxglove."

"I can't tell you how safe that makes me feel," Briar said, deliberately misunderstanding his threat. "But as you are the one causing me the most harm, I would prefer it if you found my sister instead," she added, not preferring any such thing. "She might be in danger."

"We're not in the business of protecting thieves."

Ethan caught her gaze. "But I am."

Aidan was still frowning. He bowed his head at her. "I do apologize for his behavior."

"You get what you deserve when you keep company with that lot," Ethan said.

"It's protocol," Aidan's serious eyes were wry. "Can't say keeping company with Iron Crows will do you much good either, Miss Foxglove."

"Probably not," Briar replied, the spot of blood on her throat stinging in agreement.

She stayed rooted to the spot as the Keepers collected Twyla and Aidan made another circuit of the cottage before leaving. She heard him gently close the front door.

"He'll be back," Ethan said, having not moved an inch.

A sound came from the window before Briar could find a reply. She half expected to see the rose vines cracking the glass, but it was the tap of iron scissors. *Tap, tap, tap.*

Bramble's iron scissors.

Briar surged forward, pushing her magic at the vines and the thorns hard enough that they parted. Her witch knot burned. Her swan bellowed in pain. Briar kept pushing, sweat beading under her hair.

Petal's bare feet dangled from the rooftop.

Ethan was suddenly at her side. He reached up, grabbing her sister by the hips and pulling her inside. Petal unfurled on the floor, as limp and unresponsive as she had been all along. It must have taken Herculean strength for Bramble to pull her out of the window and onto the roof. Not just strength—panic.

Bramble slipped into the bedroom, snarling and covered in bloody thorn scratches. She crouched over Petal, wielding her scissors, magic biting the air around her. Ethan towered over them, his dagger in hand.

Briar slipped between them, panting with the exhaustion of pushing her magic through whatever spell had fueled the roses, and the honey spell below. Her vision blurred around the edges. "Don't." She was speaking to both of them.

Ethan did not move, staring down at her unconscious sister. "The infamous Petal, I presume."

$$\textbf{Chapter Sixteen}$$

"*I'LL KILL YOU, Crow.*"

Bramble did not speak much, but when she did, she did not mince words.

Briar crouched to gently push Petal's hair off her face. Thorn scratches marred her cheek. "He's…" What exactly was he again? Friend? Ally? Distraction? "Well, he's Dragon, and he's not here to harm her."

Bramble glared at him, clearly inspecting him, seeing things only a rabbit witch could see. Her shoulders finally lowered and she nodded once, tersely. "He smells like that's true. And not like lemon balm." Warlocks smelled of lemon balm, a soothing, pleasant scent meant to lure you in. "But he also smells like he can't be trusted."

Ethan inclined his head, unsmiling, and in complete agreement.

Briar was not sure what to make of that.

"He wants the shields lifted," she said. "And he wants them lifted before anyone else can mess about with them. So, at least in that, our goals align."

"For now," Bramble said as though he was not standing right there.

"For now," Briar agreed, as though he was standing exactly right there. "You're exhausted," she added softly. "Sit down and rest and I'll bring you something to eat while we figure out what to do next."

"Your sister can't stay here," Ethan said.

"I know," she replied evenly. The back of her throat burned. "Don't you think I know that?"

"Has she been here the whole time?"

Briar nodded.

"You *are* a surprise."

"Not really."

"Believe me, you are."

Briar decided not to comment on that. "To move her, I would need some sort of cart. And a horse. Neither of which I have. Not to mention a place to hide her."

"I can't take her to the burrow," Bramble said. "They've already sent Keepers to watch it. Even we can't hide when there's that many of them. And our secret places are too far, too hard to reach."

"I assumed as much. And Sorcha's castle is too far from here as well, unfortunately." Sorcha lived in her family's run-down castle in the hills. It was secluded enough to be safe, but it would take hours to get Petal there, with very little cover to hide them.

Briar made a sound of frustration. There had to be somewhere else.

"You could bring her to my ship."

Both Briar and Bramble turned to stare at Ethan. There was no way to read his expression. "Pardon?" Briar asked.

"There's not a person alive who can get onto my ship without my permission."

He was serious. Bramble tilted her head, staring at him again. "Good."

Briar blinked. "*Good?*"

Ethan nodded. "Then it's settled."

"Why would you help us?" Briar had to ask. She'd be a fool not to. And a fool to believe whatever he said.

"Like you said earlier: I need to get the hell off this island. Your sister is my best chance. And I don't trust the Order."

"Or the other Crows?"

"Hell no."

It was a logical reason. One she could trust more than whatever was burning between them. Her body might want to lean toward him like a sunflower following the sun, but that was no reason to trust him with her sister's life. Even if she did, somehow.

His own self-interest was a smarter thing to trust.

"But we should trust *you*?" she asked softly, regardless.

"Hell no," he said again. "But I don't mean your sister any harm."

"You held a dagger to my throat." And why had it given her a secret thrill? She clearly needed a cleansing. A bucket of salt. Iron shavings on her breakfast oats.

"I did."

"That's it? That's all you have to say?" She was outraged all over again. There had not been even a hint of apology.

"It was necessary."

"*Necessary?*" No one had ever made her screech in quite this manner before.

His mouth twitched as if he were aware of it, as if it might amuse him.

She began to contemplate murder.

He looked as though he was aware of that too.

"Twyla would have killed you on the spot if she thought there was any kindness between us."

Was that what was between them? Kindness? She didn't think so. It was too hungry for that, untamed and more tempting than sonnets and courtship rituals and kisses on the back of her hand. The pull made her limbs feel shivery and hot.

Ethan grunted. "And then you went and released her Black Shuck and all my efforts were wasted."

"Oh." She thought she might believe him. When she glanced at Bramble, she only shrugged.

"But we'll never get her out of here unseen," Briar said, back to the matter at hand. Back to what truly mattered. Petal. "Even if we take the cliff path, there's bound to be a Keeper lurking back there. And who knows where Lord Coventry is hiding."

"Coventry is too honorable to hide outside the house of a woman alone," Ethan said. "And you've got the very earth beneath our feet answering to you," he added. "I've got the sky and the sea. They can't see through the green and the storm. Not all at once."

It could work.

It *had* to work.

It was all they had.

Briar glanced again at Bramble, who watched him quietly. "And my sisters will help."

"They will?" Briar asked.

"As they can. Petal stole the moon to prove herself to them. To be my betrothed. She is one of us now."

Briar sighed. "That's all very romantic, but I do rather wish she had written you a sonnet instead."

But no one, not villager, not Keeper, not museum curator, would ever expect Petal Foxglove to be on the Dragon's ship.

Briar could not think of any place safer.

Which was odd.

She nodded. "It's nearly twilight. That will help as well."

And it gave her the time to fetch the basket of seashells: cockles, mussels, periwinkles, and scallops. And the painted top shell she was looking for. In London they used the Tabula Rasa spell, inking messages into parchment that showed up in the receiver's journal, or sometimes on their skin. But on the island, they used seashells. Mussels wrapped in silver thread trapped voices, snippets of songs, spoken memories. If you listened hard enough, you could hear a thousand secrets. But painted top shells linked whispers together, sending them far away. Sorcha had a shell of her own, spelled and connected to Briar's. Briar whispered into hers: *Black Shuck in the hills. Find him before the others can.*

The reply came quickly, an excited squeal: *Puppy!*

"Your friend is a menace," Ethan said, standing so close behind her that her skin felt electrified even though this definitely was *not* the time for that sort of nonsense.

Briar nodded. "One of us has to be."

He raised an eyebrow incredulously. "Do you think *you're* not a menace? Woman, you took on an Iron Crow whom even I don't care to fight, armed only with a teacup full of honey and a mermaid hair you nicked from my belt. Don't think I didn't notice that. And *then* you released a *Black Shuck*. Into your parlor. And told him not to fuss."

Something about the disbelief in his tone made her feel significantly better.

She really did need a good magical cleansing.

ETHAN LEFT TO secure a cart and Briar brought Bramble a basket of pasties made with potatoes and carrots and peas, a handful of pears and cherries, early for the regular season but not for Briar's orchard. She convinced her to sleep for the couple of hours that remained until twilight. Briar spent her time pacing between the windows, watching for Keepers or Iron Crows or museum curators. When Ethan returned, shrouded in storm clouds, she was tense as a bowstring. The road had fallen into the blue shadows of dusk. Rain hit the roof, spattered the windowpanes.

It was time.

A covered wagon trundled along the lane beside the cottage. It was painted blue with cheerful pennants and garlands of bright flowers. Yellow silk birds were attached to the roof by wires so it appeared as though a flock was continuously flying overhead. The horse was a village horse, sturdy and unbothered by magic. It was perfectly suited for the Midsummer Festival. It could easily be carrying casks of strawberry wine, a soothsayer arriving to read tea leaves, a carnival troupe.

But unlikely to be housing a wanted witch and criminal.

The driver jumped down, blond curls plastered to his head. Briar vaguely recognized him from Ethan's ship. He strode toward her, all friendly smiles. Were anyone watching, they would not have looked twice.

The rain beat down harder.

Briar gave the garden a little push, encouraging the branches and leaves to tangle low, the lilac bushes to stretch out, the hydrangea to spread.

Ethan climbed out of the wagon wearing a cloak that shadowed his face. He nodded to the driver and they ducked inside the tearoom. "This is Matthias," he said. "No one ever believes he's a Crow."

Matthias grinned. "I would take offense, but I'm afraid it's entirely true."

They carried Petal down the stairs gently, but swiftly. Briar and Bramble had wrapped her in a cloak of her own. The rain came down in silver lashes as they brought her into the cart. Thunder cracked, discouraging anyone from approaching the cottage, from looking too closely.

"I've left the bonfires on the beach alone," Ethan said. "So everyone will head down there. Except for the Keeper hidden across the street. He is not having a good time."

Bramble crouched to slap her palm against the earth three times, the way rabbits thumped their hind legs to warn of danger. "My sisters and their Jacks will lure anyone away from us."

Jackrabbits were even shier than rabbit witches, and twice as feral. Short of an actual invisibility spell, which was complicated and expensive and rarely worked as intended, they could not ask for a better guard. They climbed into the covered wagon and Briar pulled the door closed, palms sweaty.

Petal lay on the bench along one side, her head in Bramble's lap. Ethan sat next to Briar, like a shadow turned sharp and deadly. The wagon rumbled along the rough path through the grass, away from the village, cutting around to the far docks. The Sea Dragons had elected to dock away from the main festivities, even before her sister stole the moon.

The ship was as impressive as she remembered, with the tinkle of bewitched sea glass and the gleam of weapons. The dragon figurehead opened its jaw and blue sparks shot over the water, discouraging any approaching kelpies with thoughts of murder, as well as mermaids, also with thoughts of murder. The crew waited on deck, fierce and suspicious.

Briar swallowed, her throat dry. Was she quite mad to trust her sister to Iron Crows? Infamous ones at that? She glanced at Bramble, who had frozen, eyes narrowed. One breath, two. Finally, she nodded at Briar and turned back to oversee Matthias when he carried Petal from the back of the cart.

The rain fell harder, blurring the ship, the sea, the sand. Anyone who might be watching would only see water.

Briar hurried after them, slowing down on the plank so she did not slip. Her hip was rather cross with her. Ethan was at her back, warm and solid, fingers pressed to her lower spine. Was he pushing her forward? Or steadying her? She honestly did not know anymore.

"We've a guest," he said.

Briar saw Anais and Maleko of the tattooed chin. There was a woman with snakes for hair, a man with the legs of a satyr. She had never heard of a satyr who chose the sea. He winked at her. Satyrs were not known for their shyness. She blushed and she wasn't even sure why. He had not done anything untoward. A wink was hardly a proposition.

"Easy, Godric," Ethan rumbled.

When Petal's hood slid free, revealing her shining auburn hair and alabaster skin, the attention shifted dramatically. One of the sailors looked as though he'd just been hit in the head. Briar was very accustomed to that expression. Ethan, clearly, was not. "Get it together, man."

"She's like a fairy princess."

"Bollocks, just get going, idiot," Anais muttered.

"It's all right," Briar said. Bramble looked resigned, but also willing to stab anyone who lingered too near. "It happens all the time."

Bramble snorted.

"Not on my ship." Ethan's tone was hard. "Focus or I'll feed your guts to a kelpie."

"And who are you, love?" the satyr asked. It took Briar a moment to realize he was speaking to her and not her sleeping sister. His voice was like the wind through a cypress tree.

"The fairy princess's sister," Briar replied.

"She's one of us," Ethan added. The sailors exchanged glances. Briar's cheeks warmed. Why did that feel like the truest compliment he would ever give another? Probably because an actual fairy princess would affect him not at all.

Inexcusably, she fell a little bit in love.

Just a little.

Not enough to matter. Infatuations came and went. They were meant to be enjoyed, not scrutinized.

Later.

Matthias had to kick another sailor who got in the way trying to help him carry Petal. Ethan shoved him over the edge of the ship and the problem was solved. No one seemed much concerned with his yelps when he hit the water and struggled to pull himself up onto the dock. Lightning struck, singeing the bottom of his boot when he was too slow. There were bloody scratches on his arms and he'd barely been in the waves. Kelpies and any number of creatures lurked beneath the surface, also trapped by the shields.

"Reach for her again," Ethan said. "I fucking dare you."

Bramble smiled at him. It was the first time Briar had seen her smile. She looked angelic. It was disconcerting.

They took Petal to a small cabin with a porthole that looked out into the ink-black sea. An eye flashed, huge teeth. Even the kelpies were taken with her. Anais pulled a curtain over the glass as Petal was laid on the narrow cot, witchlight swinging above. Her hare familiar glowed, but only faintly. Her cheeks were pale, her hair in perfect curls despite the circumstances. She looked the same. Normal. Safe.

Tears prickled in Briar's nose. Something jagged that had

been poking into her chest for hours, days now, retreated. Just a little. Enough. She caught a proper breath, and then another.

Briar handed Bramble the basket of supplies she had put together. The ship rolled under them, a gentle sway. It felt a little like a lullaby. "I should go," Briar said. "If the Order is watching me, it's not safe to linger. But I can keep them busy chasing me and not Petal."

"I'll keep her safe," Bramble said. She looked a little green from the swaying, but resolute.

"I know. And I'll fix this for her."

"I know."

There was something in the way Ethan was looking at her, hard, searching, a bit cross. She did not have the time to parse it. "Thank you," she said. "All of you," she added to Matthias and Anais and the others crowded in the hall, besotted.

Ethan sent them running with a single turn of his head. He did not say a word, only nodded to Anais and then ushered Briar back up the ladder-stairs. She felt awkward and clumsy, her skirts tangling around her ankles. Exhausted.

But relieved. Hopeful. Armed, even though she only had her usual boline knife and a packet of seeds in her pocket.

Nowhere near armed enough.

Ethan lowered his head to murmur in her ear, "We are being watched."

# Chapter Seventeen

BRIAR FROZE. "KEEPERS?"

"No, that arse from your tearoom."

Briar willed her heart to unstick from her throat. "Charles? What is he doing here?"

"Don't know. But I can fix that." Ethan was grimly certain. Always.

The rain hissed across the surface of the sea. Wood creaked as the ship shifted. A kelpie screeched, and it prickled the hairs on Briar's arms.

"Wait." She caught his arm but turned her body so it would not be visible from the docks or the beach or the cliffside. She had no idea where Charles was lurking. If he was indeed lurking and not just out for a wander. In the rain. "You can't just murder him."

Ethan did not look remotely convinced. "I think you'll find I can."

"Well, you *shouldn't*."

A grunt was her only reply, as if he found her logic unsound. She did not know why Charles was out here during a storm. He did not enjoy wet hair. Or weather. Walking. Basically, being outside. Had he followed them? Had he seen Petal? It seemed impossible.

But not impossible enough.

"You're reconsidering that murder option, aren't you?" Ethan murmured, pleased.

"No." *Maybe.* She sighed. *Probably not.* "I'm sure there's another way. This could be just a coincidence."

Ethan's gaze did not waver. His hair was tousled and damp, rainwater running down the side of his scarred jaw. Witch glass gleamed behind him, twisted into a rainbow of colors inside a clear ball. Ropes lay coiled like giant snakes. There were cannons and barrels of gunpowder, swords and sabers and magical iron. A fierce, glowering woman in the crow's nest, crossbow in hand. All of it so tempting. But ultimately not helpful.

"I can shoot him," the woman called down.

"So can I," Anais added from the quarterdeck. She sounded half bored. "It's not even a challenge."

"What do you want to do, little thorn?" Ethan asked Briar. He laughed softly at her expression. "Your choice."

"There's no good way to explain why I am on your ship."

"I *am* considered handsome by some," he said, mildly offended.

As if *handsome* was a word that suited. It was entirely too insipid. He was rugged and powerful, commanding. He was like a sword, gleaming and sharp and beautiful and dangerous.

Not the point.

"An Iron Crow as *handsome* as yourself would not spend a single minute with a spinster like me without some kind of ulterior motive. No one in their right mind would believe it." She wouldn't. Couldn't.

Wanted to.

At any rate, he did not like that. There was thunder in the clench of his jaw, lightning in the narrowing of his eyes.

"If Charles has seen me, even accidentally, then he'll have to believe he saved me," she added with a great deal of distaste. "That I owe him." Owed him her magic and her cottage and her gardens.

Ethan liked that even less. Lightning speared the sky, a glint of fire on the crossbow bolt at the top of the mast where he had once bound her, on his dragon, on witch glass and kelpie teeth and iron nails. "Like hell."

Briar was not particularly enamored with the idea either. But she knew it would work.

And Petal was just below deck. There was too much at stake for Briar to be squeamish because of her pride. And, once again, not enough time to think of another plan. What if Charles went to the Keepers? "But he can't want to tell anyone about being here," she said. "He has to want to brag that he saved me from you, but not here specifically."

"It would be much easier if you let me do this my way."

She sighed. "I know."

There was no reason for Ethan to go along with yet another mad plot. It was enough that he was protecting her sister. "I'm going to have to make this look good," he warned. "Are you ready for that?"

"Do your best."

"Don't you mean my worst?"

And then he wasn't Ethan, nor even an Iron Crow with an unsavory past, nor a captain with a small army of thieves and murderers at his beck and call. He was the Dragon. Cold, calculating. Hunting, stealing, and taking for himself what anyone else would hesitate to even ask for politely. Magic, gold, weapons.

Briar.

He had her backed to the railing between one blink and the next, looming, scarred, and ruthless. She gasped as he bent her backward. Her hair fell loose, heavy with rainwater, scattering the last of the flowers she'd woven into the knot at her nape. His hand was warm at the back of her neck, gripping hard. The rain eased, but the lightning limned his face as he lifted his head and smirked. He was an oil painting, turbulent and seething with some inner depth. A story within a story. Glowing.

He brushed his lips over her ear. "Got his attention now, little thorn. What are you going to do about it?"

She pushed against his hard chest with the palm of one hand and he allowed it, easing back.

And then she slapped him.

Hard. His head jerked to the side, his black eyes never leaving hers. She swallowed, feeling bold and shocked at herself. And nervous. Very nervous. She had to stifle a mildly hysterical giggle.

Ethan said quietly, just for her, violence and vengeance carefully leashed, "You weren't supposed to enjoy that, sweetheart."

A shiver went through her.

"And neither was I," he added.

The shiver turned hot. Hungry.

Deeply inappropriate.

But also deeply enjoyable.

How else was she supposed to react when Ethan was so near, so entirely focused on her? The rest of her might be in a panic, but her body did not seem to mind it. It was quite certain it could do more than one thing at a time.

"You! Release her at once!" Charles shouted.

Ethan sighed, his mouth ghosting over hers, denied. "I really hate that sodding git."

Briar also sighed. "Me too. And I hate this even more." She turned to face the beach. Charles was soaked through, the fur of his beaver hat spiky and ruined. There was mud on his breeches, ordered from London. "Charles?" she called out, tremulously. "Help me!"

Ethan growled.

"I'm going to make him pay for that," he added quietly.

"You release her right now!" Charles said, approaching the ship with a combination of arrogance and uneasiness. Briar knew full well that were she in actual danger, he would save himself at the first opportunity. Every time. "This is not how we do things in Haven!"

It took some work not to grimace at him. Or roll her eyes.

"I'll call the Order!"

"Not the Keepers," Ethan said flatly. That Charles thought he could intimidate such a man only showed that he was truly an idiot.

Briar shimmied free of Ethan's grasp, but he did not make it easy.

"Captain, what the hell?" Godric asked, disgusted. She had forgotten he was there. That anyone else was there at all.

"I know," Ethan muttered to the satyr, equally disgusted. "The long con, Godric."

She hurried across the plank to the dock, his gaze hot on her back. Charles waited until she was within reach before sauntering forward.

The urge to push him over the side was strong.

Too strong, apparently.

The storm suddenly lashed out, smashing waves against the wooden dock. The witchlights swung wildly. Water reached up and pulled Charles into the dark sea. He fell, screaming. There was a splash, a yelp.

Briar glared up at Ethan.

"What?" he asked as innocently as one could when bristling with weapons and questionable spell ingredients. Not to mention all that talk of murder. "I had to make it look good."

"I don't think he can swim!"

"He lives on a bloody island and he can't swim?"

"Well, even if he can, he can't fight off a herd of kelpies!" She darted to the edge of the dock, where she could hear thrashing.

"Don't you fucking dare." Ethan leapt over the side of the ship, landing beside her. He caught her by the waist, growling, "You're not going in there."

"Someone has to."

"Not you." He gave a long-suffering sigh, just before the sea tossed Charles back out like it had not enjoyed the experience any more than he had. There was blood running down one arm from a kelpie bite. He choked and groaned.

Briar backed away from Ethan.

"One more thing," he said to Briar as Charles coughed up salt water, oblivious to his audience. Anais watched from the railing and could not have looked more disgusted if she had bitten into a rotten pear.

"What is it?" Briar asked.

His eyes burned.

"If he touches you, sweetheart, he dies."

THE WALK HOME was long. The ground under her feet was muddy and riddled with puddles, but the rain did not touch her, not once.

It fell on Charles as though it hated him personally.

She did not even try not to enjoy it, though she did keep her expression calm. Not that he noticed—he was too busy moaning over the state of his shirt sleeves, his hair, and his arm, in that order.

It felt odd to leave her sister behind, to leave a ship full of witches and Iron Crows and return home to her little cottage. It was where she usually felt safest, but tonight everything was too topsy-turvy. The Midsummer fires burned, cheerful music drifting up the hillside from the beaches. Wine flowed; wishes were made. The wind was sweet and warm where they celebrated, but at the top of the hill, it was chilled with rain and there were Keepers hiding in the shadows, watching her. There were Iron Crows coming for her sister. Black Shucks roaming unbridled. Probably boggarts in her rosemary buses.

And Charles Bloody Aster where he did not belong.

But a green witch knew patience. Seasons would not be rushed. Daisies did not grow in January, no matter the magic. Seeds needed time.

Small, manageable steps, she reminded herself again. Plant, grow, harvest.

So she bade Charles goodbye and locked her front door. She pulled the bench in front of it for good measure. She swept the floor clean of broken crockery, ignoring the scorch marks and the honey residue in the center of the room, the hint of Black Shuck breath. The very thought of dragging herself up the stairs nearly undid her. She was so tired that even her arms ached, never mind her hip. And it was hardly the first time she had slept on the shop floor, tucked by the hearth.

It was, however, the first time she curled up in a circle of salt for extra protection.

And it was definitely the first time she woke to an Iron Crow glaring down at her.

She gave a start, heart hammering. "Is it Petal?"

"She's fine." The rain had stopped and Ethan had left his cloak behind. He wore his usual black trousers and lawn shirt, dry now. There was violence in every bone in his body.

"Oh." She sat up, confused. "Then why are you here?"

"Had to make sure Aster went home and stayed there. The flood in his shop ought to see to it."

"You flooded the apothecary?"

"Yes."

"But…why? He'd never have the gall to bother you again. Not after tonight."

"What about you?"

"What *about* me?"

"You didn't really think I'd let you walk home alone with him, did you?"

"Yes?" She was too tired to lie or even wonder if she ought to.

Ethan's brows, already dark and menacing, lowered. "We're going to talk about that later."

"We are?"

"Yes. But first, why are you sleeping on the bloody floor?"

She refused to be embarrassed. "My hip is not up to climbing at the moment," she said evenly. "Not that it's any of your business."

"Why do you live in a house at the top of the steepest hill in the village with a bedroom at the top of a narrow set of stairs?" Ethan asked, sounding truly angry for the first time since she had met him. And that included the time she had stabbed him with his own fork.

Briar blinked up at him. "It's home."

"Well, you're not sleeping there."

"This rug is perfectly comfortable. I braided it myself." She felt a little ridiculous, like Cinderella to his Prince Charming. Only he wasn't a prince. Nor was he charming. He would be the dragon in every fairy story.

"No."

She frowned. "That is not an answer, because I did not ask you a question. Neither did I ask for your permission." She could barely keep her eyelids open. Even her bones were weary. She may as well have been made of mist and dandelion fluff. "Go away, Mr. Swansea. I'm tired."

He crouched next to her, eyes glittering, jaw sharp. "Stop calling me that," he growled.

She sighed. "Mr. Dragon, then."

"*Ethan.*"

"Certainly not." She didn't know why that should scandalize her after everything else.

"We'll discuss it later. But you're not sleeping there," he said again.

He slid his arms under her and lifted her up. Her eyes popped open, but only briefly. "What are you doing?"

"Putting you to bed, little thorn."

"Why?"

"Because someone should." His touch was gentle. His expression was not.

He carried her down the hall and up the staircase as though this was all perfectly normal. As though he wasn't an infamous Iron Crow who made seasoned Keepers blanch and other thieves tremble. As though she wasn't a witch who made tea and grew roses.

She didn't even have it in her to argue.

"Don't murder me," she mumbled. "I'm too tired for that."

## Chapter Eighteen

Ethan Swansea did not murder her.

That was her first thought when she bolted awake. She could not say if it was because he had definitively *decided* not to, or had simply not gotten around to it.

Her second thought was that he had already gone, and she felt unaccountably cross about it.

She had slept better last night than any night in her recent memory. And her not-so-recent memory. If the scariest thing in the room decided not to murder you, what fear was there for anyone else? But then she had opened her eyes and she was alone with the knitted blanket and the tray of teacups she kept forgetting to bring back downstairs.

Her peevish mood did not improve upon having to stumble to the kitchen half awake, to get the baking started. Sorcha brought the bread and the festival rolls, but Briar was the one who made the petit fours and the profiteroles and the custard tarts. It was her least favorite chore. She always preferred to be in the garden.

She wanted to see how the jasmine clippings were faring, how the plum trees in the orchard were doing now that she had filled their roots with rock crystals. If the slugs had been well and truly convinced to abandon the lettuce. The cabbages and the leeks and the carrots would do so much better in a proper greenhouse, even with the added benefit of her magic. Slugs did not seem to care if you were a witch or not.

But first: petit fours and cake in the shape of roses and hearts and mermaids.

Midsummer Festival was no time to go lax in the baking department. Especially as the visitors were now quite literally trapped here and everyone wanted a pastry when things turned strange. Chamomile tea might soothe frayed nerves, but sweets worked miracles.

She carefully measured flour into bowls, not wasting even a pinch. Salt, honey. Dried currants for the iced buns, orange slices for the cakes. Frosting colored pink with the help of beet juice for the roses she piped onto anything that could do with a bit more decoration. Her mother had used them for love-spell cakes, but they had become tradition even without her magic.

Briar's mood was further sabotaged when there was a hesitant knock at the door. It was too early for customers this far up the hill. They tended to take their breakfast in the hotels or the coffeehouse that served coffee, and chocolate pots out on their white-painted docks. Briar wiped her hands on a towel. "Come in."

A very tall, stoop-shouldered man ducked inside. Briar's heart sank.

Mr. Crane, her solicitor.

He smiled as he took off his hat. His bald head gleamed. "Miss Foxglove."

"Good morning, Mr. Crane. Would you care for some tea?"

He shook his head. "I've come for your mother's debt, you see."

"It's not due for another two weeks, Mr. Crane. I promise you that they shall have every penny." Even if she had to sell every spoon, every flower petal. Or make a thousand marzipan doves.

He bobbed his head this time, twisting the brim of his hat. "I'm afraid I don't think it will be enough. I cannot represent you."

Briar shut her eyes briefly. "My mother hired you for her will."

"Yes, and I've seen to my duties. I was not party to the debt agreement. I would have encouraged your mother toward better terms."

"I know."

"But it's out of my hands, I'm afraid."

The mint on the windowsill wilted. "I see."

"Don't blame your mother. I too have a debt to pay," he replied. "And the terms have changed."

His debt was to Mrs. Aster and Charles, she would bet her hollyhocks on it. He was all apologies. And perspiration. He was not an unkind man, merely disinclined to fight the current in any way. And the Asters were not just a current—they were a deadly undertow.

Briar wanted to wilt like the mint. She forced herself not to. Also, not to scream. Shriek. Screech. Break something into a hundred pieces. She curled her fists, breathed in the smell of the fire, the dough, the sugared violets. Tea steeping in a pot. Rosemary from a clay pot by the door.

"I see," she said again, finally. There were no other solicitors on Lyonesse whose services she could afford. No way to fight her mother's debt. She had borrowed an ungodly sum and promised to return it within the year, using the cottage as leverage.

Briar would never make enough money to cover it in such a short time. She knew it. He knew it. The Asters knew it.

"I am sorry, Miss Foxglove," he said before taking his leave. If the lilac bushes poked a branch into the back of his head, it had nothing to do with her.

She refused to cry. It would solve nothing. They had lived here for nearly twenty years, when her mother had finally saved enough to move them to a fine cottage on the hill where she would not have to sell love charms furtively at the back door. They had lived in a cramped gatehouse before then, on the edge of the moors, at the crossroads to the main way into Haven. Briar had not minded. Her mother had minded very much. Petal would have lived in a hole if it meant people stopped staring at her face.

They might yet have to resort to that.

But, as pressing as it was, it was still a problem that would have to wait.

She needed to help Petal first. They could worry about the roof over their heads when her sister woke up, when the shields lifted. When the Keepers found her and arrested her, forcing her into an iron collar. When the London museum locked her in a dungeon, or whatever it was they did to thieves who were smarter than they were.

*No.*

That line of thought was not helpful either.

Today she would fill the glass cases with delicate petit fours and brew sun tea and hunt for the moon.

She rubbed the mint leaves between her fingers. "Sorry," she murmured. It perked her up immediately, its bright and crisp scent in her nose. A balm.

But when she glanced out of the window, her heart did not just sink—it felt as though it seized entirely in her chest.

All of the flowers in her garden had turned white.

The purple delphinium, the yellow larkspur, the red hollyhocks. The pink foxgloves, the blue cornflowers, the orange poppies.

All white, every petal and blossom. White as bone, white as salt.

Moon-white.


ETHAN WAS STILL in hell.

And it continued to be ruled by a woman who should have been plain but was, in fact, alarmingly the opposite. She was obstinate and charming and fascinating. Her curves made him sweat. And he had been in regular contact with mermaids and sirens since the age of fourteen. He was used to beauty, murderous and otherwise.

But Briar was unique. Her voice was soft, throaty. Made to moan his name.

*Hell.*

He watched her from the kitchen garden door, unnoticed. She attacked a bowl of batter as if it had personally insulted her. There was frosting all around her in bright pinks, mossy greens, lilac. Flour dusted her arms and the tip of her nose, wrinkled with concentration. There was a furrow between her brows.

He wanted to eat her up.

At least the dark smudges under her eyes had faded. He had watched her sleep until he was content that she was truly resting, not merely pretending in order to jump out of bed at the first opportunity on some other foolhardy mission to save her sister.

Miss Petal Foxglove had a lot to answer for.

Iron Crows did not cleave to their families for this reason. If you stole amulets and grimoires and magic that did not belong to you, consequences came for you—but sometimes also for those who knew you. Better to surround yourself with other thieves and troublemakers.

They knew what to do when magical cargo exploded in the hull or when Keepers and museum gits came to your door. And there were too many damned doors to this small cottage. Front, back, front shop door, side shop door, kitchen door. He'd already warded them all with iron nails and technically illegal bone dust from the Iron Witches, but he was running out of supplies. He'd have to go back to the ship, where Anais and the others had already caught a Crow and two tourists attempting to climb aboard.

Needless to say, they did not make it.

And climbing anything at all would not be possible for them for some time.

Haven might consider itself the epitome of civilized behavior and graceful living, but that only meant it would be the first to devolve into chaos and cruelty when fear and scarcity truly hit. He had seen it before. When the pearls and the freckle lotions and the glamours weakened, everything would change.

He watched as Briar crossed to the window where a fat bumblebee knocked against the glass, disoriented on its quest to get back to the garden. She lifted the latch, scolding gently when it veered toward her, confused. She cupped her hands, leaning out to place it on the rosebushes invading the side of the cottage.

Then she went back to icing little cakes with yellow roses. She did not look particularly impressed with her work, which was delicate and fussy. Not at all words he associated with her. Where was the spark in her eye, the one she had when she tossed a teacup spell at two Keepers? The flash of a grin when she sent ivy and brambles and thorns on little errands? Did she even realize how she smiled then? As if she were full of sunlight.

But this cottage kitchen, her wayward sister, this bloody sparkling village… They were stealing something vital from her.

And he did not care for it.

Even if she was a softness he couldn't have. Shouldn't want.

Desperately craved.

Might yet commit murder to protect.


THERE WAS A reasonably large crowd of customers when Briar finally opened her doors, which was a relief, considering Mr. Crane's visit. Ethan had returned without a word, sitting in a chair and sharpening his knife on a whetstone. It was most uncivilized.

Briar could not have said why she found it so comforting.

The tall, scarred Iron Crow, the grim set of his jaw, the repetitive scrape of metal on stone. A teashop should be full of whispers and birdsong and the light tinkling music of a harp.

Which sounded dreadfully boring all of a sudden.

When he moved on to whittling a chunk of wood, he did not look any more refined.

She served strong tea and scones with clotted cream and strawberries. The queen cakes were popular, decorated with tiny marzipan swans. Children were allowed barley sugar candy and chocolate drops and candy comfits, even though it was still early in the day. Her customers were more nervous than they had been yesterday, even the locals. The dropped shields and circulating Keepers were beginning to take their toll. Problems with Lyonesse's magical barriers were usually mended more quickly than this.

Aidan returned, frowning at the white flowers. Of course he had noticed. And of course he was suspicious.

Everybody wanted answers and no one had any to give. In its absence, gossip would do. It was clear in the way people sat, shoulders tight, glances flickering. There were a lot more iron-nail pendants, which had never been popular in Haven. They weren't nearly pretty enough. Some enterprising soul had already begun to sell them ornamented with pearls and rock crystal.

Briar brought Ethan a pot of tea, even though he had not asked for it. She added a marzipan dove because it amused her that a grim-jawed Iron Crow might eat a pink bird of peace. He held her gaze and devoured it in two easy bites.

Something warmed in her belly. Something most inconvenient. The struggle not to blush was real.

"Charles Bloody Aster is lurking in the bushes," Sorcha announced not long after, and with deep distaste, as she marched into the shop. The tip of her nose was red from the sun. She had been walking the moors again. Briar hoped she had found the Black Shuck. "And it's dodgy, even for him."

"Wonderful." Briar sighed. She was not surprised, not after yesterday. But she had hoped the damage to Charles's favorite hat might have put him off.

"And there's some other bloke very carefully circling your peonies." She lowered her voice. "Which are all white now. Why are all of your flowers white?"

"I don't know," Briar whispered back. "They were like that when I woke up this morning."

"I told Old Man Harlow out on his stoop that you did it for the festival."

"I can't turn an entire garden's worth of flowers white."

Sorcha shrugged. "He doesn't know that. And he's stopped

making the sign against evil toward your front door. Someone else already painted an evil eye on the street outside your cottage."

"Wonderful." Briar sighed again. "Have a cup of tea—the evil eye is free, on the house."

Her friend snorted. "Nothing's free in Haven."

Briar snorted back. "True enough."

Sorcha leaned against the wooden counter and plucked a chocolate drop from a jar, crunching it between her teeth, the colorful sugar sprinkles catching the light. "Why are these so good?"

"They're even better when you let them melt on your tongue instead of chomping away like a badger."

Sorcha waved a hand. "Who has the patience? We could all die tomorrow."

"You're very cheerful."

She grinned. "I like any excuse to eat more chocolate."

"I am aware." Briar grinned back. She smacked her friend's hand when it returned to the jar. "Eat the broken ones, you savage." She brought out the plate she had already put aside for her.

Sorcha ate half the pile before raising her eyebrows meaningfully in Ethan's direction. "He's still here, is he?"

"He's been…helpful."

"Excellent. Now I don't have to murder him. I'd hate to get blood on my chocolate."

"I'm relieved to hear it," Ethan said drily, not looking up from his dagger. The chunk of linden wood in his hand was taking the shape of a swan.

Sorcha choked on a chocolate drop. "Oops. Good morning, Dragon."

"I'm not sure he wants people to know he's the Dragon," Briar murmured, watching one of the gentlemen nearby give a full-body start. He was pale as boiled milk.

"Then he shouldn't have let his very large dragon take a nap on your roof."

"What?" Briar stepped out and squinted against the sun. Ethan's familiar was indeed curled up on her roof. He barely fit. His scaled tail was wrapped around the gargoyle crouched on the corner. He glowed, not like fireflies and starlight, but like sunlight off the sea. Like knives. He was menacing and beautiful. So much like Ethan.

"He's protecting you," Sorcha said smugly. "Ethan."

"He's protecting his path to the moon egg."

"Well, you're in the middle of that path, so I'm glad you have someone keeping an eye out." She shook her head at Aidan, who really was staring at a moon-white peony blossom. He was dressed exactly as one would expect from an earl who worked in a museum: tidy, a bit formal. Expensive. "Who is he, really?" Sorcha asked under her breath.

"He works for the London Museum of Magic. He came yesterday with two Keepers."

Her eyes narrowed to slits. Outrage and worry sparked off her. Her crow flew out of her chest, screeching a warning.

"You probably can't eat his eyeballs," Briar pointed out mildly.

"Spoilsport. You can't just let him poke around."

"I don't like it either, but I only look guiltier if I don't."

Sorcha huffed out a breath. "I suppose. Luckily, I don't have that problem. Oi!" she added with a sharp whistle. "You!"

Aidan straightened, his serious-scholar face a combination of arrogance and curiosity. Sorcha marched right up to him, her red tangled hair in its unfashionable plait, no bonnet to be seen. One would never guess her grandfather had been a duke. Disgraced, of course. But still a duke. Her green eyes flashed.

"You gave him something to eat?" Sorcha said to Briar before he could say anything at all. She shook her head, even more outraged with Aidan after a glance inside the paper bag. "And *you* chose *marzipan*?"

Aidan frowned. "Yes."

"The worst of the sweets. The most *boring*."

"I was not aware there was a hierarchy."

"That seemed unlikely." Sorcha scoffed. Aidan blinked. He did not seem the type accustomed to women who scoffed. Or shouted "Oi" at him over the hollyhocks.

Briar was not sure if she should save him or throw him to the wolves. "Sorcha Beauregard, this is Lord Coventry."

Sorcha snorted. Aidan appeared both bewildered and irritated. A common reaction to Sorcha, truth be told.

"It's not polite to trample about in a lady's garden," Sorcha pointed out.

"I assure you, I was not trampling." Aidan was so serious, so courteous. Briar almost felt sorry for him. Sorcha would find it irresistible to needle him until he turned purple and possibly exploded. He bowed stiffly in Briar's direction. "I shall be in the orchard for the rest of my inspection."

Sorcha crossed her arms. "I am coming with you."

"I do not need assistance."

She rolled her eyes. "I'm not *helping* you. I'm keeping an eye on you."

"I assure you, miss, there is nothing unseemly about this," he said stiffly. "I am on museum business."

A snake slithered from behind a pot of thyme. It ought to have been green, but it was white.

Moon-white.

Briar stifled a squeak. White flowers and white snakes would not endear her to a museum curator hunting for the effects of his tracking spell on a moon charm.

Worse yet, the snake was curled around something that flashed silver, edged with pearls and crystal. Exactly where Bramble had dragged Petal into the garden.

Around a part of the moon charm.

It had clearly broken, as this looked to be the bottom cap, seed pearls dangling.

Sorcha followed her gaze and then immediately snapped it

back to Aidan. "It's *Lady* Sorcha, actually," she said forcefully.

"Pardon?" Aidan asked, too taken aback by her general demeanor to notice Briar gently dragging her foot back, hiding the silver and pearls under her heel.

She kept her smile placid. The roses perfumed the air. A bee arrived to investigate. An acorn dropped on her head. "Stop that," she murmured to them.

"I'm not *miss*," Sorcha continued. "I'm *Lady* Sorcha. Technically."

Aidan was surprised, as expected, but clearly too polite to remark upon it. And when she marched ahead into the orchard, he naturally followed. Sorcha was a force of nature.

She had taken him away from the white snake—and the white snails Briar had also just noticed on the gravel walk.

Away from the piece of the moon charm, which she crouched to scoop into her palm. It seared her witch knot. She slipped it into her apron just as Aidan said, quite stiffly, "After you, Lady Sorcha."

"Keep up, Lord Coventry," Sorcha returned, with a cackle.

Briar exchanged what could only be called a commiserating glance with the dragon on her roof.

# Chapter Nineteen

I T WAS TRADITION, during the Midsummer Festival, to step into
the sea at midnight for good luck.

As Briar could use all of the luck she could beg, borrow, or
outright steal, she would also dunk her whole head underwater if
it would help.

She avoided the main beach with its bonfires and stalls of
spiced ale and tart lemonade and Pegasus rides. The villagers and
visitors would splash into the sea and bob about like so many
jewels. There would be stolen kisses, shrieks of laughter, songs
sung.

Tonight, Briar preferred the secret cove, bathed in moonlight,
with wild roses growing over the short cliff rocks above. She did
not remember seeing them growing there before. She kicked off
her shoes and stepped out of her dress, the breeze ruffling her
thin chemise. She had placed a flower wreath on her hair, even
though there was no one to see it. It was braided with St. John's
wort, lavender, and daisies.

The sea was ruffled like a black velvet dress trimmed with
white lace ribbons. The sound of the waves was soft and
constant, overlaid with the occasional snippet of violins and flutes
from other celebrations. The stars were bright, eating up the
darkness.

And then Ethan was there, leaning silently against the rocks.

She had not seen him arrive, but she was not surprised. He
had appointed himself her bodyguard. Or more accurately, the

bodyguard of his best chance at getting to the moon charm before anyone else. He needed her. And she needed him to keep the others off her trail.

But what would happen if they found it? *When* they found it? Would he try to steal it from her? Would he let her wake her sister and see if that was enough to lift the shields? What if it was not? What then?

As Briar had no answers and no method of getting them, she settled for the push and pull of the waves, the shifting sand under her toes. And Ethan at her back, her very own bloodthirsty shadow. Honest but untrustworthy. Protective but dangerous. Treacherous as the ocean, as unyielding as fire. A dragon to his core.

Briar turned back to the sea, her neck prickling with the knowledge that he watched her. He made it feel like he was right there next to her. As if he was touching her. Her body reacted, a slow, hot throb of awareness between her thighs.

She counted the waves as they crashed and foamed around her knees. The seventh was the one that brought good luck. Her swan settled on the water, bobbing happily. Her sister was as safe as she could be. Briar had a moment to catch her breath. She would need a clear head to see them through the rest. She had part of the moon charm, but that meant there were more pieces littered about. And too many others hunting for them. They did not know it was in pieces, though. That was to her advantage.

She caught a glimpse of kelpie teeth just as Ethan whistled sharply, stalking into the water behind her. The moonlight caught his many daggers, the silver ring on his thumb. The kelpies raced closer, with that haunting, piercing cry that fueled the nightmares of everyone on Lyonesse. They had the heads and front legs of horses, tapering to fish tails with the strength of a hundred steel-tipped whips. Frequently the water around them roiled with blood.

Ethan, grim faced, used his magic to push the waves against them, their muscular bodies churning the water in defiance.

Fennel and burning salt mingled with the roses above them.

The kelpies snapped their teeth, and it was too easy to imagine them dripping blood and seaweed, to hear the crunch of her own bones. They did not, as a rule, stay close to Haven. They were too cruel and hungry, pulling the unwary under to drown them and eat them, and not necessarily in that order. The locking of the shields must have trapped them closer to the beach than was comfortable for anyone.

"Mine," Ethan growled when one of them tried to circle around to nip at Briar's swan.

Snapdragon slapped the water with a fierce wing. Ethan had claimed her before, in front of Twyla. Briar knew it was just a figure of speech, a warning that had more to do with rivalries over magic and stolen moon eggs.

So she tried not to like it.

And failed, decided that what made her tingle in the privacy of her own mind was nobody's business. It was Midsummer, after all. The rules were different. Some leeway was given.

Ethan sliced an iron dagger across the water as his dragon unfurled giant, scaled wings above her. He breathed fire that was not fire but effective all the same. One of the kelpies shrieked. "*Go*," Ethan ordered them.

They moved as a herd, turning toward Haven's crowded beach. The bonfires flickered like beacons. "Not there," he added sharply. "You can try your luck in Holdfast."

They keened again, and Briar's ears rang. It was the sound of breaking glass, metal screeching against metal, bones shattering. The kelpies knew they had no chance with the Iron Witches of Holdfast and swam away to sulk in the shadows.

"Thank you," Briar said, her chemise tangling around her knees.

He glanced down at her, eyes dark and fathomless, mouth absurdly sultry against the rugged clench of his jaw. He was in his element, standing in the shadows of the sea at midnight. Briar, on the other hand, wobbled, trying to find purchase in the slippery sand when a particularly rough wave jostled her. Ethan reached out and steadied her, splaying his hand across her lower back. The water pushed her closer to him and she did not fight it, could not.

Did not want to.

He had pushed his dagger against her throat.

But in all fairness, she had stabbed him with a fork first.

Some alliances weren't meant to be simple, even if they felt deceptively easy. Natural.

They stood there for a long moment, gazes snarled on each other.

And then it wasn't the tide that brought them together, nor gravity, nor chance. It was need. Desire so keen it scorched through the hesitation, through perfectly reasonable arguments and warnings. Wisdom. Everything.

All she knew was that Ethan's mouth was on hers. *Finally.*

His fingers tightened at the nape of her neck, holding her steady. Holding her still for him. The kiss started slow and deep, making her knees weak. His tongue stroked against hers, and when he pulled back to let her catch her breath, he nipped at her bottom lip, dragged his teeth along her jaw, across her throat. She had never been kissed like this before. There was nothing delicate or polite about it. He was ravenous, not just for her touch, but for her pleasure. She felt it in the way he groaned when she pressed closer to him, when she gasped.

Was it wise?

Probably not.

Was it necessary?

Most definitely.

Taking risks with her own safety, her own heart and body, was far easier than risking her sister. This was something she could do for herself. Just for herself.

His knee slid between her legs, and she gasped at the pressure against her sensitive, heated flesh. It wasn't enough, but even then it was perfect. A tease, a taunt. She moaned again, frustrated.

"What's the matter, little thorn?" he asked, darkly amused, breath ragged in her ear. "Is there something you want? Something you need?"

She squirmed against him, pulsing with need for his touch.

"Say it," he ordered her quietly. "Say it and you get what you want. We both get what we want."

She tried to wriggle closer, to find a rhythm. Friction.

He pinned her in place. "I asked you a question, Briar."

She narrowed her eyes, feeling far more frantic than she could have predicted.

"What do you want?" he asked again.

She huffed out a desperate breath. *"You*, you monster."

He closed his hands over her bottom with a low laugh and lifted her up against his body. Her legs locked around him instinctively and he rocked into her softness, sending bolts of sensations up her thighs and into her core. Her nipples tightened, pressed against his chest. He kissed her throat, just this side of rough. "The things I'm going to do to you," he said. "But this doesn't lead to handfastings and sonnets, little thorn."

She knew what he was saying, knew that he meant it with his own gentlemanly sort of honor. Nights like these often led to compromised reputations, to handfastings and wedding breakfasts. Marriage was supposed to be a prize, a goal. But Midsummer nights, much like Beltane Eve, was a thing on all its own. The rules bent, broke.

And even if they did not, Briar was not a fool. One did not shackle a Black Shuck, or a ship's captain. Some creatures were meant to stay wild.

Still, she rolled her eyes at him, because, wild or not, Ethan Swansea did not require additional fuel for his ego. "Obviously," she said. She had her pride, after all. "Or babies," she added. "I take a moon tea." Most witches on the island did the same. It was a simple tincture of herbs, with a dash of magic. No one talked about it, but every witch Briar had ever met knew how to ask for it or make it for themselves.

He tilted his head, searching, suddenly ravenous. "If you were wise, you'd tell me to go."

"And if I don't?"

"Then God help us both." He walked her out of the sea, his mouth on hers, grinding her against his hardness, fingers splayed, dimpling her flesh. "Not here," he muttered.

"I'm not delicate," she argued.

"I'd rather not be murdered by a kelpie." He released her, letting her drag along the length of him until her bare toes touched the sand. He grabbed her chin. "I have plans for you, little thorn."

She fumbled with her dress ties, feeling clumsy, on fire. Everything. When he dropped her blanket over her shoulders, she abandoned her dress entirely. He helped her up the cliff steps, toward the cottage. The villagers danced below, bonfires burning. A phoenix streaked past, tail leaving sparks that formed sunwheels and roses and spirals.

They crossed the gardens, the peonies blooming so fast it rained petals as they passed. They kissed against the oak tree, her back pressed to the bark. Lichens bloomed. They kissed against the door, rattling the windows. They kissed and kissed and kissed.

And then Briar found herself sitting on the steps that led to her room, Ethan caging her in with his hard, scarred body. "I'm not waiting a moment longer," he vowed. "Open your legs for me, sweetheart."

The filthy cadence of his voice, the flare of his eyes, had her core clenching, her legs parting. He stepped between them, nudging them wider, staring down hard at her until she had to lean back to keep his gaze, her breath catching. He pulled his lawn shirt over his head, revealing the hair-dusted chest tattooed with swallows, the faded scars, the glint of silver and thick, padded muscles. She reached out to touch him as he bent over her, dragging her nails over the planes and ridges. He folded his shirt and placed it under her head to cushion it, smiling wickedly. "Get comfortable, sweetheart. I need my mouth on you."

She exhaled shakily, her skirts pushed up to her thighs, her cheeks flushed. Wanton. She felt wanton.

And wasn't that lovely?

Miss Briar Foxglove, wanted and wanton.

"Hurry," she begged. "There are things I want to do to you, too."

He cursed, but it was reverent, holy.

He knelt in front of her, and it was nearly too much—and he was barely touching her yet. His gaze was a fiery, alive thing, brushing over her skin, leaving streaks of tingling sensations. He drew his palms up her legs, dragging her skirts higher. She felt swollen and slick. Desperate. But he was patient, methodical, as if committing every second to memory. She was squirming by the time his mouth touched the inside of her knee. A sucking kiss, a scrape of teeth. His breath was hot against her.

When he finally reached her center, licking softly with the flat of his tongue, she jerked in his grasp. His fingers dug into her hips, holding her in place. There was no pain, only command. Not just an expectation but the certainty of being obeyed.

She loved it.

She didn't know what that might say about her, and she did not care.

The heat gathering in her belly shot through her, down her thighs, up to her breasts. He licked again and again, up to her bud, around it, sliding through her folds, making sounds indicating that he found her delicious. He slid his fingers into her, only up to the first knuckle, pressing down but no further. The pressure, the taunt of more, threatened to make her mad. She moaned, waves of her release tingling in her lower belly, building but not cresting.

Ethan smiled against her. "Do you need more, sweetheart?"

She nodded helplessly.

"You can have it all."

She might not survive it. He closed his lips over her, sucking her bud into his warm, wet mouth. His fingers stroked deeper,

deeper. Her thigh muscles began to shake. He was relentless, patient, inexorable. When she came, waves of sensations worked up from her inner thighs, over her quim, making her clench around his fingers. Her back arched off the steps. He didn't stop his work, still licking and sucking, until she was whimpering. When he pulled away his smile was darkly satisfied. She could only blink at him, mildly stupefied. Her bones were made of molten silver, her blood turned to starlight.

Since when did she resort to poetry, even inside her own head?

Oh, he was a dangerous one.

He wiped his mouth, eyes glittering. "Come on, sweetheart," he said, rough and gravelly. "I'm not nearly done with you."

Only they never made it up the stairs.

The moment shattered.

Briar gave serious consideration to cursing everyone in Haven with boils. Or a tail. Maybe two.

Her sister might get a boil on her nose as well.

This kind of magical interruption was unacceptable. If there was a Keeper at her door, he would be sorely surprised by his welcome. She knew a spell that would cover his tongue in goat fur.

Another thrum of magic. It was disconcerting, like a skittering under the skin. Briar's breath clogged her throat. Her heart sped up.

The sharp feeling of unease was immediately washed away by a soft, lilting voice.

It was the most beautiful thing she had ever heard. Felt.

"What is that?" Briar breathed.

"A grimsong," Ethan replied. Rain hit the roof in a steady, loud patter. Not enough to cover the song, but enough to mask it slightly. Briar found the interruption irritating. What was wrong with him? This was no time for rain.

"It's so beautiful," she said.

"And deadly."

The cottage gleamed and glittered with the song. That lilting voice drew them out into the back garden, under the stars, to a woman with pale, waist-length hair, floating as though she were underwater. She shone like mother-of-pearl. Her eyes were the blue of sea glass—no, the green of a summer pond. She had wings that shimmered like abalone and mother-of-pearl.

When she smiled, she had the pointed, sharpened teeth of a shark.

It did not take away from her beauty. Nor from the dangerous allure of the song wrapping around Briar like seaweed. She would have drowned already, were they any closer to the sea. And she would not have minded.

"Who is she?" Briar whispered, awed.

"A siren," Ethan ground out. "Sent by a warlock or an Iron Crow. See the threads?"

Briar could, now that she knew to look for them. She had to squint, but the shimmer of threads floated from the siren. She continued to sing, clear and bright. A sparrow dropped from the plum tree.

Briar frowned, but it was hard to move. The gossamer threads of the song pulled at her, wrapped around her ankles and her knees. The siren shone like starlight. Even Snapdragon was utterly mesmerized, frozen in the grass. Briar's witch knot burned, but she barely noticed. Everything was the siren and her song. A grimsong was the wrong thing to call it. It was too perfect, too angelic.

But she was very near Ethan now. His jaw clenched. A vein on his temple throbbed. He was fighting some invisible battle.

And if she drew any nearer to him, he might lose.

Rain fell harder, muffling the song. But Briar did not know if it was enough. She was barely outside the tearoom, had only taken a few steps outside, and she already felt like she would drop to her knees, if asked. She would bleed into the grass. Give her last breath. *Anything.*

Ethan set a large chunk of jet down between them. It siphoned some of the magic, but not enough. Not nearly enough.

Thunder cracked, along with the jet. The siren paused, eyes glowing acidic with ire.

Ethan had an iron dagger in his hand. His dragon circled above them. He looked like a nightmare one would never want to face.

But he was still stepping closer to the siren, closer and closer.

As was Briar. The song called to her, urged her to follow, follow, follow.

The siren drifted backward, over the garden wall, into the fields that led to the cliff's edge. The moon touched the water, a dark, vast expanse below them. Briar tripped over a clump of twisted grass, her hip jolting with pain.

It cleared her mind, if only briefly. Very briefly.

But long enough to realize that walking off a cliff was a very, very bad idea.

When Briar fought the pull, the siren opened her mouth and the soft chains of her song tightened. The longer she stood still, the more painful the song felt. Invisible barbs latched on to Briar's skin. But she was used to moving through pain, used to thorns and brambles biting at her, used to her hip joint refusing to cooperate. A few threads of magic, however sharp and sticky, would not stop her. She crouched slowly, gathering moss from a boulder by the cliff's edge, then rolled it into little balls and stuffed them into her ears.

Ethan had stopped when she stopped, and now a gale of otherworldly wind pushed at his back. The siren's song was turning hungry, impatient, insistent. There was blood coming from his ears. His boots dragged in the dirt, struggling to find purchase. Charms tumbled from his pockets, daggers, iron nails, a small glass vial filled with teeth.

Briar slipped closer, the moss and the steady beat of the rain shredding some of the gossamer threads that tangled her up. Her limbs still felt heavy, her head light. But the siren was locked in a battle of wills with Ethan and had stopped paying attention to her.

Briar was beginning to think that being underestimated was a very useful weapon indeed.

She lowered to her knees, as if in awe. It was not entirely pretense. The siren was even more formidable up close. Her song reached into Briar's chest. She could smell roses and hot tea and baking bread. Earth. Pine sap. Mint leaves. All the things she loved.

Her swan shuddered in pain.

A boggart cackled from the shadows.

An animal cried out from the distant moors.

Briar dug her fingers into the grass and the dandelions and the blossoms of sea pinks and down into the earth. She urged it all to grow, the weeds, the flowers. She tasted mint and salt on her tongue. The grass grew thick, snaring Ethan's boots, slowing his drag toward the siren.

He glanced down at Briar. "Run," he ordered her, pain and resolve so visceral, even through the moss in her ears muffling sounds, that she could almost *see* it wrap around his words. His dragon struggled to stay aloft. "Run, *now*."

She shook her head. A drop of blood fell from his earlobe. Briar whispered to the grass until it parted, revealing the iron nails that had fallen from Ethan's pocket as he struggled. She found one and crawled forward, stabbing it down through the siren's ghostly foot.

The siren choked on her song.

The silence was cool as water on a hot day. Soothing.

Too brief.

Briar jabbed another iron nail through her other foot, the icy jolt scalding her fingertips. Her nails turned blue, aching. It was not enough to banish the siren entirely but it was enough to distract her, to weaken her.

Just long enough for Ethan to sever the connection to the Iron Crow who had sent her. He had a dagger inlaid with abalone shell, reflecting all the pastel hues of a sunrise over the ocean. He slashed it down through the gossamer threads that clung to him, and to Briar, from the siren, who had more threads trailing off to link her to the one who had sent her. The shell dagger came down again and again, severing the magic that compelled and connected them.

The last note of her song hung on the breeze, a piercing lament.

The siren, though not quite corporeal, shattered. The force of it flattened the fields under an unnatural wind. One of the last charms hanging from Ethan's pockets burst. He curled around Briar, taking the brunt of the explosion. Feathers burned; the very air sharpened.

And then the siren was gone.

Silence stretched, finally punctured by the call of a nightingale, the trill of crickets. The rain stopped.

"Fucking Iron Crows," Ethan grunted.

# Chapter Twenty

I F BRIAR HAD thought the siren and her grimsong would be the deadliest part of her evening, she had underestimated the force of Ethan's fury.

They went back to the cottage, pulling the wooden shutters closed, locking the doors. Inside, the tearoom was cozy and dark.

Until it wasn't.

Ethan sauntered toward Briar, eyes blazing. "You put yourself in danger," he said with a lethal kind of softness that she already knew to ignore at her own peril. The treacherous sea was in his eyes. A storm brewed on the horizon outside the cottage in reply.

She swallowed as he bent closer, invading her space. She inched backward. "You're welcome?"

Wrong thing to say.

He closed his hand around her throat, gently but inexorably, halting her escape. "You do not put yourself in danger. Not for me."

Her body was a riot of conflicting feeling: weary from the battle but also oddly revitalized, as if she had drunk an entire carafe of coffee or eaten all of the rock candy in the jar. She was aware of every single thing—the wind pushing the roses against the shutters, the thinness of her chemise, the soft touch of Ethan's breath on her cheek, making her skin tingle all the way down to her knees. The feeling of being prey to Ethan's predator and liking it.

*Loving* it.

Stern, silent Ethan with his scars and tattoos and lethal black eyes that saw everything. Every part of her, yearning and desperate. His usual control was chipped, something more than fierceness in those eyes. There was a growl in his throat. She was wet with only his fingers at her neck. But she knew what it was to be touched by him now.

"Are you listening, little thorn?"

She nodded, or tried to.

"I don't think you were." His voice was quiet but hard. His accent thickened.

"I…"

"You. Don't. Put. Yourself. In. Danger."

*Oh.* That.

He waited, eyebrow raised. "Say it."

She felt mutinous. So desperate for him to touch her. A little bit more cowed than she'd like. But also so tempted to push, just to see how serious he was.

"Don't," he said pleasantly, as if reading her mind. "I'd like to let you come tonight." His mouth brushed her ear, a nip at her lobe, a devious smile against her skin. "You want to come again, don't you, sweetheart? And again?"

She gasped when he pulled up her skirts, her thighs already parting for him. With the fingers of one hand still clasped around her throat, he plunged the others rhythmically in and out of her quim until she was quaking. Heat raced up and down her legs.

He slowed his ministrations until she whimpered. And still he gave no quarter, only tsked as if disappointed. "A shame." His fingers stilled, palm against her bud adding pressure but nothing else. Sweat dampened the top of her spine. "And you're so close, aren't you?"

"Ethan, please."

His grip on her throat was the only thing holding her up. She felt feverish. Feral. He stayed silent, demanding. A ship's captain through and through. Orders had been given.

She swallowed again, whispering, "I don't put myself in danger for you."

"Good girl," he said, as inevitable as the churn of a whirlpool.

And then his fingers stroked deep inside, dragged out to circle her bud, in that steady, patient pattern that made her toes curl. "Give me your pleasure," he urged. "It's *mine*."

He kissed her, capturing her cries when she came, hard and fast as a lightning strike. The bedroom was full of shadows and the heavy perfume of mint and the white roses swallowing the cottage. The waves of her climax seemed endless, receding like the tide, only to crash over her again when Ethan fit his cock against her. She pushed down to draw him in, too far gone to be embarrassed at her eagerness. He swore, but it was low and soft, like a prayer.

"I knew you'd feel like this," he said, then groaned. "Perfect."

He slid into her only a little and with excruciating slowness. She bit his shoulder, impatient, demanding. He grinned softly, but the tendons in his neck were in sharp relief.

"Slowly," he said.

"Faster," she demanded instead. "More."

She wriggled under him, but he was bigger, stronger, even more determined. His jaw clenched on a low groan. "Patience."

She glowered at him, her blood on fire. "No."

He chuckled, dark and tender. "I don't want to hurt you, little thorn."

He slid in a little deeper. There was an ache as her body strove to accommodate him. It wasn't pain, exactly. She angled her hips and squeezed around him. *More.* She wanted more. She wanted all of him. But he was merciless, even in his care for her.

"You're taking me so well," he said, and she gasped, his words a spark that lit fires deep in her belly. He kissed her deeply, still taking his time, still torturing them both. His tongue touched hers and she felt it everywhere. Her nipples tightened and he bent his head to suck one into his hot mouth. A deep pull, the swirl of his tongue. Her quim fluttered. He kissed her again, and she lifted her knees to take him deeper; every inch he slid into her made her gasp and whimper. "You are perfect," he said, breath ragged.

She dragged her fingers through his hair, gently. And that gentleness seemed to be his undoing. He stilled, eyes flaring. She stroked her thumb along his jawline, finding a new scar. He turned his head slightly, dangerously close to nuzzling her palm.

And then he drove into her like she was everything. Like she was home.

When he came, their gazes tangled and held.

She came again. And again.


WHEN BRIAR WOKE the next morning, Ethan was gone and there was a man in her kitchen.

Singing a sea shanty.

Badly.

Briar blinked at him. "Matthias?"

Matthias, with his tousled blond hair and shining smile, sang like a wet, thoroughly disgruntled cat. "Good morning!"

"Is Petal all right?"

"Perfectly fine," he assured her, and the instinctual panic receded. "Some of the crew have taken to bringing her flowers."

"Of course they have." She nodded through a yawn, thoroughly unsurprised. He had a towel over one shoulder, jam on his shirt, and he was stirring batter in a heavy ceramic bowl. Something delicious bubbled in a pot over the fire. Rows of freshly baked eclairs watched her from the windowsill where they cooled. She had only ever attempted them once. They took ages and were so fussy. "Matthias?"

"Yes?"

"What are you doing?"

"Your kitchen is enormous!" He beamed.

It really, really wasn't. It was a cramped and smoky cottage kitchen with a single worktable, a long bench, and a cupboard for supplies, which was mostly stacked with canisters of dried flowers for tea. The whitewashed walls were streaked with soot. There was a stone by the hearth that stood up at an odd angle, just enough to stub a toe. Repeatedly.

"I'm used to a galley kitchen," Matthia added when he caught her dubious expression. "Barely room enough for me, and it always smells like onions, no matter what I do."

"Oh." She really did not know what else to say. Except… "Matthias?"

"Yes, Miss Foxglove?"

"Why are you in my enormous kitchen baking… Is that a croquembouche? And raspberry-rose flummery?"

"It is. My specialty." He grinned, tossing a blond curl off his forehead. His cheeks were flushed with the heat. Ethan was right—he did not look like an Iron Crow. "Dragon sent for me."

"Because he wanted a pink flummery?"

He laughed. "No, he prefers the madeleines."

"Duly noted."

"He sent me to… Erm…"

"To…erm?" she repeated when he trailed off, looking deeply uncomfortable.

"To keep an eye on you." He proceeded to flinch with his whole body.

"What are you doing now?" she asked when it looked like he was having some sort of fit.

He opened one eye. "If I told Anais that I was sent to watch her, she would stab me. Repeatedly. Until her arm got tired, and then she would kick me in the stones. A lot."

"I'm not going to stab you," Briar said wearily, dropping onto the end of the bench not currently stacked with cooling muffins. "Or kick you. Not before I've had my tea, anyway."

"Your tea!" Matthias scrambled for the kettle, pouring the boiling water into a teapot already filled with leaves. The soothing aroma of tea and bergamot competed with the tart sweetness of strawberry compote bubbling away.

"What is Ethan afraid I'm going to do, exactly?" Briar asked when he slid a cup toward her, along with the honey jar and a dish of cream. She refused to feel any which way about Ethan leaving and setting another Iron Crow in his place. He did not trust her. And he had told her she should not trust him. The things they had done to each other in the darkness did not change that.

"Not *you*," Matthias assured her, then paused, rather ruining the effect. "Well, not exactly. He needed to go find some supplies and said there were Keepers about. And Crows. Can't trust a Crow, you know."

"So I hear."

"He didn't want to leave you unguarded."

"I see."

"And he sent me because not only am I handsome"—he winked—"and more handsome than that satyr, don't let him fool you—but also because Dragon said you don't care for baking."

Her teacup froze halfway to her mouth. "He said that?"

"He did. And I've always wanted to make petit fours and a croquembouche in an actual kitchen with actual ingredients instead of pickling vegetables and hoping butter will soften the hardtack. It never does. Nothing makes hardtack edible. Believe me."

"I never told him I don't enjoy baking," she said softly. He was quite right, though. Baking was not her favorite, but it was a necessity. Especially as everything Petal baked turned to the consistency of a rock. Or soup. Painfully salty soup. With rocks.

Matthias winced. "Was he wrong? Am I invading your space? I would murder someone if I found them in my kitchen." He shoved a plate of sugar-dusted madeleines at her as if disarming a bomb. "Try these."

"He wasn't wrong, exactly," she allowed, still wondering what it meant. If anything.

"He said he wanted you to have time in your garden."

"Oh." She softened. Unacceptably so. She couldn't fight Keepers and Iron Crows and Charles bloody Aster if she went soft. She took a hasty bite of the madeleine before she could do something mortifying, like sigh into her teacup. Or blush. Again. More.

"Does he do this sort of thing often?" she asked.

"Like this? Not exactly."

"It's rather high-handed." And surprisingly sweet. Though he would definitely scoff at being called sweet.

Matthias also scoffed. "Are you asking me if the captain of a ship of Iron Crows is likely to ask permission before he does things?"

She wrinkled her nose. "I suppose not." She took another bite. "Matthias?"

"Yes?

"This is the best thing I've ever eaten."

BRIAR HATED TO admit it, but spending several hours with the sun on her shoulders and her fingers in the dirt was exactly what she had needed. She felt stronger, brighter. Replenished. Magic did not have an inexhaustible supply. Nor did a calm state of being. They had to be cultivated, just like hollyhocks.

There was the ever-present danger of burning out your magic. Briar had never had to worry about it before now. Coddling rosebushes, encouraging plum trees, and bewitching violet petals did not take much from her.

Black Shucks and boggarts and sirens, on the other hand…

Not to mention the heavy weight of worry for her sister. It was taking its toll. Her hip was not the only part of her that needed a rest. And nothing was more restful, more soothing, than deadheading hydrangeas, murmuring to bumblebees, scolding slugs. She filled a basket with rosemary, another with mint. Three more with roses, foxgloves, and stalks of lavender.

She harvested dandelion heads for wine, the purple thistle nearby catching its spikes in her hair and pulling. "Rude." She reached for her trowel. "We talked about this," she murmured to the thistle, before gently prying its roots loose. "I don't believe in weeds—all plants have a purpose—but you grow too fast and too strong for this little patch. You're a bit of a bully, you know."

She carried it to the edge of the garden, just on the other side of the low stone wall. It took only a few minutes to dig a hole and plant it in its new spot. "There. Try to be more polite."

A shadow fell over her.

She glanced up, a tall, dark figure blocking out the sun. She stumbled back onto her bottom, skin prickling with fear before she recognized the slant of the jaw, the muscled forearm tattooed with an anchor. The silver rings.

"Mr. Swansea."

He narrowed his dark, fathomless eyes at her. The prickle of fear turned into a thrill. "Miss Foxglove," he returned pointedly.

*Oh.* He had been right to be cross when she called him Mr. Swansea. She did not care for it at all either. It was formal and polite and not at all *Dragon.* The pointed lift of his eyebrow was entirely of the Dragon, however. As was his presence, looming over her.

Also, the blood on his chest, the deep scratches on his left hand.

She shot to her feet, scowling. "You're wounded!"

He shrugged. "It's nothing."

"You're bleeding on my hydrangeas," Briar pointed out. "So it's not nothing. Come with me."

When she grabbed his hand and pulled him into the garden, he let her. She led him to a table and hurried off to fetch water and the basket of supplies she kept under the counter. Matthias was busy charming three elderly ladies who were suddenly in desperate need of lemon possets and bergamot tea and pink flummery.

"What happened to you?" Briar demanded of Ethan when she returned. He was sprawled in the sun very like a pirate king on a throne. Except for the pink forget-me-nots around his boots. They danced on their green stalks. "Where did you go?"

"I needed kelpie teeth and more mermaid hair." He shot her an accusatory sidelong glance. "Someone stole mine."

Briar shrugged, very much as he had shrugged. "I needed it."

He pulled a small glass bottle from his pocket and handed it to her. Inside curled a shimmering strand of seaweed-dark hair. It felt like a posy of wildflowers. A song sung outside her window under the full moon. *Calm down, Briar.*

"Thank you," she said. "I'll keep my hands to myself, then."

He frowned. "Let's not get drastic."

A laugh bubbled out of her. How she could laugh when he sat glowering and covered in blood after having done only the gods-knew-what? Right after leaving her bed before the sun.

"Did you find out who sent the grimsong?" she asked.

He scrubbed a hand over his face. "An Iron Crow who likes to dabble in baneful magic, as expected. A friend of Twyla's, also as expected."

"And?"

"And what?"

"And where is he now?"

"He's thinking about what he's done."

"Where? At the bottom of the ocean?"

Ethan did not reply, but he did smile. Just a little.

It was not a reassuring smile.

She washed his cuts and applied a comfrey salve to them, as well as to his bruises. The knuckles of his hand were both cut *and* bruised. He sat very still as she ministered to him. When was the last time someone had tended to his wounds? She assumed by his scars that he was often hurt, but by his demeanor that it was not something he let others see. The moment stretched between them, warm as a cup of chocolate on a midwinter night.

Followed by a swig of whiskey.

The man did pack a punch.

Even sitting idly, menace and command fairly emanated from him. It didn't help that she knew exactly what he could do with his hands now. His mouth.

She cleared her throat. "I never told you that baking is my least favorite thing about the tearoom," she said.

"You didn't have to. You get a little line right here between your brows when you bake." He pressed a finger to the spot.

"And when you think someone is being rude."

"I do?"

"It's very fearsome, I assure you."

"You're making fun of me."

"I only make fun of things that scare me."

She scowled. "Now you really *are* mocking me."

"I wouldn't dare."

She rolled her eyes. "As if *I* scare you."

"More than you know, little thorn." His voice was quiet, as if he were speaking to himself. "More than you know."


Briar stayed in the garden a little longer.

Which was her first mistake.

Ethan went inside to talk to Matthias, and she took a turn in the orchard, murmuring to the plums and the pears ripening on the branches. Bumblebees hovered, drunk on pollen and sweetness. The heat between her and Ethan had not been banked by their night together. Not at all. If anything, it was growing more complicated.

She felt flushed just knowing he was nearby.

He was probably used to that reaction. She saw the way people looked at him down in the village. She could not blame them. She was absolutely certain she looked at him the very same way. It was difficult not to, and that was even before she knew the sound of his breaths growing ragged in her ear. The lick of heat when he pinned her down to use his tongue and teeth. The—

"Miss Foxglove."

She could not think of a more unwelcome visitor than Charles bloody Aster.

Any interruption of the pleasant reminiscence she had been having about the feel of Ethan's mouth on her skin ought to be a criminal offense. Clap a Keeper's iron collar on him. Posthaste. Let a kelpie eat his liver.

Alas, if the Keepers were still watching her, they were not

very interested in Mr. Charles Aster.

She could hardly blame them.

She was not interested in him either.

And her fountain was not large enough for a kelpie.

"Mr. Aster," she said evenly. She knew Ethan could not see her from the kitchen window. She was not sure where his dragon was. Snapdragon flapped its wings, beak open to show tiny, vicious teeth.

"Control your swan," Charles said.

Briar smiled. "No."

He blinked, taken aback. "I saved you, Miss Foxglove. I think I deserve a little courtesy."

"What do you want, Mr. Aster?" She did not put worms down his shirt or ask a bee to bite his backside. If that was not courtesy, then what was?

"I know where your sister is, Miss Foxglove."

A cold stone dropped into the pit of her belly and lodged there. She was half surprised her teeth did not chatter when she spoke.

He had not happened by the ship after all.

She had known it was too much to hope for.

"Do you?" she said, positively dripping politeness. She blinked as though she were a little confused. Couldn't possibly know what he was hinting at. She was only a green witch, after all, with a limp and marigolds in her apron. "That's a relief, as I assure you, no one else does."

He was spiteful and spoiled. And unfortunately, not stupid. *More's the pity.*

She could call out for Ethan, but what would that do but confirm any suspicions Charles might have of him, of where Petal was hidden? Perhaps he was bluffing.

Unlikely, but not impossible.

Charles remained on the other side of the shields Briar knew Ethan had worked at the borders of her gardens. Iron and rowanberries and bonedust. She did not know if it was dumb luck or mindfulness that kept Charles from triggering them. He did not mean her well, that much was obvious. But he was unlikely to physically hurt her. He did not like to get dirty by mud or blood or magic. That was for others to do on his behalf. His mother. Mr. Crane.

"Don't cross me again, Miss Foxglove. We will have this land, and you *will* keep it hale for us." He ducked under a branch and walked away, crossing onto the cobblestone street, whistling. For some reason, that enraged her most of all.

Briar was still frozen in place. He could be lying. He might suspect something, but that was not the same as actually knowing something he should not, something he could use to hurt Petal. And it was not as if he would be welcomed on the Sea Dragon ship to snoop around. Not him nor any other.

She had to stay calm.

Tell that to her trembling hands. Her stuttered breathing.

Was it her panic that triggered Ethan's wards? Or something else? She did not know. She only knew that one moment she was standing in the sun feeling cold to her bones, and the next, Ethan was stalking through the orchard.

But it wasn't Charles he hauled out of the lilacs on the other side of the pear tree by the shirtfront. It was an Iron Crow. This one appeared to be an ordinary brute with flat, angry eyes. He had no Black Shuck, no siren. Only fists the size of hams.

They did not save him from Ethan's wrath.

Every one of Ethan's blows landed with vicious precision. A fist to the jaw, the stomach. An elbow to the back of the head. The Crow dropped like a stone, gagging on pain. Ethan pressed his boot to the man's chest. Blood stained the side of the Iron Crow's lips, dripping from his nose. "She's *mine*."

The Crow coughed, groaning when it tore at what must be a set of cracked ribs.

"Understand?" Ethan did not remove his boot. He tilted his head as though he were listening carefully. His left eyebrow rose. "I said, do you understand?"

His dragon snapped at the Crow's familiar: a wasp with a glowing stinger. He clawed at Ethan's ankle. "I understand."

"Good. I'm going to leave you with just enough of your teeth so you can tell the others."

AND AFTER ALL of that, it was the white roses shedding petals that stuck to Ethan's hair that did it.

The cold stone in her belly melted. Her witch knot flared. She tasted mint and roses and fennel. She jumped to her feet. "I have to go."

Ethan's hand around her wrist stopped her dead. "Not alone."

"Yes, alone. Just down to the village." She pulled but could not break his hold. Not that she had expected to.

"Briar, perhaps you failed to notice, but there was a Crow here not five minutes ago. And he was here for *you*. So if you're going, I'm going with you."

"You can't."

His expression hardened. "Pardon, sweetheart?"

"You can't," she repeated with a huff of impatience. If she was right, she needed to hurry. "No one will notice me on my own. But if I go strolling through the square with the Dragon…"

"Yes, that's the point."

"I can't be noticed, Ethan."

"I'm a Crow. I think I can handle it."

She snorted. "You are not exactly easy to ignore."

He snorted back. "And you think you are?"

"I have nearly thirty years that prove it." Her voice softened. "Please, Ethan."

His gaze snapped to her mouth, eyes darkening. "Hell."

She tugged her arm free.

"My dragon will circle. That's not negotiable."

"Fine, fine." She darted away before he could stop her, possibilities whirling in her head. Was she onto something? Could she be right about this?

"You have ten minutes, and then I'm coming after you."

She nodded at him, ducking under a mulberry tree, distract-ed, impatient.

"Briar?" His tone was so quiet it lashed around her, unexpect-edly restraining.

She stumbled to a halt. "Yes?"

"Make it five."

# Chapter Twenty-One

B RIAR STOPPED ONLY long enough to take her driftwood cane and the basket she usually took to market. It swung from her arm as she hurried down the hill like any other witch looking to buy potatoes for stew or golden bells for solstice charms. The rooftop gargoyles watched her, wearing their flower crowns. Tourists ate lemon ices under the sun. A Pegasus trotted down the center of the road, golden wings gleaming. Children chased after him, hoping for a fallen feather for luck.

Briar stopped at the grocer for cheese she could not afford, and at the charm shop for black salt and an iron nail tipped with a tiny shell. She kept her pace easy and unhurried even as everything inside her screamed, *Go, go, go.*

She bought a bottle of strawberry cordial even though she preferred dandelion wine.

She traded bundles of rosemary for water from the healing baths in a blue bottle. She tied gold bells on red ribbons around her basket handle. She avoided Aster Apothecary, for obvious reasons.

The shop specializing in grimoires refused to sell to her, sliding panicked glances at Charles outside, bowing to all of the ladies and charming them into trying lotions that would stop sun freckles.

Briar snuck glances at the portal. The red door was still locked, the garland flowers starting to wilt. The daisies had drooped; the Queen Anne's lace had shed its petals. All but the white roses.

Three Keepers stood at attention, observing the crowd who stared curiously back, whispering, on their way to the beach. There were even more iron charms and red rowanberry necklaces than Briar had seen yesterday. Ethan's dragon circled above, trailing sparks of light and gathering cries of wonder from below.

While the dragon pulled gaze after gaze, Briar pondered the red door. If Petal had come through the portal, how had she made it up the hill to the cottage garden without being seen? She could not have taken the main road. She would have had to circle behind, either dropping down into the sand dunes or running behind the last row of houses. How had she managed to stay hidden when the Midsummer crowds were everywhere?

Briar cut through the alley between two shops, sending her magic out like vines of ivy, searching, searching.

As it turned out, she did not need witchcraft. Only eyes.

Even the alleys and back gardens of Haven were picturesque, whitewashed and dripping flowers. There were pots of geraniums and rosemary for protection. Red poppies, blue irises, pink sweet peas.

And white roses.

Just there, bursting in a froth of petals and thorns, choking the spaces between the wooden gate and a white-gravel walkway. They spilled from the inn's stable roof, wound around a nearby water trough, tangled over the stone wall.

Her witch knot tingled, green magic waking.

White roses where Petal had lain in the garden. White roses climbing up the side of the cottage to crawl through her bedroom window. White roses on the cliffside near Ethan's ship.

White roses here, where a witch might keep to the shadows on her way home.

It could not be a coincidence.

Briar bent over the roses, plucking flowers for her basket in case anyone happened to glance in her direction. A dove cooed from a nearby rooftop, perched on a gargoyle's head. Her heart thumped in her chest as she peered among the roots, dragging the toe of her shoe through the dirt. Nothing but leaf matter, ants, a surprised worm to whom she apologized. The petals shivered under a breeze off the sea.

She dug deeper, the back of her neck prickling. She waited for someone to jump out of the alley, to shout at her from a window. A Keeper to descend on her with iron chains.

But it was only the roses growing where they shouldn't be and her tingling witch knot.

And there, just there…

The glint of silver. The sheen of a small seed pearl.

White as bone, white as salt.

White as the moon.

She pulled it from the ground, anticipation racing through her.

The other half of the moon charm.

She tucked it into her stays, down between her breasts, and straightened. Wandering slowly back to the main square, her basket bursting with flowers, was the hardest thing she had ever done. She wanted to run up the hill. But Miss Briar Foxglove galloping up the road with a mad grin would be noticed. And she could not afford that.

Bad enough that Charles Aster noticed her. Again.

The bastard. Why was he suddenly everywhere? He smiled in her direction. She whirled on her heel. Better to be seen running than stay here.

"Miss Foxglove."

Too late. She froze, cursing under her breath.

"Miss Foxglove, have you any news of your sister?" he called out loudly.

Heads turned, attention sharpening.

"How odd that she should go missing at the same time as the shields dropping."

Someone gasped.

Briar vowed to put something in his next cup of tea to induce a rash. Or he could do with a few sores. Painful ones.

"Magic is unpredictable," Briar returned calmly. Serenely, even. He wanted a reaction from her—they all did.

They would not get one.

"Even the Keepers fear the shields have trapped her in the between," she added over her shoulder, hurrying away. "Thank you so much for your concern, Mr. Aster. How gentlemanly of you."

"That's not what I heard."

She wanted to keep walking, but others had drifted into her path, frowning. A cat familiar swiped at her leg. Charles sauntered closer. His cravat points were perfectly starched. She hoped fervently that they poked him right in the eyeball.

"There have been Keepers at your tearoom," he said. "And *Iron Crows.*"

The shocked whispers made her grind her back teeth. As she needed customers, she could not even threaten to poison anyone.

"*Very* suspicious, don't you think?" Charles asked the gathering crowd.

"Is this true?" someone shouted. She did not recognize him. "Are you why I'm stuck here?"

"No," Briar said. "My sister is missing. She didn't drop the shields."

Well, not on *purpose*, anyway.

Briar did not think anyone currently glaring at her would care for the distinction. This was precisely the sort of attention and delay that she could not afford. If Charles really did know where Petal was, she had to swallow her ire. Vengeance sang in her heart. But it would have to wait. "I assure you, we know nothing about the shields." She added, "I am only worried for my sister."

"I think you do know!"

"Why else would Keepers care about a tearoom?"

"Where is she?"

Someone shoved her. She was a small woman, but strong.

And angry. Briar stumbled, not expecting it. Her cane stuttered on the cobbles.

"I want to go home!"

"Bring her to the Keepers!"

"Put her in an iron collar until she tells us how to get home!"

Another shove, this one hard enough to take Briar's legs out from under her. She landed awkwardly, her basket spilling bright flowers at everyone's feet. The golden bells for good luck rang.

The Keepers were tracking the moon charm. Worse, Lord Coventry was tracking it. It would only be a matter of minutes before they came for her if she stayed here much longer, tourists and villagers yelling at her, a stolen amulet piece between her breasts. The wild dance of magic from so many revelers would only hide her for so long. Especially with Charles trying to prove a point, showing his power, such as it was.

But he had miscalculated. Briar was perfectly willing to be pushed around if it meant keeping her sister safe.

The Dragon was not.

A clap of thunder rattled the sky. The sound reverberated, sharp as needles. It scraped the inside of the skull like a single, giant iron bell. Everyone froze, a tableau of angry witches in a circle around Briar.

Ethan did not have to raise his voice. "Get the hell away from her. *Now.*"

Briar sat up, pushing her hair off her face as the others scurried away.

"Not fast enough," Ethan added, silkily. Menacingly.

A bolt of lightning seared the perfect blue summer sky, slamming into the ground. Someone screamed. The smell of burning ozone and cobblestone was thick.

Another bolt hit just outside the apothecary. The window shattered into dust. Keepers ran into the square. Ethan did not even spare them a glance. He stared at Charles, who had gone red, then pale. His throat bobbed as he struggled to swallow.

"I won't tell you again," Ethan said.

The violence that came off him was enough to send three more tourists running and a cat up a tree. Charles was not that brave. He backed away, sweating. The fire from the lightning strike licked at the apothecary door.

Ethan reached down to help Briar up. His usually impassive expression was as mutable as a summer storm. Lightning changes, thunderous fury, and something softer. Something she could not name.

"You said you'd let me go alone." Briar frowned at him.

He grunted. "I lied."

She nearly smiled despite the bruises on her hip, the shocked stares, the whispers already traveling from shop to shop.

Ethan glared at Charles over his shoulder. "Still here?"

And then he tossed him something small and green. Charles was too slow, too stunned with fear. He caught it out of reflex. It was a bundle of coltsfoot leaves, also known as horse hoof, wrapped with a strand from a white horse's mane, and red thread. A curse.

Ethan finally smiled. "Enjoy your nightmares."

The charm sent seven nights of nightmares. Charles dropped it like it had stung him, wiping his fingers on his fine breeches. But it was too late. He stumbled back a step, another, before turning and dashing back to the apothecary.

"It would be so much easier if you let me murder him," Ethan grumbled.


HALFWAY HOME, BRIAR'S cane splintered. Ethan tossed the pieces of driftwood into a bush with a sound of pure disgust. It was the same derisive sound that old dowagers reserved for newfangled, fashionable hemlines that were too short and familiars that ran wild at formal dinner parties. "You need a proper walking stick."

"I know," she admitted. "My mother thought white driftwood would fit Haven. She thought it was pretty." Briar had drawn the line at the loops of pearls and opals that they could not afford and only cut into her skin anyway.

"Driftwood is not strong enough. And this design is ridiculous." He nearly growled. "This whole bloody town is ridiculous."

"No argument here." Briar shrugged. "But it's home."

Ethan frowned at her as she darted under the metal teacup sign of the Rose and Petal. "You're very cheerful."

"And that offends you?" She dropped onto the bench inside the hall, not wanting to wait one more moment.

"Ladies who are pushed to the ground by a mob of idiots are not usually so cheerful about it," he pointed out. He did not sound cheerful at all. "I half expected them to bring out the pitchforks."

"Oh, *that*."

"Yes. That." That lethal bite to his voice again. The gleam of magic sparking from a dagger at his belt.

She wouldn't pretend that it had not frightened her—the thought of the iron collar and a Keeper's cart. The thought of associating her tearoom with the locked shields and losing her customers and eventually her home. Her broken cane from being manhandled. She had another, but it was a bit too short for her. Her mother really had chosen them for the aesthetic value. She had no idea what was needed for a useful cane. But even so, Briar now had something in her possession that made it all worth it.

Ethan tilted his head. "What have you done, little thorn?"

She grinned, reaching into her stays and pulling out the amulet. The silver was warm from her skin.

Ethan took a step closer. "You found it."

She beamed, smug and uncaring as to what that said about her character. Haven preferred haughty. Confident. But she had smugness. "I did."

"You'd make a decent Iron Crow."

"Thank you. I think?"

The twists of decorated silver and the iridescent pearls looked so innocuous, just sitting in her palm.

"Now we just need to find the other half," he said.

"As to that…"

Ethan lifted her chin, forcing her to meet his gaze. "You've been keeping secrets." Censure and warning and something close to pride were in his eyes. Also something that promised consequences. Punishment.

It wasn't just Ethan watching her so intently, but also Dragon. The Iron Crow who had killed three warlocks last year alone, according to rumors he'd neither denied nor confirmed. But she could easily believe it. He was dark as the waves, the lulling song of the tides, the sudden undercurrent that pulled you under. The line between water that saved you from dying of thirst and water that drowned you was very thin indeed.

She found she did not mind it at all.

She rather liked it, actually.

And by the way his eyes narrowed consideringly, he knew full well. "Tell me," he commanded.

If it had been over anything less important, she would have pushed back just to see the line of his jaw clench. To see his eyes flare. To feel that delicious thrill, half warning, half anticipation.

Instead, she rose to her feet and led him to the kitchen. Matthias was in the tearoom, convincing customers to try his croquembouche. The windows were open to birdsong and the familiar tinkling of the teacup wind chimes. The fire had died down but the wall was still warm as Briar wedged her finger under a loose brick near the top of the hearth.

She pulled out the other half of the amulet triumphantly.

Ethan cursed, softly, admiringly. "You really do have everyone fooled, don't you? Serving tea and pink-frosted cakes with daisies in your hair."

She couldn't stop a small smile at that. "I'm sure I don't know what you mean."

He was behind her now, crowding into her, breath against her ear. His mouth brushed her hair. "I see you, little thorn." It was a warning, a promise.

She swayed backward against his heat, couldn't help herself.

A rush of desire tingled through her. She had to clear her throat before speaking. "Only the moonstone is missing."

"How did you find this?"

"I followed the white roses."

"Clever little green witch." He sounded impressed but also implacable. He reached up, closing his fingers around the base of her throat. Her breath stuttered. Heat bloomed up her thighs. "You kept this from me."

"I…"

His grip tightened, just a little. Just enough. "Do you really want to make it worse by lying to me, sweetheart?" he asked softly.

"But…"

"And then you put yourself in danger again, just now, in the village." He clicked his tongue in lazy recrimination. "I know I was clear about that."

"I needed—"

"You *needed?*" His other hand slipped lower, dragging her skirts up. His knuckles brushed her quim. She whimpered, already so sensitive it made her feel a little drunk. "I know what you need, sweetheart."

He stroked her, lightly, teasingly. Slowly, as though an entire tearoom was not just on the other side of the wall, chatting politely, asking for more cucumber-watercress on biscuits. As though someone could not walk by the window. As though none of that mattered because he had her pinned against his chest, his for the claiming.

"Don't I?" he asked.

She tried to chase his hand, but he still had her throat in his grip. His erection pressed against her and she pushed back, wanting to touch him. *Needing* to touch him. To be touched.

"I asked you a question, Briar." His voice hardened and his fingers stilled. Her pulse fluttered against his palm. The combination was too perfect. Too much. She made a sound she was not proud of.

"Yes," she breathed out.

"Yes what?" He was patient, unforgiving.

"Yes, you know what I need—Ah!" She broke off on a gasp when he plunged two fingers inside of her, stroking deep. His thumb brushed her bud. He pressed against the little hood at the top and it made her buck. She was already lightheaded with pleasure. He really was a menace to good society.

*Thank the moon.*

He curled his fingers, still deep in her channel, dragging against her intimate flesh. She fluttered around him. "So wet for me," he whispered roughly. "So perfect."

Deeper, slower, until she was again whimpering.

"Are you going to come, sweetheart?"

She moaned, "Yes."

"Right here? In your kitchen, where anyone might see you?"

"Yes. *Please.*"

"And are you going to be more careful?" he asked.

"Yes!" She was very close to babbling. She would have said anything. He was working her closer and closer to a release she knew would burn right through her. Her thighs trembled in anticipation.

He sighed, disappointed. "I'm not convinced." He stilled his hand again.

The waves of her release retreated. "*What?*"

"Convince me."

She was helpless, throat in his grip, heat racing under her skin. He was in control. And she loved it.

Still. It was the principle of the thing. And the fact that she was still squirming with unmet desire.

"Ethan Swansea, so help me, I'll do it myself." Her fingertips barely brushed over her own slick and swollen folds when he stopped her. He gripped her wrist hard, his forearm pinning her ruthlessly against his body. His hardness slipped between her buttocks, another tease. She was a butterfly tacked to a board. Sensations ran through her and she could not chase any of them. "Ethan!"

He shook his head with false sympathy. "Only good girls get to come."

The names she called him were not generally used by genteel spinsters who lived in pink cottages.

His answering laugh was dark and merciless.

When she finally came, the pears in the tree just outside the kitchen ripened all at once.


HER CUSTOMERS WENT missing at the same time as the pieces of the broken moon charm.

It was mere hours later and word had traveled fast that Petal was missing and might be involved with the shields, and that Briar was keeping company with a notorious Iron Crow.

As predicted, it was not good for business.

When she asked the tea leaves about it, she swore she heard them laugh at her.

"Fine, then," she muttered, pushing the cup away and ducking out into the garden. Charles might well have been making empty threats when he said he knew where Petal was, but he meant every word when he said his family would have the cottage and her gardens. It was the only thing they wanted. They didn't care about the shields.

And no customers meant no money.

No money meant she would never be able to pay off her mother's debt.

The sun was sinking into the ocean, turning the air every shade of blue. It was still warm, with butterflies congregating in the yarrow. The outdoor tables should be filled with chattering customers, the walkways with couples wanting a romantic moment. She ought to be running out of sunwheel cookies, rose-petal honey, scones in the shape of oak leaves. Sachets of St. John's wort and lavender to burn at the bonfires for blessings, water gathered last solstice in tiny glass bottles, painted acorns, rowanberries strong on red thread.

"Where is everyone?" Ethan asked, appearing in the doorway.

He was starting to look as though he belonged here, even though he was a yew tree in a sea of roses.

She liked having him in her home. That was going to be a problem.

"Everyone is too scared to risk coming here," Briar said instead, with an annoyed sigh. "Charles convinced them that they might look guilty by association."

"I can make it look like an accident."

She smiled.

"I'm very good at what I do," he insisted.

"I'm sure you are."

"I don't understand you. You are letting them walk all over you. Him especially."

"It's complicated."

"Is it? Because Petal is safe on my ship."

"I know that." She did know that, and it was still a wonder to her. Because she believed him. Petal was safe. "But when the shields lift again and Petal wakes up, I still have to live here."

"But *he* doesn't."

She had to admit, it was a lovely feeling to have someone so dangerous grumbling over her. Something she could never have imagined. Something she would remember and cherish when she was old, gathering her flowers. "The Asters have power in Haven."

He snorted. "That's not real power."

"I know. But it's more than I have at present." She shrugged when he scowled. "It's true. Anyway, no one's going to go against them for the sake of a cup of tea and a frosted biscuit." She paused. "Perhaps they'll come for the notoriety when they get bored. Although if Matthias's eclairs aren't enough to lure them back, nothing will be."

But it wouldn't be enough to pay off her mother's debt. Not nearly. Not in time.

He shook his head. "Fucking Haven."

"Haven," she agreed. "Anyway, Matthias took the rest of his

baking to sell at the beach. It would be a shame for it to go to waste. He worked so hard and was so pleased with himself."

"And you?"

"I'm just waiting for the next Iron Crow or the next Keeper to break in and start smashing more teacups." She reached for the amulet pieces tucked into her stays to reassure herself.

But she was not reassured.

Because she found only cotton and ribbons and skin.

No moon charm.

# Chapter Twenty-Two

W HEN BRIAR TOUCHED the space between her breasts and gave a choked gasp, Ethan knew exactly why.

He wanted to run his tongue where her fingers touched, but he also knew that was not why she had gasped.

Not yet, anyway.

"Ethan," she said, and there was smug satisfaction that she had used his name, uncorrected.

He needed to hear her moan it. Scream it.

Soon.

Although he had a feeling she was about to scream it in a much-less-enjoyable manner. His little poison berry. God, what she did to him. The things he wanted to do to *her*.

"The amulet is gone."

He could have feigned innocence. She would have believed him. But it did not suit his purpose. It had nothing to do with not wanting to lie to her. Not wanting her to be upset in any way, for any length of time. Ever. It was the long con, as he had told Godric. He needed to get his crew home. He had promises to keep, the kind that would come for more than just himself if they were broken.

Even if he *had* considered staying put a little longer for the first time in his life.

He had never cared for gardens or garden walls, tea in pink cups, rose petals in his honey. Not until now. Not until Briar.

But it made no difference. Not in the end.

"I have it," he said calmly, pulling the loops of silver and pearls from his pocket.

Briar stilled, her eyes going wide. She looked betrayed. "You *stole* it?"

He twirled the pieces once just to watch the temper flare in her gray eyes. Magnificent. How anyone confused her for a mild-mannered spinster was beyond him. "I did," he confirmed lazily.

"When did you even—" She stopped. "In the kitchen!" Accusation made her voice husky, her cheeks pink.

Delicious.

Distracting.

She poked him in the chest, hard enough to bruise. It made him want to grin, but he thought it might make her combust.

"I never agreed to exchange orgasms for amulets!" she exclaimed hotly.

He shook his head in mock outrage. "The things you say, Miss Foxglove."

"*Mr.* Swansea."

His eyes narrowed. He was a great deal less amused now. "Briar."

"Give them back."

"They are safer with me."

Her own eyes narrowed so quickly she probably gave herself a headache. "Give them back, now."

"Convince me," he said, echoing his words in the kitchen when she'd come apart on his fingers. The way she had whimpered, the soft gasp of lust when his hand closed around her throat.

"How about I witch a rash on your—"

She was clearly not reliving the moment alongside with him.

"Tsk, that's not very ladylike."

She looked like she might start shrieking like a kelpie. It should not have been adorable. None of this should be. He crowded her, leaning down to meet her gaze, which was incensed and then instantly wary. It did things to him; he wasn't too proud to admit it. He liked knowing he could affect her.

But there were other factors involved. And they threatened to break him out in hives every time he considered them. Which was often. Always. Every damn minute. "You broke your promise to me to not to put yourself in danger," he reminded her, low and absolute.

He had made a man wet himself with a less-threatening tone of voice.

Briar might have balked at it a week ago. Tonight, she scoffed.

She actually *scoffed*.

God, it made him want to laugh. And to turn her over his knee and spank her until her delectable bottom was as pink as the wildflowers in her hair.

But he didn't. Couldn't. It was too easy to remember the way that Keeper sneered at her, the way the villagers had surrounded her sprawled on the ground. The way Twyla could have killed her, the way the grimsong could have sung her into the sea. The way her only defense against this blasted island was a driftwood cane he could break with one hand and her stubborn, indomitable spirit. He wanted it to be enough. Knew too much about the witching world to believe it was.

Her scoff faltered when he did not drop her gaze, did not soften his jaw. "Is that what this is about?" she demanded.

"You are too reckless."

She laughed. It burst out of her, clearly unbidden. "This, coming from you?"

"Exactly. Imagine how bad the situation is," he said drily, "when an Iron Crow finds you too reckless."

She glared at him. He could all but see the wheels turning in her head. The vengeance brewing. He welcomed it. It was simple. Clear.

When nothing else was.

With a sound better suited to an enraged cat, she lunged for the amulet dangling from his fingers. He held it up out of her reach easily. "Don't trust me yet, little thorn?" he asked, humor fading. His voice changed again; he could feel the ice of it in his throat. "Good."

"Is this what this is about? To prove something to me?" she growled.

Adorable.

"Or to yourself?" she continued.

Less adorable, because it might well be the truth.

She was too sharp and too astute for her own good.

"You are vexing," she added through her teeth. Very astute. "And I do trust you, you ass. I trust you with *my sister*."

A privilege he would never admit rocked him to his very core.

Trusting an Iron Crow was unwise. Trusting Dragon was downright foolhardy.

But she had. Did. And he'd be damned, but it filled him with something too akin to pride. Satisfaction. Duty.

*Fucking hell.*

He gave her the amulet. Her exhale was tremulous, relieved. Happy. He felt like a king.

Or an idiot.

Briar tucked it back into her stays, from where it would be his honor to steal it again. "I know a spell to turn your entire ship as pink as my cottage. I am sorely tempted."

"Godric would love it. Anais would come for you in the dead of night. So let me tempt you into something else," he said, because he could not bloody well help himself.

Definitely an idiot.

"A stroll, Miss Foxglove," he said when she shot him a look. "What a wicked turn of thought you have."


Briar had never punched a man in the nose in her entire life.

Or cursed him with a rash, or turned his mighty, dreaded warship pink.

But she was currently considering all three with a great deal of enthusiasm. She was twisted up with irritation, uncertainty, and an unhealthy lick of desire.

Damn the man.

He had stolen the amulet right out of her stays. She was mildly impressed. She supposed it was easy work for a Crow. It was what they did, after all. Stealing things like a murder of crows. She wondered if she should feel more betrayed. But mostly she just felt the need for revenge. Something that would make him want her as much as she wanted him, that would twist him up so she would not be alone with these uncomfortable feelings.

Because although he had stolen from her, he had not bothered lying about it. He could have taken off with the amulet, continued his own investigation. Held her sister hostage. A frisson of fear went through her, but she dismissed it. Her instinct said she could trust him with this. Her swan agreed. The tea leaves. Even Bramble. And Bramble did not even entirely trust Briar.

And he'd already had many chances to trip her up but had not done so. Instead he'd carried her up the stairs to bed when she could not manage the stairs. He'd flooded Charles's shop and then set it on fire. He'd broken a man's ribs in her orchard.

And he had given the amulet back.

She was under no illusion that she could have physically forced him to do so. With her magic, perhaps, given enough time. And a proper batch of stinging nettle or deadly nightshade vines. And she realized he could just steal it back at any point in time.

But he'd been truly proud of her when she admitted she had found both pieces. She had seen it in his face.

"Where are you going?" he asked when she turned away from the cottage.

"For a walk."

"Alone?" he demanded.

She pointed above her head, without having to look up. "He's coming with me."

Ethan's dragon circled over her. She would not even need a lantern. His glow, added to the moonlight, silvered the ground under her feet. Ethan nodded once. He faded into the shadows, all except for the glint of his eyes and his weapons. He looked fierce, severe. Ruthless, even just standing there.

Alone.

She sighed. "Well? Are you coming?"

He fell into step beside her without a word. Her body tingled at his nearness when he opened the wooden gate for her. It creaked on its hinges. "On the night before the solstice, we count fireflies," she said.

"Why's that?"

"For good luck until the winter solstice," she explained. "And I clearly need all of the luck I can get," she muttered. Of course, the last time she had followed a Haven tradition for luck, she had walked into a herd of kelpies.

They crossed the fields, the long grass dotted with stonecrop and yellow gorse. It smelled like earth and flowers and the salt of the sea. Like home. The pond she took him to was a shallow mirror, tucked into a small valley. No one bothered to come out here much, which suited Briar just fine. A toad plopped into the water, disgruntled at the interruption. Ethan frowned, keeping his body angled between Briar and the water. "Any Shellycoats in these hills?" he asked.

Shellycoats were cousins to kelpies who preferred rivers to the sea, but had the same penchant for murdering unwary swimmers who crossed into their territories. They wore coats covered with shells that clacked when they pounced. Some were said to be friendly, but you could never be certain until it was too late.

"They mostly stick to the edges of the moors and down by Hallow," she replied. "The most dangerous thing I've ever seen here is a duck."

And Ethan, of course. He was dangerous in so many ways.

"Any unicorns? They do like to do some damage with those horns."

"They prefer Holdfast," Briar said. "This is a sleepy little pond no one bothers with very much. It's too quiet. Boring."

His dragon circled once more before settling onto a hillock, head raised and alert. Snapdragon streaked behind him, finally settling on the dragon's back as though it was a perfectly normal thing to do. Briar's cheeks warmed and she refused to look at Ethan. Familiars weren't supposed to flirt with each other, for the moon's sake. Were they? But her swan had never looked more comfortable. And the dragon did not try to swallow it whole in retribution, so she supposed it was fine.

Embarrassing, but fine.

She turned back to the pond, waiting for the fireflies to come out of hiding. The arrival of a dragon, corporeal or not, sent most living creatures scurrying for cover. It was not long before a yellow-green flash of light drifted from the grasses, from the marsh marigolds. One, then two, then a hundred.

Every year, when the nights turned hot, the fireflies came. And it never failed to amaze her. She followed their trail of lights as they darted in and out of the shadows. She counted twenty-seven before she turned to Ethan, but he was watching her, not the fireflies. "Aren't you counting?" she asked.

"I don't need luck," he said quietly, eyes still on her.

"What *do* you need?"

"Careful, little thorn. Or I might answer."

She couldn't pretend not to know what he meant, but she did not press him either. The pull between them was alive, full of its own magic. He might have tried to warn her away earlier with his little trick, but he couldn't pretend to be indifferent. Not fully.

And she had a few tricks of her own.

"I thought a captain would be more superstitious," she said. "Don't ships have all those rules? Don't set sail on a Friday? Never kill an albatross?"

"Matthias hangs a hot cross bun in the galley to prevent fires," he admitted. "And I have rules," he added. "Those aren't them."

He didn't elaborate.

"There's nothing you do for luck? Pick four-leaf clovers? Make a wish on dandelions?" That was a favorite of hers. "Wear daisies in your hair?"

"How did you guess?"

"You seem the type. So frivolous."

His mouth twitched with amusement. "Do I?"

She grinned. "I could make you a daisy crown. It would be very fearsome. King of the Iron Crows."

"As fearsome as you?"

"Oh, at the very *least*."

"Best not risk it. Not sure Haven could handle it."

She sat at the edge of the pond when her hip began to protest the uneven ground. Ethan sat next to her, lithe and graceful. "Your hip is bothering you."

She shrugged. "It comes and goes."

"Did someone…hurt you?" The question was both gentle and rough. Patient but commanding. A dagger through the still night air. Pure Ethan.

She shook her head. "It's always been like that. Sometimes it's perfectly fine and then other times it does not like to stay in its place. The doctors all say the joint is weak, or loose."

"And the witches?"

"No spell for this kind of thing. It is what it is."

"Hmm." He didn't say anything else, not for a long moment, until he added, "Look up."

She did as he asked, expecting his dragon to be showing off, or a swallow to be diving for insects. But it was only the night sky, on fire with stars and magical in its own way.

"I count stars," he said. "My mother told me they would bring me luck when I was a boy."

"She did? Oh, I like that. It means I don't have to wait for the fireflies. Sometimes I need luck in January too." She slid him a sidelong glance. "Where is your mother now?"

"She died a long, long time ago."

"I'm sorry."

"My father left soon after, but that was for the best. I hopped on the first ship that would have me."

"How old were you?"

"Eight."

"*Eight years old?*" She sounded as scandalized as she was. When she was eight years old, she was building twig houses for snails and trying to catch fireflies and then releasing them immediately when she felt bad for putting them in a jar.

He shrugged one shoulder, faintly amused at her outburst. "My father was gone, thank God, and I loved the sea and that was good enough for me."

It made sense for a boy who had power over water. She still hated it on his behalf. He ought to have had birthday cakes and holidays at the beach and someone to make him tea when he was cold.

"And then Granny Gallows claimed me and it wasn't so bad."

"Who is Granny Gallows?"

"She was an ornery old weather witch who could make any man cry at ten paces. She bullied everyone. She would have bullied the king if she'd met him."

Briar smiled at the image and the softness to his tone when he spoke of her. "I'll make dandelion wishes on her behalf," she said, and then instantly felt silly. He did not need her prayers. "I never met my father," she added. "He died a year after Petal and I were born, but my mother liked to tell stories of how he rode into the village on a gold Pegasus. Or how he called all the bluebirds from the sky on her birthday." She wrinkled her nose. "I'm not sure any of them are true."

"My father tossed me in the well on my birthday because he made a wager over my powers. Keep your stories. They're not harming anyone."

"That rat. Where is he now? I have a lovely tea blend in mind, just for him."

Ethan did smile then. "If I can't murder Aster, it doesn't seem fair that you get to murder my father."

"I suppose," she grumbled. "But I could make his nose bleed stinging nettles. Or give him violent stomach cramps."

"If my mother never managed to murder him, I'm not sure anyone could," he said wryly. "She was not an easy woman, but she did her best by me." He frowned. "I haven't spoken about any of them in years."

She slipped her hand into his because she understood perfectly well that sometimes families were complicated. You could love them and still find it easier to be on your own, all while your chest cracked with the grief of missing them.

They stayed like that for a long moment, lying in the warm grass, the stars glittering above.

❧

# Chapter Twenty-Three

B RIAR COULD NOT help but wonder if Ethan had ever known softness. There were soft beds and soft hands and soft silks, but they were not the same thing. Briar's own mother was also not an easy woman, but Briar had Petal and she had flowers and hot tea and honeybees at the window. What did Ethan have, so young on a ship as a cabin boy? And then as a captain and the Dragon. He had fear and respect and envy, but not softness.

She began to gather the sea pinks and campion flowers and water mint that grew around them, the feverfew and the clovers and the daisies. She tucked some around his head like a crown.

"What are you doing, little thorn?" he asked.

She sprinkled petals over him. Tucked a foxglove into the scabbard with his favorite dagger. Tiny forget-me-nots in his boots. More in his pockets when it occurred to her that she really, really did not want him to forget her. When she was still not satisfied, she straddled him, feeling bold. She picked a dandelion gone white and fluffy and held it up. "Make a wish," she whispered.

"I don't believe in—"

She frowned at him in disapproval. "Don't argue with a green witch."

"Yes, ma'am." He blew on the dandelion, sending the fluffy seeds floating in every direction. Fireflies drifted closer, flashing green. A star fell behind him.

She found pineapple weed and wrapped a dandelion leaf

around it. "Now try this."

He arched a brow. "You want me to eat weeds?"

"Yes, please." She was still straddling him. She never wanted to stop. He was all warm, padded muscle between her thighs.

"Is this how you poison your suitors?"

"Well, I'm sure you've noticed I don't exactly have a line waiting at my front door."

"I've said it before, Briar. Haven is full of idiots."

She rolled her eyes at the blatant flattery, but it made her cheeks pink all the same. He brushed his thumb over her cheekbone. "You're trying to distract me," she accused, but her voice was softer than she liked.

He raised his eyebrows. "Is it working?"

Yes. "No." She sent him a severe glance. "You refused to eat your peas as a boy, didn't you?"

"I was the model of proper behavior."

"Ha."

"You wound me."

"Ha again. Just try it."

He crossed his arms behind his head, smirking dangerously. "Convince me, sweetheart."

A thrill shot through her. She had a dangerous and powerful man between her thighs and was allowed to touch him. She was allowed to want him to have to catch his breath. To make him groan. To make him whimper with need. She wasn't supposed to want these things. But she did. Desperately.

She wiggled, settling herself. He went very still.

Oh, this was going to be fun.

She bent her head and let her voice go soft in his ear. "Please, Ethan."

His jaw tightened, breath catching. Just once. She felt like a queen. And she would quite like to make him her throne.

"What's that gleam in your eye?" he asked, rough and deep. Knowing.

She kissed his cheek lightly, innocently. Which was not at all how she felt. Then she kissed his other cheek, his brow. The tip of his nose. The tension in him changed, ebbed.

"What are you doing?" he asked.

"What I like."

"You're trying to undo me," he said hoarsely when she kissed him again and scored her nails through the pelt of hair on his chest. She rocked closer, holding him in the cradle of her thighs. She moaned at the pressure against her quim, the hardness of him. He lifted his hips and she moaned again, threatening to lose control of the moment. His hands flexed on her thighs. She kissed him again and again, soft, teasing. Reverent even as her hips promised something darker, something deeper. The combination made her squirm. Made him curse.

She eased away slightly, panting. The crushed flowers between them scented the air. "Convinced?"

His eyes flared greedily. "Not even close, sweetheart."

She reared back, pouting.

"Unfair tactic," he groaned. "I have fucking *dreams* about that mouth."

She brightened. "You do?" She'd dreamt about him as well. The sharp line of his jaw, the way he scraped his teeth over her neck. The smell of the sea that clung to him. His fingers stroking into her.

He groaned again in defeat. "Give me the damn greens. Eating the damned lawn for you like a bloody goat."

She was grinning as she whispered a spell to the leaves, one she had devised purely out of self-preservation when she was very little. Her mother had *not* been a good cook. Ethan watched her mouth and she felt powerful. She offered him the leaves and he took them, nipping at her fingertip. Heat bolted into her center.

He chewed, swallowed, his eyes on her. He blinked. "It tastes like cake," he said, surprised.

"Green witch, remember?" He would have his birthday cake, even if she had to sneak it to him.

"I would have eaten all of my vegetables if I'd known you as a lad."

"I do make a brisk business in winter spelling cabbages to taste like raspberry tarts."

"I'd rather taste *you*," he said, closing his fingers around her waist and tugging her forward. She braced herself, palms on his chest. She could feel his heart beating. "Sweeter than cake." He gripped the back of her neck and brought her closer still, close enough to capture her mouth with his. It was a slow, deep kiss, full of heat that lingered. "Are you done torturing me, sweetheart?"

"Not even close." She slid down his body, reaching for his buttons. His erection sprang free. He was hard, silky. For her. She licked him, swirling her tongue around the tip.

"Briar." A soft warning. She licked him again, and then took as much of him into her mouth as she could. He groaned, breath stuttering. "That fucking *mouth*."

The filthy encouragement made her wet, and she sucked him deeper. She used her tongue to stroke the underside, flicking and hollowing her cheeks until he bucked.

When her eyes drifted shut, his fist tightened in her hair. "Eyes on me, sweetheart."

She looked up at him, suddenly feeling so needy that she had to squeeze her thighs together. Her quim fluttered, swollen and aching. She sucked harder, deeper, watching him watch her. His eyes glittered and he was every bit the Dragon that witches feared. *Her* Dragon. At least for tonight. For now. When she gripped the base of him, his curses were as reverent as her kisses had been.

A gleam in his eye was her only warning.

One moment she was moaning around the hot length of him, and the next he had flipped her onto her back and was pushing between her legs to loom over her. He used his mouth to devour her—her lips, her throat, her nipples. She felt it everywhere.

"You're not trying to undo me," he growled against her damp and flushed skin. "You're trying to fucking break me. Aren't you?"

He pulled her skirts up, baring her glistening quim. She squirmed, trying to get closer. He dragged his cock through her folds, then stopped.

"I asked you a question, little thorn." She reached for him, but he pinned her wrists in the dandelions. "Answer me."

"I need you," she said, not even caring if it sounded like she was begging. "Please, Ethan."

He transferred the hold on her wrist to one hand and slipped his fingers between her slick folds so lightly that she whimpered. "You're playing with fire, little thorn. And there's always a price."

The price included slow, soft touches that threatened to steal her sanity. A build to something that shimmered and sparkled and then a retreat, like the ocean he loved. He brought her closer and closer, never quite giving her enough. His kisses promised vengeance. She was a mess and he was so amused, almost condescending.

"What's that, sweetheart? I can't quite hear you."

"You bastard," she panted. It should not have made her toes curl, but it did.

His laugh was dark, soft. "Convince me," he said again, all taunts even as the tendons in his neck stood out in stark relief. He was not unaffected. It made the desperation all that much sweeter. She still couldn't touch him, with her hands trapped, her body pinned.

She writhed, dampness sliding her along the tip of his cock, just enough to torture them both. His fingers closed around her throat, firm but not squeezing. It anchored her further into her body and she came close to release right then and there.

"What do you say, little thorn?"

She met his hungry gaze with her own, pressing up against his grip.

"Convince *me*," she dared him.

He went still. She had a moment to wonder if she had pushed him too far and that was part of the pleasure. A soft spinster made of flowers and the Crow that everyone whispered about.

"Open your legs for me." She parted her knees, pressing further into the grass. "That's it, sweetheart." He surged into her and she gasped, rising to meet him. Her intimate muscles stretched to accommodate him; a twinge of discomfort and then it felt so good she was afraid she might start babbling.

They were frantic, lost to the sweat and the moans and the panting for breath. The slide of their bodies, the way he thrust into her, murmuring soft, filthy things into her ear. The way he came, hips stuttering and dragging her with him all because he demanded it. "Come with me, Briar. Come. Right now."

And she did. Somehow he ordered it and she obeyed, promptly fluttering around him, gasping.

When he collapsed beside her in the grass, they were both gleaming with sweat.

"You really are a thief," she murmured. "I think you just stole my virtue and I did not have it to begin with."

A soft chuckle. He used a square of cloth from a pouch on his belt to clean her up. "Well, I *am* an Iron Crow. We steal things."

"Magic, witch's bones, maidenly virtues. Amulets that don't belong to you," she added pointedly.

"Next you'll say I stole your heart?" he asked drily, getting to his feet to pull up his trousers.

It was a jest, a throwaway comment. And she took it as such.

Only the words still shimmered between them despite her determination.

"No," she scoffed to drain those words of their power. "Not your heart." Her hair had fallen out of its pins and tangled down her back. She was not a petal like her sister—she was a thorn. "Your ship."

She held up the tin charm in the shape of a ship that she had stolen from his cross-belt, smug and preening. Snapdragon preened just as hard next to her, teeth full of starlight. Briar tossed Ethan her most wicked grin over her shoulder and took off at a run through the long grass, laughing. Her hip did not even twinge. His dragon followed her without a backward glance. She did not know if dragon familiars could chortle, but it certainly seemed like it.

"Traitor," Ethan muttered.

BRIAR DID NOT make it back to the cottage.

She was rushing down the path, still grinning, flushed with a heady mixture of pleasure and victory, when she caught her heel on the edge of a mound. The old hillfort temple dated back centuries, all the way to when the Romans tried to take Lyonesse. They'd never managed it. The witches had chanted day and night, sending storms and kelpies and phoenixes. The temples had long ago been reduced to stone outlines and patches of grass that never grew quite right, but the old magic still lingered.

It was the same place where Petal used to dig holes to hide her rock candy the summer she decided she would become a pirate queen. And the summer after that, when she stole all of the green ribbons from the hatmaker when he sneered at Briar's limp. The gold candlesticks from the vicar's house when he insisted Petal should marry him to save her soul.

Petal had always been a thief, now that Briar really thought about it. She had once hidden the last of the candied pineapple from Mrs. Aster and concealed it in her mouth. She had refused to confess even with her cheeks comically stretched. And Petal hated pineapple, no matter how fashionable it was.

Briar froze.

Dragon and swan circled her, dragging starlight, vigilant.

Her heart thumped loudly in her ears, drowning out the ever-present murmuration of the sea, the distant shriek of a kelpie, the toads croaking once more from the pond.

She knew where the moonstone was.

She wanted to shout at Ethan to hurry, hearing his footsteps. But she was suddenly suspicious of the thistles, the blackberry hedge, the boulder to their left. A Keeper or an Iron Crow or even a villager might well lurk in the shadows. A rabbit in a burrow, a fox in a den, all could answer to a witch. The very grass might tell her secrets despite its best intentions. She did not think Charles was brave enough to follow her when Ethan was nearby, but she was not going to take any chances.

In the end, it did not matter.

# Chapter Twenty-Four

T HE ORDER OF the Iron Nail had come for her.

And that meant they were here for Ethan as well, just for being in her vicinity.

And if they came for Ethan, they would come for Petal.

Briar had no doubt that Anais was more than capable as his first mate, and the rest of the crew. But the ship belonged to Ethan. He was the Dragon. Petal needed his ruthlessness but also his reputation. More than she needed Briar.

Ethan would not agree. His dragon would not agree.

And she had mere moments to take the decision out of his hands. If he was captured—or worse, shot—because of her, she would never forgive herself. She might not even forgive Petal.

There was only one thing to be done. When the ants swarmed the peonies, you harvested the flowers before they fully bloomed. You set up protective barriers.

You gave them something else to devour.

Briar had to move fast. There were grasses and mosses and lichen, but not enough of them to send her magic to trip Ethan up. No trees to beg for help. Only those wild roses inching closer, thorns gleaming.

She moved as quickly as she could, and as silently, so as not to alert Ethan. His dragon sharpened above her head, starlight fire streaming from his nostrils. He knew something was happening. Could he see the Keepers? They were at the edge of the field near her gardens. She didn't have much time. Any time at all.

She could try to hide, but she knew that Ethan would find her. He was an Iron Crow. He was *Ethan*. And she already knew they were here for *her*. The roses had told her, whispering, whispering, *Run*. She nearly choked on the warning bite of mint at the back of her throat. Her gardens shivered, leaves shaking. Bees filled the air.

Ethan was behind her. He would close the distance between them in moments. His dragon was already screeching.

Now or never.

Briar ran faster, faster. Panic clawed at her ribs. Her hip pulsed with pain. None of that mattered. She could not hide from the Keepers, so she would do the only thing that would keep Petal safe. Ethan safe.

He was going to be so furious.

The sweet summer air seared her lungs as she pushed a little faster. She stumbled over an anthill, and could not catch her balance. She slid down the rest of the swell of the field, tumbling to a stop in an undignified sprawl at the feet of the Keepers' horses.

She looked up at them, gasping for breath. Her shopkeeper's smile was firm. "Good evening, gentlemen."

Ethan caught the moonlight on the daisies in Briar's hair as she began to run.

He had pleasant enough thought of chasing her down, hearing her gasp and giggle when he caught her.

Until his dragon sent a stab of light through his chest. The silver crow claw around his neck frosted, searing into him.

Briar was in danger.

How had she managed to find danger in the handful of minutes since she had bolted, laughing over her shoulders, eyes bright, cheeks pink? The fields were full of fireflies.

Why the hell was she running away from him instead of toward him?

And then she was suddenly scooped onto the back of a Keeper's horse and he was still too far away to stop it. And he already knew exactly what it looked like when she kidnapped herself. Little martyr.

Ethan hurled his dagger and nicked Oliver's arm, biting through his sleeve and slicing through his skin. He recognized the bloody Keeper, if not his two companions. He had several more daggers to throw and would dearly have loved to aim for that blighter's head, but the horses were moving and the light had faded and he could not take the chance he might accidentally hit Briar.

He was perfectly willing and able to kill them all for threatening her. Threatening his little thorn.

But not at any risk to her.

No time to go back to the ship for reinforcements. Any message he sent would be intercepted, that much he could assume. The Order was closing ranks around Briar. They must be getting desperate. And he didn't trust a Keeper at the best of times. A desperate Keeper was a real threat.

But he was worse.

So much worse.

Briar had told him Matthias was at the bonfires. Ethan sent his dragon after him, knowing that when Matthias spotted the familiar, he would follow. In the meantime, Ethan would tail the Keepers.

He shadowed them through the village, where they were not even trying to be circumspect.

Not a good sign.

Fury was a lick of cold fire in his chest. Rain pattered the ground, hard as coins.

Briar in a Keeper's cart, or a cell, however makeshift. At the mercy of the Order.

Without warning, the rain turned to hail, hard as musket fire.


BRIAR HAD NEVER been inside the island headquarters of the Order.

She supposed it was better than the infamous dungeons of Holdfast, but she had not been there either.

The headquarters were stationed in a long wooden building that had once been an inn of some repute. It was painted white, naturally, with a row of gargoyles on the roof. Roses grew in a thicket between the red door of the portal and the front door toward which Briar was marched. The horses were taken by a stable boy who stared at her, eyes round. The headquarters mostly saw Keepers, travelers who had drunk too much goblin ale or tried to steal from one of the shops. The occasional witch whose familiar would not behave.

The rain turned to hail, and she knew what that meant. Ethan was near.

If the bloody, ragged tear in Oliver's sleeve was not proof enough already.

She was not sure the headquarters had ever seen the likes of an Iron Crow. It might not yet. She threw more magic at the roses, at the trees shaking their leaves in sympathy over her head. Ethan was meant to go back to the ship and protect her sister, not come after *her*. He must know that.

"I wish you wouldn't," Bear said quietly. He had been very courteous, if unyielding. "Bewitching the roses will not win you any friends, Miss Foxglove."

She frowned, blinking water out of her eyelashes. "I am not feeling particularly friendly, Mr. Bear."

He smiled briefly before leading her inside and showing her to a chair. There were iron chains attached to the back wall and three cells with iron bars studded with black jet. Jars of salt sat in every corner. Ropes of rowanberries hung from the ceiling, painted with white sigils against baneful magics. Even the Order had to ascribe to the aesthetic in Haven.

"Lock her up," Oliver fumed. "I'm *bleeding*."

"She didn't cut you," Bear said, quiet dignity turned to stone. "What your sleeve tells me is that you need more training."

Oliver's brow lowered. His companion laughed. There were

two more Keepers, one who seemed to be rummaging around making tea in the back kitchen, another who held a pendulum over a map of Lyonesse.

Searching for Petal. Briar would bet her gardens on it.

She perched on the chair, Snapdragon tucked safely away, and twisted her fingers together so no one would see them tremble. She did not know what they planned to do with her but could not imagine it would be pleasant. She knew no charms to help her against a Keeper's spells, no tricks. She began to feel quite sick to her stomach. What if she told them where Petal was hidden while under a witch binding?

"Miss Foxglove," Bear said, "I do apologize for the manner of your arrival."

Briar swallowed. "I don't know where my sister is."

"Would you tell us if you did?"

She stayed silent.

"I thought not. In any case, this is not just about your sister's whereabouts."

"It isn't?"

"This is also about the roses."

She blinked. "The roses?" Was she here as a green witch? Did they know what she had found beneath the white roses?

"Yes. As a green witch, you must have noticed them."

"It's the summer solstice," she hedged. "All of the flowers are plentiful. And the business with the shields has muddled the magic some."

"Not like this. So now I am afraid we really do need that moon charm," he said. "And we were given information that suggests you know more than you are letting on."

By whom? Certainly not Ethan or Sorcha. Who, then? Someone who had seen her digging under the rosebushes? Unlikely. She was always digging in the dirt. There was nothing out of the ordinary about that.

Which left Charles *Bloody* Aster.

"Is this because of Charles?" Briar asked, incensed all over again. "He has a personal quarrel with my family and can hardly be trusted as impartial."

"We take all evidence seriously," one of the other Keepers said. "If you've nothing to hide, you've nothing to be afraid of, do you?"

"That has not been my experience," she said calmly, though she did not feel calm.

The Keeper at the table strewn with maps and scatterings of salt dropped the brass pendulum with an irritated grunt. "It keeps pointing to the roses, and the Foxglove cottage. And just now to headquarters since Miss Foxglove arrived. But nothing else."

Not the ship. Bless Bramble and her rabbit magic and the Sea Dragons. Briar could only hope her own magic was as strong.

"Search her," Oliver said, hauling Briar up by her elbow. He shook her once as if expecting the moon charm to fall from her person.

"That is enough," Bear snapped.

"Sir, she needs searching."

"Not like that. We are not Crows. And I was assured *you* were a gentleman. Act like it, damn it."

Oliver released her, but the look he gave her sent a shudder through her.

"Miss Foxglove, I do apologize for him," Bear added. "Once again."

Briar nodded silently.

"We must search you for the charm," he continued. "I am sure you understand."

Her mouth went dry. She nodded again. She wasn't sure what else to do. There were no plants nearby to appeal to for help, and the rowanberries on the ceiling were already charged with a magical purpose not easily altered. There was the tea in the canister, a jar of rosemary on the far table. Nothing that could get her out of this.

Bear approached her. "If you could stand, please?"

She stood, thoughts racing. She consoled herself that every

moment they spent interrogating her was one fewer moment with Petal in their sights. Yes, she had stolen from the museum, and yes, it had triggered unfortunate and unforeseen events, but it did not warrant the things they would do to her. Trap her familiar, bleed her dry at the portal. Any number of spells with no guarantee of success.

Bear had a charm made of two crossed iron nails wrapped in red thread and piercing two rowanberries. A standard charm to either amplify or break witchcraft. It was secured to a small bottle in which a wasp buzzed against the glass. It would track any magic on Briar's person and neutralize it, bound to the Keeper's charm. She had heard of such a spell, but had never seen one. Or been the subject of one. Her legs tensed with the instinct to run. She noticed her chair sat in a circle of iron nails driven into the floorboards.

Bear pressed the charm over her witch knot. There was an immediate jolt of power, the smell of fennel, the taste of salt. Bear released the wasp. It buzzed around her head in an angry halo before widening its circle, bumping into a daisy still tangled in her hair, infused with the magic of the firefly wishes by the pond. The pink quartz stone in her ring, spelled by her mother for general beauty and very common to Haven. The strawberry vines she had embroidered on her sleeves for sweetness and abundance.

The wasp crawled along her neckline, and she held her breath. What did it do when it found something it did not like? Would it sting her? She had an understanding with the wasps in her garden. This one did not seem amenable to conversation.

When its wings tickled her skin above her stays, it took a great deal of effort to remain still.

The wasp buzzed again, waving its stinger. Briar flinched.

And then the wasp merely returned to the bottle she still held in her palm.

Because the moon charm was not tucked into her stays where it should be.

Ethan had nicked it again.

*Thank all the spirits.*

There was nothing to find on her person, no wayward magic, no moon charm. Briar exhaled slowly.

Bear nodded, reclaiming the charm bottle. "Thank you."

"She's hidden it somewhere," Oliver snapped.

"Possibly," Bear said.

"Sir, she's been consorting with Crows."

"Just the one," Briar said. "And what does that have to do with anything?" Everything. *Everything.* "He's very handsome." Hardly the point. "You've already searched my house. Twice."

"And we will keep searching until we find what we are looking for."

"We really do need to stop the roses," Bear said quietly. "They are overtaking the village."

Briar frowned. "I have not spelled anyone's roses. For Midsummer, people prefer to focus on sunflowers and marigolds. Or St. John's wort for luck. I convinced a rosebush to abandon someone's pea plants and cut them back from the well, but that's it."

"This is a different kind of witchery. It's hungry."

The door swung open and yet another Keeper appeared, hair wet with rain. "Some bloody idiots are trying to use a battering ram on the portal."

"I'll see to it." Bear sighed. "Before they trigger another counterspell. That's all we need."

"I knocked one on his ass, but they're gathering a crowd."

"Barnaby, with me," Bear said. The Keeper with the pendulum followed them out.

Briar was left alone with Oliver and one other Keeper. "Ambrose, get the truth spell," he said, smiling an oily kind of smile at her.

She tried to take a step back, but there was nowhere to go. The chair blocked her; the circle of iron nails flared molten hot. Ambrose returned with the charm of herbs and ashes from solstice bonfires. She did not know what other ingredients went into the spell. Only that it was not gentle.

"I saw Petal Foxglove once. She's a beauty. A true pocket Venus," Ambrose said. "If we save her from the Order and the Museum, do you think she'd be grateful? How grateful?"

"Never mind that," Oliver snapped. "We have the island to protect."

"We can do both."

"Just hurry up before Bear comes back."

Briar, not knowing what else to do, shoved the chair at Ambrose. He staggered back, grunting with surprise.

But it wasn't enough. Not nearly.

Oliver was already moving. He grabbed her and clapped the spell bundle over her mouth, nearly smothering her in the process. Her tooth cut into her bottom lip. She choked on the taste of blood and witchcraft.

The truth spell crawled through her brain, scraping like thorns, needles, lightning.

She screamed.

"Shut her up," Ambrose said.

Oliver gripped her face, fingers digging into her jaw. His eyes bored into hers. Her swan hissed but she refused to release it. The danger that it might get trapped was too great.

She gasped as Oliver clawed through her memories, as careless and violent as a housebreaker after heirloom jewels. Paintings crashed to the floor; drawers were upended, clothing pulled from trunks. Teacups smashed, again and again. Moonlight pierced her skull.

Briar screamed again.


AT BRIAR'S FIRST scream of pain, Ethan's blood ran cold.

Fury gripped him in a way that ought to have cracked the entire island like an egg. He'd never felt its like before. The sea rose against the beach, the bonfires, past the walls, lapping at the houses. The water in the fountain froze.

Ethan lit the first fire.

At her second cry, he dove through the back window of the Order headquarters, smashing through glass and barking at Matthias as he shot past him. "Now, goddamn it."

Matthias closed his eyes.

"What the hell?" someone yelped. "I can't see."

"Me either!"

Matthias, young and kind and obsessed with the proper consistency of coddled eggs, wielded magic that blinded those around him. Literally. Ethan's hagstone kept his eyes clear. But it wouldn't have mattered—he would have found Briar without his eyes, his ears, his very hands. The blinding spell had the added benefit of fogging her vision, cutting the connection Oliver was relying on. *Amateur. Thank the Kraken.*

Ethan took note of the layout of the room, the chains, the sigils, the ropes of rowanberries, but all he truly saw was Briar.

Oliver had his hands on her face.

Ethan broke his left wrist, tossing him aside like a bucket of kitchen slop. Oliver howled, also blinded by Matthias's magic. Ethan tossed the other Keeper into the wall and he crumpled, unconscious.

When Ethan slipped a hagstone into Briar's palm, she blinked at him. "Ethan." Her voice was strangled, hoarse.

It made the Dragon in him want to burn the world.

He ushered her toward the window, pausing only to knock an oil lamp onto the floor. The oil spilled, the flames spreading.

"You can't murder two Keepers," Briar protested when she paused and he nudged her to keep going.

"You really have to stop saying that to me." He did not have the time for murder, at any rate. But he'd be coming back for those two bastards. If they survived the night, they wouldn't survive him. But first, he needed to get Briar the hell away from this place and this magic. "Someone will come get them."

He helped her out of the window, still protesting, but weakly. She looked tired, scared. He almost went back right then and there. But the need to get her away was stronger.

"Run, little thorn."

He whistled once, a warning to Matthias. Fire ate at the hay he had stolen from the inn's stables and bundled at the side of the headquarters. Flames were already licking out of the window. When the fires met, the headquarters would burn. Someone rang the alarm bell. But it was too late.

They had taken Briar, tried to hurt her. There wasn't a water drop on the island that would put out that fire until Ethan decided it was time.

Briar's eyes were wide, the fire reflected in her pupils. "You have fire magic too?"

He grunted. "I have matchsticks."

# Chapter Twenty-Five

MATTHIAS MET THEM behind the inn and they ducked into the fields, the long grasses and shadows keeping them hidden. All eyes, now that they could see again, were directed at the fire.

"Keepers already got their mates out," Matthias told them, sounding harder than he looked.

Briar only nodded toward the path where it curved away, leading down the craggy steps toward Ethan's ship. The moon caught the metal of a cannon, the white of a rolled-up and secured sail. His brow lowered as he followed her, hand hovering by his dagger. Her head pounded and her throat was sore from screaming, but she couldn't stop. Not now. The Keepers would come for her again, as soon as they could. The fire would not distract them forever.

The steps were uneven and not particularly safe to maneuver over in the dark, but they couldn't very well use the village stairs, made of white marble and edged with columns. Ethan stayed close and she felt the coiled tension in him, ready to reach out if she slipped or her hip gave out. White roses choked the cliff, clinging tenaciously to sandy ground where they had no business thriving. Their perfume rivaled the salt breezes. Petals scattered like stars underfoot.

The sand was warm and welcoming, the docks painted with sigils that had not been there before. Anais waited at the railing. "Captain," she said.

"Any trouble?"

"Not yet."

"Well, get ready. It's coming."

"He didn't get to any real memories," Briar said. "Nothing about the ship or the charm. Just flashes of the cottage, the fireflies I chased as a girl. Our cat before he ran away. They're fuzzy now, as if they belong to someone else. Is that normal?"

"Truth spell from the Order," Ethan explained tightly to Anais. She swore.

"Unsanctioned," Briar pointed out. "Bear did not know."

"Oliver and his friend will pay the price."

She was too tired to talk him out of murder again.

She crossed the gangplank. The witch glass rang. Magic swirled, so close to the locked shields, flashes of light, curls of mist that were not quite natural. Eyes where there should be no eyes. She knew better than to look back. She ducked her head and hurried down the stairs below deck where her sister waited. Ethan was a grim, watchful shadow at her back. The crew melted out of her way.

Matthias had not exaggerated when he said the crew had taken to Petal. She lay in a bower of white roses clearly picked from the nearby cliffside. They were scattered over her blanket, caught in her hair, piled in the hall outside the room. Briar felt some of them growing vines even without earth or water to sustain them. Their magic called to hers, making her momentarily dizzy. Ethan's hand pressed to her lower back.

Bramble stood when Briar kicked the roses out of her way. "Has it always been like this?" she asked.

"Always," Briar replied. Sometimes people brought Petal candy or butterflies in jars—which Briar always released—pearls they stole, more poems than any one person should have to suffer, pressed-tin medallions in every style of heart, and once, memorably, a donkey. And a pie filled with blueberries and pearls. Which the donkey ate. But usually, it was flowers.

Petal, despite her name and her green witch sister, did not

particularly care for flowers. She preferred lemons and solitude and rabbit girls.

Bramble's nose twitched. "What is it? What happened to you?"

"The Order happened to her," Ethan said, his voice odd. "And I will be happening to the Order."

"They don't know Petal is here," Briar assured them both.

"This isn't about Petal," he bit out, sounding even angrier.

"It doesn't matter," Briar whispered as Ethan shut the door. "I know where the moonstone is and they do not."

Anais stayed in the hall, barking orders. "Not one more fucking flower. I swear to God, I cannot sneeze anymore. There's more pollen than seawater on this blasted ship. Get to your posts. *Now.*"

Hurrying footsteps echoed on the other side of the wall as Briar approached her sister. *Please let me be right.* She had been so sure before the Keepers came for her. "You searched her for the amulet?"

"Of course," Bramble replied. "Her pockets, even her shoes. And my sisters sent rabbits to your garden but found nothing."

Briar had already found that piece, she reckoned, under Lord Coventry's nose.

But her sister did like to hide things.

"Check under her tongue."

Bramble stared for a moment and then darted to Petal's side. "I'm sorry, love," she murmured before kneeling next to Petal in the roses and forcing her jaw open lightly. A pause. An inhalation.

And then the moonstone in Bramble's palm.

Elation shot through Briar, quickly followed by panic. There were no guarantees that this would work. But Petal could not stay like this, and anyone who might know how to help her would probably turn her into the Order. And after tonight, Briar knew they were out of time.

She extended a hand toward Ethan without looking at him, waiting. Pieces of the amulet dropped into her palm. She took the moonstone from Bramble. It fit perfectly in the silver-and-pearl-studded cage. A whisper of magic rustled the rose petals. A kelpie's eye filled the portal window, flashing a threat.

"Are you sure about this?" Ethan asked.

"No."

And then Briar fit the pieces together over the moonstone.

For a long moment, nothing happened. Petal did not wake. There was only the lap of the waves against the hull, Briar's pulse in her ears. The moon egg was just a piece of jewelry, pretty but ultimately insignificant, with no real power. It could have been one of the rosebuds for all that the curse changed.

Until there was a tickle, a curl of glittering power.

And suddenly, a crashing boom that Briar felt more than heard. It slapped through the ether, shaking the lamps, shattering the witch glass on deck, shooting like silver daggers through the ocean. A kelpie screamed.

Briar might have screamed too, but there was no air left in her lungs.

The flash of white light blinded her, seared into her brain. Her skin prickled. The white roses around her feet seared to ash, smelling of salt and fennel and magic.

And then Petal opened her eyes, groggy.

"Why am I covered in flowers?" She sneezed once, daintily. "Did I die again?"


BRIAR DID NOT know if she was laughing or crying.

Bramble had hauled Petal into her arms, kissing her fiercely. Petal kissed her back, her hare familiar bounding through the room like a shooting star, finally free. It was dizzying. Petal finally stood and reached for her sister. The hug was fierce and Briar was not sure who was holding who up.

Ethan did not say a word, merely leaned against the wall, coldly watchful.

The magic that had pushed through the sea returned, jostling them hard. Petal stumbled. "Are we on a ship?"

Briar nodded. "Yes."

"Why?"

"Because you stole the bloody moon, you idiot."

Petal winced. "Right. That."

"Yes, *that*."

"I stole the moon for my beloved." Petal glanced at Bramble. "Is it done?"

Bramble inclined her head.

Petal grinned. "Absolutely worth it, then."

"I'm glad you think so," Ethan said icily. "Your sister was the one paying the price, not you."

Petal stared at him. "Who is that?" she whispered.

"The Dragon," Briar replied. "He kept you safe. He and his whole crew."

"Thank you." Petal smiled, the smile that had won her countless marriage proposals and an offer from a king. Her teeth were small and perfect, gleaming white. She did not have a slightly crooked incisor, like Briar did. Another little thorn. Her smile was a work of art.

Ethan did not look particularly impressed.

Petal smiled wider. "Oh, I like him."

He only grunted.

"But what does he mean, you paid the price?" she demanded. "You were nowhere near me, and I didn't tell you what I was doing for a reason."

"Yes, about that…" Briar replied.

"You would have tried to stop me."

"Or she might have been prepared," Ethan snapped.

Petal frowned. "Prepared for what?"

Briar waved her hand. "Nothing. He's exaggerating."

"You are lucky not to be in a Keeper's iron collar," Ethan insisted. "That blighter reached into your fucking head."

He wasn't wrong. But he had come for her. He had burned down the headquarters of the Order. She promised herself an inappropriate little swoon about it later.

He scowled. "*And* they broke your teacups."

Petal gaped. "What the hell? That museum curator came after you? Instead of me?"

"The spell he put on the amulet found me instead," Briar said. "A twin thing, I imagine."

Her sister cursed. "I'm sorry." She pressed a hand to her stomach. "And I am *starving*." She winced in pain.

"You've been asleep for days," Briar explained as Bramble handed Petal an apple from the basket of food.

Petal took a large bite. "I don't remember anything except coming through the portal and feeling awful. I had to crawl home. If I hadn't had your lemon candies for the solstice dawn ceremony, I don't think I would have made it."

"Are you the one who broke the moon charm?"

She tilted her head, trying to remember. "Yes! That curator followed me. He wasn't supposed to be able to even see me. I had rabbit magic."

"Lord Coventry, yes."

She winced. "He's a lord, too?"

"I'm afraid so."

"Am I going to have to smile at him?" She shuddered. "Or flirt?"

"No," Ethan cut in. "Coventry is too dedicated to his work for that."

She looked relieved as she finished the apple and ate a hunk of cheese, and three rolls sprinkled with dill, before she could manage another word. "Can we go up top? I think I might be dying for fresh air. It stinks of roses in here."

She moved slowly and carefully, like someone only just re-covered from a fever. Bramble hovered.

Briar smiled at Ethan. "We did it."

"*You* did it."

"You helped me not get murdered along the way," she point-ed out. "And now the shields are unlocked. I think?"

Her smile faltered. She turned away so he would not see it. If the spell was broken, then Ethan would be leaving. He had only ever been honest about that. The fact she would miss him enough that her chest already ached was her own problem to deal with. She would not let it tarnish the night's victory.

She followed Petal and Bramble up the ladder, sternly informing her eyeballs that if they watered, she would toss them in the sea to be eaten by kelpies. No crying. Not here.

The crew were gathered on deck, shards of witch glass glittering under their boots. There was the definite burn of magic to the air. When Petal teetered, four sailors and a satyr instantly appeared to help her. Godric still managed to wink at Briar before he noticed Ethan glowering. Bramble bared her teeth at them all. Rabbit magic wrapped around her and Petal, swallowing them in a misty blurriness.

"Back off," Ethan sighed.

His crew dispersed, starry-eyed but cowed.

Petal frowned at her sister. "Um, Briar?"

"Yes?"

"When did you start glowing?"

Briar blinked at her. "What?" Then down at herself. "Oh."

She was, indeed, glowing.

It was like the moon was touching her. Only her. It gilded her in silver, shining on her hair, her grass-stained dress. The darkness deepened around her. She was salt-white, bone-white. Moon-white.

"That's probably not a good thing."

Ethan cursed and sent the clouds scurrying over the moon.

It did not help.

Nor did the rain he called down, or the blanket her sister tossed on top of her head. Even Bramble's rabbit magic had no effect whatsoever.

The moon had found her.

And so had Aidan Hunt, Lord Coventry.

ETHAN'S DRAGON TRIED to eat the museum curator without any

prompting from Ethan.

Briar was glowing like the moon, bright and beautiful and so vulnerable it made his teeth hurt. He tried to unclench his jaw but it was not happening, not with Briar in danger. Maybe not ever again. The sound of her screams echoed in his skull.

So when Aidan stepped out of the rose-scented shadows of the cliff and said her name, just her name, Ethan exploded. His hands were full of daggers between one breath and the next. There was no thinking, no planning.

Only the soul-deep certainty that anyone coming for Briar would have to go through him first.

And his dragon. His ship, his crew. A herd of kelpies.

Anais had her sword out and Cosette pointed her crossbow at the earl.

Aidan held up his hands, solemn as a scholar. He did not look as terrified as Ethan would have liked. He wanted the man to piss himself in fear if he even considered taking a single step closer to Briar. She, for her part, only peeked around Ethan and looked at Aidan as though she were prepared to offer him tea. There were still flowers in her tangled hair.

Hard to drink tea without a throat.

Ethan's dragon roared, lightning slashing at the sky. He had no idea what Aidan's familiar was but, sparrow or shark, his dragon would feast.

"Swansea," Aidan said. Ethan realized it was not the first time he had said his name when Briar tried to edge around him, her hand on his arm. The blood faded from his vision and he tucked her back where she was safe. "I'm not going to hurt her."

"I know," Ethan said. Icicles of magic shot from his dragon, slamming into the ground between Aidan and the ship. Between Aidan and Briar. They glowed, sharp as swords and full of menace.

"Good evening, Lord Coventry," Briar called out.

"Don't talk to him like he's a friend," Ethan muttered.

Briar ignored him.

No one ignored him. *Especially* when he was in an icy rage. There were men he had never met who whispered stories about him like threats. There were no fewer than three bounties on his head.

And the little witch who lived in the pink cottage ignored him.

It made him want to kiss her senseless.

"Lord Coventry," she said again, Ethan's arm across her waist when she tried to step too far away from him. He wasn't having it. His every instinct was seething to toss her over his shoulder and hide her away. "Is your tracking spell causing me to glow?"

"Yes."

"Get it the hell off her," Ethan ordered him darkly.

"I can't."

"Wrong answer."

A dagger hit the ground between Aidan's shoes, digging into the sand. Ethan had another ready before it landed.

"Ethan!" Briar said. "That's a bit dramatic."

"Just wait," he promised.

"You'll leave my sister alone," Petal added, "or I'll eat your spleen."

She looked perfectly ready, willing, and able to do it. It made Ethan like her a bit more. He wasn't feeling forgiving about the trouble she had brought to her sister's doorstep—anything that brought the Dragon to your door was not a good thing—but he did appreciate a good threat.

"I'm afraid it's too late for that," Aidan said. "May I come aboard? I don't think you want me shouting this for all and sundry to hear, and we haven't much time."

The wind tore at the roses, sending petals drifting down like snow. For some reason it made Briar frown. Her magic curled like vines up her arms. "Please, Ethan."

Ethan nodded once. "Fine. One wrong move and you'll get an arrow to the throat, Coventry."

"I am aware."

He was a calm one—Ethan would give him that. Spending all of his time cooped up with dusty artifacts had not dulled him.

But it would not save him, either.

"Miss Foxglove, I assume you have found the amulet." His calm, dry gaze settled on Petal briefly. "And the thief."

Briar scowled at him ferociously even as she held on to the rail to steady herself as the ship rolled. "You're not taking her."

"She broke several laws."

Briar sniffed. "I don't care."

Aidan sighed, clearly aware of every weapon currently trained on him, both obvious and camouflaged. "Yes, I gathered as much. That's not what I wanted to talk about, although I'd like to come back to that, Miss Petal. You should not have been able to do what you did."

Petal only shrugged.

"Get on with it," Ethan said. "Reverse your damned spell."

Aidan winced. "I'm afraid I cannot."

"Then I don't see what's keeping me from murdering you. *That* might do it."

Briar pinched the bridge of her nose, before pointing at him and her sister. "Both of you are not helping." She pointed at Aidan next. Rose vines crawled across the sand behind him, thorns gleaming in the moonlight. "Why can't you remove the spell?"

"I *should* be able to," he admitted. "I made it so it would lead me to any stolen amulet, preferably within a few feet of the museum, *and* with the thief conveniently asleep."

"However?"

"However, the magic of the portal interfered when your sister managed to make it through. Rather a lot, I'm sorry to say."

"What does that mean?"

"It means that the shields finally unlocked when you fit the amulet pieces together, but they aren't fully open. Not yet. And I believe that the moon will continue to track you until everything is as it was."

"And how do we fix the shields?" Briar asked, sounding exhausted. And exasperated. Ethan didn't blame her. This should be done with. The bloody moon charm was back in the hands of the museum—or near one of its curators, anyway. That should be good enough. Briar should be out of it now. *Safe.*

"I'm afraid the amulet must go to Holdfast. The Iron Witches work the shields, as you know, and only they can truly fix them."

"Take it, then, and begone," Ethan said.

"I can't. Only Miss Foxglove can. The magic is too tied up with hers—there's no undoing it now. There isn't time to unpick the threads. It would take hours, days. And you burned down the Order's headquarters. They are not feeling patient."

"They hit her with a truth spell," Ethan said.

"It was *not* pleasant." Briar rubbed her brow wearily and Ethan saw red all over again.

"I am truly sorry, Miss Foxglove."

She waved it away, but Ethan swore they would be coming back around to that. Violently. "I don't want the moon charm. I never did," Briar said.

"And that's why it has to be you," Ethan said between his teeth, catching Aidan's expression. "*Because* you don't want it. And every Keeper and Iron Crow does. Fucking hell."

"But surely they want off the island like everyone else? And they could get to Holdfast much quicker than me."

Despite the fierceness in her that no one else seemed to truly recognize, there was also a streak of sweetness that it would be his honor to protect for the rest of his days.

"I can promise you that every Iron Crow on this bloody island would hold that damn thing hostage for power or wealth or both."

She blinked. "Oh. And you?"

"I have enough problems." It wasn't the answer she wanted. It wasn't even the answer he wished he could give her. But it was the only answer at the moment. Especially while they were being watched by his smirking crew and her feral sister.

He didn't like to think of the way the Iron Crows would come for her now. It would be so much worse. The power in that amulet, the way it could be used to control the shields—the sheer extortion one could have at one's fingertips... Hell, it *was* tempting.

But not at this cost. Never at this cost.

Ethan already did not like the way Briar's cheeks were pale. Her hip was paining her, that much was obvious. And then that fucking truth spell.

She sighed. "I suppose I must go to Holdfast, then."

"*We* are going to fucking Holdfast," he corrected her.

# Chapter Twenty-Six

BRIAR DID NOT want to go to Holdfast.

She wanted a nap. And a cup of tea. Willow-bark powder for her head. And a mountain of scones with butter.

But no. Instead, Holdfast with its rocky beaches and unforgiving witches and slippery cobblestones.

Still, Briar could not help a small flutter of relief. Ethan would not be sailing away before the sunrise. Which was rather beside the point. Village in peril, etcetera, etcetera.

She felt as though she were moving through treacle while everyone around her sped about like they were being shot from cannons. Ethan barked orders to his crew, before disappearing briefly into his quarters. Petal and Bramble held hands, whispering furiously. Aidan stepped off the gangplank onto the beach.

Briar followed him because there was something odd about the roses. The moonlight touched them the way it touched her, which was curious enough. But they were growing too fast and strong, tangled like a thicket. Bear was right to be concerned about them. They *were* hungry. Ravenous. Magic glittered between the vines. She watched for a long moment until Ethan appeared at the rails, scowling.

"I told you to wait for me," he said grimly. She could only see one extra sword strapped to his back, but she knew full well there would be dozens of daggers and magical curses stuffed in every pocket and pouch. In his boots, even. He held a stick, which he handed to her when he'd crossed the sand. "This won't snap like driftwood."

The stick was actually a cane. He had whittled roses into sturdy blackthorn, sharpening some of the thorns into lethal points. It was beautiful, but more importantly, it was the exact right height for her and it was strong and deadly.

"Did you do this?" she asked, running her fingers over a petal and remembering the small, carved seals and mermaids and dragons in his quarters, the swan he had carved while sitting at her table.

"Aye."

"Thank you."

"You could bash a bloke's kneecaps in with that," he added. "Start with Oliver. Then Aster."

Because the gesture threatened to make her eyes water, and one could not fight off Iron Crows while blubbering, she forced a smile. "You're not expecting me to use it to prop myself up and wait for you to come rescue me if there's trouble?"

"Woman, I expect you to do as much damage as you can."

It was such a lovely thing to do, to say, that her swan purred in her ear. She had not even known swans *could* purr.

Petal crossed to them, linking her arm through Briar's. "Are we ready?"

"You're not coming," Ethan said calmly.

"I am not leaving my sister," Petal shot back. Her chest mottled pink with outrage. Even that was beautiful on her. Her hare shot out of her ribcage, snarling. "Choke on it, Iron Crow."

Briar frowned. "Why can't Petal come with us?"

Ethan merely extended his arm and poked Petal in the shoulder, not particularly hard. She stumbled back, equilibrium dodgy. Bramble shot to her side.

"You've been out cold for days," he said. "You'll slow us down."

Petal opened her mouth, then snapped it shut. "Damn it. I would have a better argument if there weren't two of you." She rubbed her eyes.

"You can distract the Keepers," Ethan suggested. "Let them see you just enough to keep their attention."

Petal nodded. "I can do that." She turned to Briar, squinting. "I think you're getting brighter. And why do you keep frowning at those roses?"

"There's something off about them." Briar glanced at Aidan. "Is it a part of your tracking spell?"

"No, it isn't."

Still frowning, Briar climbed the rough-hewn steps to the top of the cliff, Ethan right behind her, followed by Petal and Bramble and Aidan. The moonlight glinted off the water, and the flowers, but mostly Briar. She shivered, feeling very exposed.

The roses glowed at her feet. The vines crept down the cliff, reaching the wet sand. They crept across the field leading toward Haven. They crept toward the moors.

They were everywhere.

They grew into sharp, thorned thickets, choking the grasses and the thistles even as she watched. Briar already knew they would stand against sword and dagger and witch's boline. The smell of roses was thick with salt and fennel.

She tried every counterspell she could think of—she pushed salt into the roots, burned rose petals, sang a song about barren stone fields, winter ice. She tore at the vines until her fingers were slick with sweat and blood. Her swan attacked with its sharp beak.

None of it worked.

The spell would not answer to her. The magic had gone too wild, fed by too many other hands. She found a sparrow trapped in a tangle of thorns and carefully set him free, knuckles and fingertips scraped and cut.

"I don't understand what's happeni—Unless." She sat back, still kneeling on the prickly ground. Ethan speared a vine when it tried to wrap around her ankle. The burn of green witch magic stung.

"Unless what?" Petal demanded.

"When we had to hide you from the Keepers that first night, I stashed you in the rosebushes. I asked them to grow so thick no one would ever find you." Briar picked up a petal, and it made her witch knot tingle, magic racing through her palm. She dropped it when it reminded her too much of the truth spell electrifying her brain. "You had the moonstone on you then, only I didn't know it. I think the roses followed you here to find you for the tracking spell, but also to protect you for me. And that must be why there were white roses where I found the amulet pieces, as well. It's all tangled together."

Aidan looked down toward Haven, grimly serious. "Your spell is going to take over all of Lyonesse in order to hide your sister."

She could see it too. It would swallow all of Haven, trapping people in their homes, in the streets. It would pierce skin and bone. Then it would travel to Hallow and Holdfast. It would strangle Ethan's ship, bringing down the masts, stuffing the cannons with leaves and thorns and pale, moon-colored petals.

"Blast," she said. "I never meant to do this!"

"This is not your fault," Ethan said sharply. "There are too many damn spells at work here."

She made a fist, the blood from her pricked thumb smearing onto a rose.

It paused.

Then it recoiled.

Paused again.

Briar let out a breath.

Ethan cursed. "If anyone mentions this, they die. Are you hearing me, Coventry?"

Aidan nodded. "You have my word."

Briar was still staring at her blood on the petals.

Her blood could stop the roses.

She knew as well as anyone that if the information reached the Iron Crows or the Keepers or anyone on Lyonesse, they would drain her dry if that was what it took.

And she might not blame them. They were about to be strangled to death by white roses.

She stood up, using her new cane to steady herself, and
looked at Ethan. "Let's go."

"Wait," Petal said. "I have an idea."

Bramble was the only one who did not shudder in fear.


WHEN THEY WERE little, Briar and Petal had loved building
scarecrows in the vegetable garden. They wove willow twigs into
knights and sorceresses and mighty queens, all draped with roses
and daisies and wild mint. Crowns of clover and dandelion were
braided together; foxglove swords were crafted. They protected
the cabbages and the onions and the carrots and the crab apples in
the orchard.

And when a particularly persistent suitor would not leave
Petal alone, Briar made a poppet of him and stuffed it with rue
and stinging nettle. He had developed such a nasty rash that he
left the island altogether to search for a cure in London. No one
had tried to touch her sister again for a very long time after that.

Tonight, Petal helped her make poppets of thorny roses,
smeared with Briar's blood to distribute throughout the village.
Ethan hissed out a warning, clearly displeased. But if nothing else
worked, Aidan could gather all of the villagers at the bonfires and
make a protective circle with the poppets. It should keep the roses
at bay long enough for Briar and Ethan to reach Holdfast and help
the Iron Witches put things to rights.

But Briar was not only the twin sister to a moon charm thief
or the most beautiful witch in Britain.

She was also a green witch.

She would not be undone by roses.

Her magic might not work on them, but her blood did. So
she would think practically, blood and bone and breath. Roots
and branches and blossoms. She would tend to it like a garden.
She would never let mint or lilacs take over, draining the soil of
nutrients. She would not plant roses near a walnut tree—they did

not get along. But she would plant marigolds to deter pests. There were hundreds of secret conversations in every patch of flowers.

Sun, shade. Predator. Only instead of keeping out the predators, this time she would invite them in.

Ethan, another predator, already invited, watched her steadily. "What are you thinking, little thorn?"

"I need club moss," she declared, already scrounging through the grasses and the stony outcrop for the thick green fingers of the plant.

"You heard her," Ethan said, and everyone in earshot scrambled to obey.

"Oh, I love it when she does this." Petal grinned, her hands already full. This had been a favorite game when they were young. When Briar whispered to plants, they listened. Fillet of fenny snake became serpents; rabbit's foot clover became rabbits; wolfsbane became a wolf. "Why club moss?" she asked.

"Because its witch name is Stag's Horn," Briar replied.

"And?" Petal pressed when the others just blinked at her.

"Stags eat roses," Briar explained, placing her witch knot down over the small pile of club moss. "Deer can decimate a rose garden within hours. They eat everything, even the thorns."

She pushed the green magic through her body, listening for the whispers, connecting to them before she bent her head to whisper back. She whispered of flashing hooves, of the stately crown of antlers, of dark liquid eyes. Of the taste of green leaves between strong teeth.

The club moss began to glow, faintly at first, then stronger.

Her witch knot burned as she pushed more and more power through herself.

Stags made of pale, shimmering mist formed, emerging tall and majestic and pulsing with witchcraft. Spirit stags, fairy stags. White as bone, white as salt.

White as the moon.

Some of the herd stampeded down the hill toward Haven,

glowing like ghosts, trampling petals and scattering thorns. The others stayed closer, dipping their heads, and began to feast.

They nibbled and chewed through the magic that fed the roses, that pushed the curse across Lyonesse. They ate blossom and thorn and vine. The roses gleamed, sharpening in retaliation. Briar smeared more of her blood, until she began to feel a little lightheaded.

"That's enough," Ethan said.

"I can do more," she insisted.

"And you will. But not here. You need to keep some for Holdfast."

Anais thundered toward them on the horse Ethan had sent her to steal. Briar recognized him as Goliath, belonging to the wheelwright. "He's a beast, but he can run." Her eyebrows rose at the herd of spirit deer, glowing fur rippling as they ate and ate and ate. Salt and fennel bit at the air. "What happened here?"

"Briar happened," Petal replied proudly.

"Any trouble?" Ethan asked.

Anais shook her head. "Most everyone is already in their cups or off finding secret corners for secret deeds. The village fountain is literally running with honey mead, though I hear it was frozen for a bit."

"Keepers?"

She shrugged and slid from the saddle. "Bemoaning the charred remains of their house. Unfortunately, the ones you really have to watch out for were already on patrol. So you'd best get moving."

"I'll go too," Aidan said, holding the blood-smeared poppets.

"What will you tell them?" Briar asked.

"He's an earl from a prominent witching family," Ethan said. "It doesn't matter what he tells them; they'll listen."

"Bear is too clever for that," Briar warned. He had been kind when they searched her house that first time, but also eagle-eyed.

"He is," Aidan agreed.

"He didn't know about the truth spell."

"Noted." Aidan bowed, incongruously polite considering the circumstances and the roses gleaming with her blood around his boots. "Safe travels."

Ethan waited by Goliath, who was stomping on rose vines that inched too near his hooves. "Good lad," Ethan said.

"Don't get caught," Petal said.

"You either," Briar returned.

Petal scoffed. "As if they could catch us. I've got myself a rabbit-witch wife, don't I?"

Briar blinked, momentarily distracted. "Wait, you're already married? Don't you need to jump the broom or handfast?" Handfastings on the island were old-fashioned: ribbons tying your wrists together, or hands clasped through a hole in one of the standing stones up on the moors, but they were binding.

"Stealing the moon was our ceremony," Petal explained. "I'm a rabbit girl now."

Briar hugged her. "I'm so happy for you."

"Maybe we could continue this when Iron Crows aren't on their way to kill you both?" Ethan suggested coolly.

He wasn't wrong, but Briar couldn't help a snort. "When you put it like that, we might never get the chance. This Midsummer Festival *has* been a little eventful, if I'm honest."

Petal winced. "I really am sorry."

"I know. You stole the moon, but I'm the one who might strangle everyone in Haven to death with roses."

"The Foxglove sisters strike again," Petal said. "Briar?"

"Yes?"

"Start with Charles."

Ethan grunted his immediate approval. "Finally, something we agree on."


As Briar clutched at Goliath's mane and hoped she wouldn't fall right off and crack her skull open, she did not exactly feel like a heroine in a storybook, the village witch come to save the day.

She felt bruised and achy and her hands hurt, cuts opening as her knuckles whitened with her tight grasp on the mane. The glow of the moonlight was disconcerting. It tracked her like an unblinking eye, cold on her skin. White roses and white deer burned behind them.

Ethan's chest was solid and warm at her back, his strong thighs bracketing hers. He slipped an arm around her waist. "I've got you, little thorn," he murmured, his breath on the back of her neck. His presence, as merciless and dangerous as he was, was a comfort.

The road to Holdfast was more of a suggestion, not often taken. Holdfast was not popular with tourists; it was too cold and stark for that, too sharp with magic. They preferred the confectioneries of Haven, the bookshops and academies of Hallow.

Briar had only been to Holdfast a few times, once to have her dreams read and then again after her mother died to have her bones gilded for the ossuary caves. Witches preferred funerary pyres outside of Lyonesse, but the island demanded everything from its witches, including their bones to power the shields that kept them safe and invisible.

It was not soft, or welcoming.

But neither was the island stretching out behind them, swiftly being devoured by roses.

They choked the road, crawling after them like a hulking shadow with a thousand shining claws.

# Chapter Twenty-Seven

HOLDFAST BELONGED TO the Iron Witches.

From the thatched black cottages to the cobblestones, from the rowan groves to the storm brewing overhead. And to the Iron Witches themselves, usually doing their work while wrapped in their plaids, white hair tangled by the breezes. The sea was merciless on the coast, threatening to fill the bone caves below, which stored so much magic that the very air felt strange. Otherworldly. Wild. It tasted of salt and iron and fennel.

Stone gargoyles had taken flight, awakened by the curse. They circled over the houses, gobbling up stray magic, but it wasn't enough. They did not look down on Briar and Ethan with any fondness.

Briar also expected the Iron Witches to be waiting for her, and to be rather cross about it.

Instead, there were white roses. So many roses, already overtaking the village.

No one was safe, not the fishing folk or the salt farmers who made up the rest of the population. Not even the Iron Witches.

The roses climbed down from the hills and up from the beaches. They flowed down the steep roads like the pale froth of a waterfall. Thorns gleamed like silver knives.

Goliath came to a stop with a snort that could only be translated as, *Absolutely bloody not.* And Briar could not blame him. Ethan cursed softly.

There were thirteen Iron Witches in total, but Briar only

counted twelve here. They lay where they had dropped into sleep, vines curling around them. A cradle and a coffin.

The villagers lay in similar repose, caught by the curse. A woman had collapsed over the butter churn outside her front door. A man lay sprawled, an axe in his hand. An old woman slumped out of her bedroom window. They must have stumbled out of their homes when the curse tightened its hold, waking them only to drop them back into sleep. Behind them, kelpies churned the water, teeth snapping. The roses had not reached them yet. How long until they dragged themselves out of the water in search of defenseless villagers?

It was roses and kelpies as far as the eye could see.

But the Iron Witches had fallen still in service to Lyonesse. They lined the road, white hair catching the moonlight almost as much as Briar did. They wore their sea-gray dresses and their silver torcs and the spiral tattoos of their station. Though they hailed from countries all over the world, those torcs and tattoos marked them as witches with powers beyond the ordinary.

And the curse had taken them all.

"Now what do we do?" Briar said, guilt and fear raw in her belly. She had thought getting here would be the hard part. Then she could hand over the amulet and the Iron Witches could do whatever it was that Iron Witches did.

Petals filled the air. They whirled, sticking to window panes and gargoyles on the rooftops, clogging the grooves between the cobblestones.

Goliath, being a wise horse, immediately took off into the fields.

Briar clenched her fists, the smell of roses thick and heavy in her nose. "What do I do?"

One of the Iron Witches twitched.

Briar jumped. "Did you see that?" she asked Ethan.

He nodded, looking even grimmer, if possible.

As Briar approached the Iron Witch, the sound of his sword sliding from its scabbard cut through the song of the waves and the creak of door hinges caught in the wind. Briar crouched and smeared her blood on the nearest rose to the Iron Witch. She already knew it was beyond her to stop all of the roses in Holdfast. There wasn't enough blood in her body. "Can you hear me? I have the amulet to fix the shields. What do I do?"

The roses shivered, thorns spiking sharper in displeasure. They did not like for their work to be interrupted. Sweat gathered at Briar's nape as she forced her magic against theirs.

The Iron Witch moved, just a little. A shift, a turn of her wrist. The others did the same around her until, to a person, the Iron Witches pointed to the white stone tower on a small isle at the end of the stony promontory.

Briar shivered. "I take that to mean they want me to bring the amulet to the tower."

Ethan did not look pleased. "Aye. Looks that way." He frowned at the sea, the lick of the moonlight on Briar's bloody hands. "I'll do it."

Briar half smiled. "I don't think it works that way."

"We'll *make* it work that way."

"It's my spell," she pointed out. "My problem."

"*Our* problem, woman."

The Iron Witches scattered around them were bad enough.

Worse yet, one of them was still awake. Her eyes were open, furious, flaring green. Roses pinned her to the ground. She struggled, thorns scraping her skin. She tried to speak but her mouth filled with rose petals. Briar hurried to pull them loose.

When the Iron Witch also finally pointed, like her sisters, it was in another direction.

Behind Briar and Ethan.

It was the only warning they had.

THE ARROW CUT through the petal-choked air, hitting its target with brutal efficiency.

Ethan.

He stumbled back, blood oozing down his arm. The stink of

burning fennel joined the smell of flowers and salt. Not just an arrow. A spelled arrow. Loosed by a Keeper.

*Oliver.*

Ethan had already dragged Briar behind him, even as he gritted his teeth against the pain. He yanked the arrow out, more blood soaking into his torn sleeve. He grunted in pain, shoving salt and iron dust from his pocket into the wound. Briar did not know what magic was coursing through him, only that they were lucky he was not already dead. Keepers were not particularly careful with Iron Crows.

Nor particularly smart. Killing Ethan would have been smarter. Safer.

Terror made Briar's throat dry. Oliver would realize that soon enough. Or Ambrose would—he was currently at Oliver's side, holding Sorcha bound with rope on his horse. He held an iron dagger to her side.

"Don't move, Briar Foxglove, or the baker and the Iron Crow die," Oliver called.

That was why he had not killed Ethan outright. He made for better leverage. She was not heartened to realize that Oliver was not an idiot.

"Where the hell is Coventry?" Ethan said. "He ordered you to stand down."

"I haven't seen Lord Coventry. We were following a lead that Petal Foxglove was spotted. And then we saw the roses. You owe me, Crow." There was a burn on the side of his neck, and his sleeve was charred.

"I owe you a slow and painful death."

"I'm not the one with the poisoned arrow wound."

"I'm only here to break the spell," Briar said, as soothingly as she knew how. She called on the calming qualities of chamomile and lemon balm and vervain. She already knew it would not be enough.

"I won't fall for your lies," Oliver seethed. "I might not be able to find your sister, but I've got *you* now. And I'll break the curse by breaking you. You won't escape me again."

"Kick him in the stones, Briar!" Sorcha shouted loudly enough that the horse beneath her and Ambrose shifted nervously.

"I have the only antidote for that poison currently infecting your Iron Crow," Oliver said haughtily. He had donned some kind of armor over his charred shirt, as though he were a knight in a fairy story. He gleamed in Briar's reflected moonlight.

She vastly preferred the dragon.

Dark green lines were already stabbing out from Ethan's wound, riddled with baneful magic. There would be iron powder, for a Keeper's poison. Salt. He had already used those. What else? She could not create her own cure in time; she did not have enough herbs on hand, no ashes of solstice bonfires or honey. No comfrey.

She had moonlight and roses.

Hopelessness clawed at her.

*No.*

She lifted her chin. "I am only here to break the spell, Oliver," she said again, willing him to believe her. "Just let them go."

He snorted. "A likely story. I'll break the curse myself as soon as you're in an iron collar."

Briar swallowed. Petals thickened the air.

"Come here," Oliver demanded, "or he gets another arrow."

"Don't you fucking dare," Ethan bit out.

"The Iron Crow or the baker, Miss Foxglove. Or you."

There was little time for deliberation, but no deliberation was required. She would never sacrifice Sorcha and Ethan. And Ethan was leaning against a post, turning an alarming shade of gray. The Iron Witch tangled in thorns near his boots bared her teeth.

Briar stepped forward.

"Don't!" Sorcha said, but it ended in a choked yelp when the blade pierced through her dress. Even through the rose petals and the shadows, Briar could see the spot of blood.

She hurried closer to Oliver. "Don't hurt them!"

He slid off his horse. "I do this for the good of Lyonesse."

He believed it, and nothing she could say would dissuade him. Nothing else would save Sorcha and Ethan.

So Briar stood still as Oliver lifted the iron collar.

It was a flattened crescent, marked with lines and dots, like the ancient stone circles. It looked more like a necklace than something that would rip into her soul and shred it to pieces.

Ethan stumbled, trying to reach her, seething with fury and poison. "I'll fucking kill you, Keeper," he promised, his dragon breathing daggers of fiery light around him like a crown.

The clasp locked around her neck.

The pain was immediate.

It spread through her like veins of fire and acid, burning through everything that made her Briar. It stole her breath, her every thought. Her magic. It crawled through her like some monstrous beast, all teeth and claws, shredding away every necessary thing. Snapdragon fought, hissing and flapping his wings so that feathers of light joined the white rose petals.

When the pain receded, Briar could not feel her swan at all. He was no longer thrashing inside her, but was still. Too still. Tears pricked her eyes. She felt empty, hollow.

Oliver smirked, but he had no time to revel in his satisfaction.

It was hard to revel in anything when two hundred pounds of Black Shuck shot out of the shadows.

Oliver went down hard, screaming when vicious teeth vised around his arm. Blood dripped from the ragged wound.

"Good puppy!" Sorcha shouted.

Ethan didn't say anything at all, as he was still slumped against a post, but he was smiling.

Briar really did have rather violent friends.

She hurried to the Black Shuck, as Sorcha took his example and bit the hand of the Keeper holding her until he dropped his dagger.

"Don't kill him," Briar said, getting as close to the Black Shuck as she dared. Oliver was struggling, gasping. "We might still need him if he was lying about the antidote." She had no idea if he understood her, but there was something frantic enough in her voice that the Black Shuck sat back on its haunches and growled. "Thank you."

Oliver was sweating and shuddering with pain. A thorn poked into his wound to add insult to injury. The roses, as predicted, cared little for her iron collar. They had already been set loose—she was no longer needed.

"The antidote, if you please," Briar demanded, standing over him dispassionately. "Or I'll let him eat you. Well, parts of you, anyway."

"I'm with the Order!" he panted. "It's your duty to help me."

"Oh, sod off," Sorcha muttered. "Give us the antidote and the key to the collar or I'll stomp on your balls." Direct, clear. To the point. And undeniably something Sorcha would follow through on. With a smile.

"Blue bottle," Oliver whimpered. "In my left coat pocket."

Briar dove for it, prying the cork loose. It smelled of herbs and fire and vinegar. "Does he drink it or does it go on his wound?" Oliver's eyes were starting to roll back in his head. She squeezed his arm, above the wound. "Answer me!"

He groaned with pain. "On…his…cut."

"Wrap his wound, would you?" Briar asked her friend. "In case we still need him."

Sorcha looked disgusted but did as she was asked. Briar had to fight through the vines to reach Ethan. His dragon curled behind him, flickering like a candle gutting out. She already missed her swan. *Not now, Briar.*

She dumped the contents of the vial into Ethan's raw wound, wincing when the blood bristled with hoarfrost in response, delicate and sharp in the moonlight.

His eyes popped open. "Son of a *bitch.*"

Briar laughed in relief. He smiled at her softly until his eyes fell on the iron around her neck.

His gaze hardened, turned deadly. "I'll kill him. No talking me out of it now, sweetheart."

"Later," Briar said. She pushed a rose off her ankle. "I need to get the amulet to the tower."

At least, she hoped that was what she needed to do. The fact that the Iron Witches were all pointing in its direction was the only thing she had to go on. She supposed it was better than nothing.

With any luck.

She stood, the weight of the iron around her neck heavy and suffocating. She felt like she could not get a deep breath, but she knew it was about her magic, not the physical collar. She could still taste charred fennel and salt. And roses. She was certain everyone could taste the roses. She was hollow. If she thought about it too long, she would start clawing at the collar and never stop.

"Be careful," Sorcha said. "I'll stay here and make sure this prat doesn't make a run for it. Charles told them to use me. We *all* survive this, so I can punch him *very* hard in the throat."

Ethan nodded at her. "I'll help."

It took some time to pick their way through the thickets, down the cobblestone path to the beach. Ethan lifted Briar up in his arms, and she squeaked. "Your wound!"

He only grunted and kicked through the roses, refusing to let Briar lose any more of her blood. She wasn't even sure it would work now that her magic was as trapped as the island of Lyonesse.

The white tower stood on a tiny islet, only big enough to house it and a few feet of rocky ground all around it. The moonlight showed dark water, a pier that did not quite reach across, and the teeth of kelpies.

No rowboat. No other boat at all. No bridge.

Only roses following them, curling through the sand hungri-ly.

The iron collar grew cold around her throat.

# Chapter Twenty-Eight

BRIAR KNEW SHE could not swim through those dark and churning waters. She would be pulled under within moments. She considered making a rope of rose vines, hoping it would reach the tower. All she could see were kelpies, with their burning eyes and impossibly muscular jaws.

"Have you ever ridden a kelpie?" she asked Ethan.

"Yes," he replied grimly.

"I don't see any other way across."

He cursed.

"I can do it alone," Briar added hastily. He had done so much already. No need to ride a murder-horse with a poisoned wound still healing on his arm.

"The hell you are," he answered, low and dangerous.

"You've risked enough."

He gripped her chin. "Look at me." His eyes were so intense that she swallowed. "We do this together or not at all." He kissed her hard and then waded into the frothing ocean, whistling.

Kelpies rushed toward them, shrieking.

Briar stumbled back a step before she could stop herself. She wondered if this was like wild dogs or unicorns, where one wasn't supposed to show fear.

Too late.

Far, far too late.

Ethan calmed the waves around them, his dragon snapping at the kelpies he decided were too rambunctious. The water became a dark glass, reflecting the moon, the white tower. A kelpie snapped at her, far too close for comfort. Ethan turned the water to icicles. The kelpie nickered and swam away, seaweed clinging to his mane, pinpricks of blood on his side.

The next kelpie had better manners. It was also the size of two large horses. Briar tried not to look at its teeth too closely. "You're very handsome," she said, gulping.

Kelpies could sometimes be controlled with ropes of ivy-wrapped widdershins around iron chains. Briar had white roses and rowanberries.

Ethan had fish bones wrapped in gold thread.

"They like them." He shrugged when she stared at him. Other men fed horses and dogs and kittens. Ethan kept treats for murder-horses among his magical tools.

He gripped her waist and placed her on the kelpie's back. She held on to the mane, knuckles going red, then pale. It was softer than she would have guessed, and thick as a fisherman's rope. The salt water stung in her multitude of cuts.

"If you drop her, try to drown her, so much as turn your head for a nibble, I will boil the sea around you," Ethan promised savagely. "Are we clear?"

He stared the kelpie in the eye for a long moment before turning to mount his own steed.

Briar Foxglove, the witch in the pink cottage, was riding a kelpie.

And riding a kelpie was invigorating. Bracing. Unique.

Also terrifying.

She clung to its wide neck, her thighs tightening. His torso and back went from draft horse to sea serpent. Holding on was tricky business. So was not panicking. Not choking on saltwater spray as it went up her nose.

Ethan charged through the sea beside her, looking as though he was born to it, his dark hair tangled with salt, the muscles of his forearms contracting, silver rings glinting. The waves around him churned and frothed, but they gentled to a lap around Briar's knees. It must have taken an enormous amount of magic.

Behind them, the roses continued to eat the island. They covered the beach and chased them into the sea.

The tower loomed ahead with its jagged, rocky coast.


ETHAN FINALLY HELPED her off the kelpie's back, steadying her when her hip shot pain all the way down her leg. "Thank you," she told the water horse politely. "But I don't ever want to do that again."

Ethan's teeth flashed in a grin. The kelpies dove under the waves, slapping their tails on the surface before disappearing.

The climb to the tower did not take long. The stones were slippery, but the steps were gritty with salt and mussel shells. Iron Witches were powerful enough that Briar could still see the glimmer of magic in the air but could no longer feel it. The iron pressed against her collarbones. Someone's familiar in the shape of a crane perched on the crenelations.

The wind howled through the arched doorway, pushing them inside. Rowanberries were scattered on the ground. Red ribbons and witch glass dangled in the windows, tinkling as the globes swung together. Lanterns lined the edges of the space in a circle of warm flickering light. In the center was a brazier with a fire of rowan wood burning hot.

The last Iron Witch also waited inside. She was slumped on the stones, her plaid wrapped around her shoulders. She wore a crown of rowan over her white hair and the silver torc of her office. Her fingers were tattooed, joined by dots high on her brow and the triple spiral of Lyonesse at the base of her neck. They were sworn to the island and its protection.

"You've come at last," she struggled to say, blood on her lips.

"I have the amulet," Briar said softly. "Tell me what to do."

"Take that shell there and fill it with salt and rowanberries."

Briar did as she was bidden, scooping salt from a large glass jar and rowanberries from a willow basket.

"Now the amulet." The Iron Witch coughed and it sounded

painful. Her eyelids were only half open.

Briar did not even check her stays for the amulet. She merely held out her hand until Ethan dropped it in her palm, on top of her dead, faded witch knot, without a word. "I don't have magic anymore," she told the other woman. "They took my craft."

"We don't need your magic—we have mine. We need your blood."

Ethan hissed out a warning breath.

The Iron Witch chuckled weakly. "Easy, Dragon."

"What's the price?" Ethan demanded.

Briar frowned at him. "What do you mean?"

"There's always a price." He kept his glare on the Iron Witch.

"He's right," she agreed hoarsely.

"It doesn't matter. I'll pay it," Briar said. "This is my fault."

Ethan clapped a hand over her mouth, silencing her. "No." He tucked her up against his chest protectively. "That was no oath, witch."

Briar had to pull on his arm with her full strength to get him to lower it. "We don't have time for this. I made this mess, however unintentionally. So I'll do what needs to be done."

"Your sister ought to pay the price."

"She's not here. I am." She stepped toward the Iron Witch, holding the bowl of salt and rowanberries. The moonstone of the amulet drank in the moonlight, pulling it through the windows and the doorway and from Briar herself. "Now what do I do?"

"We need your blood, as well as mine, delivered by a rose thorn."

That was easy enough to fulfill. The roses were already rushing up the stone steps and her scrapes were still bleeding. One of the vines had tangled in her hair and stuck there, so she pulled it loose for the Iron Witch. She used it to draw blood from her fingertip, as well as her own.

Their blood dripped over the amulet.

"And now?" Briar asked as a storm of rose petals blew inside the tower and caught in a whirlwind. One of the witch globes crashed to the ground and splintered. The sound was like a thousand bird wings, a thousand trees cracked by lightning, a thousand earthquakes underfoot.

"Burn it."

Aidan was going to be incensed over the burning of an ancient artifact. Were the Foxgloves a fine family from the peerage, they might have offered donations to assuage the museum over the loss. Briar could only offer him a nice, soothing tea. A recipe against slugs in the cabbages. Rose-petal honey.

A broken curse.

When she approached the fire, the wind intensified. Petals and dirt and debris bit at exposed skin. The fire flickered wildly but did not go out. The rowan wood sparked. A keening sounded in her ears. The iron collar grew colder, stinging her skin. Icicles formed like dangling silver spikes. Her teeth chattered. She tried to ignore the mounting pain, stumbled—but she did not fall. Her hip throbbed, and the cuts all over her hands and arms burned. The collar tightened.

But she did not fall.

"Briar, let me." Ethan was nearly horizontal as he pushed against the wind.

"It has to be her." The Iron Witch tried to sit up, but could not.

"It's *hurting* her."

"What did you expect?" spat the Iron Witch. "Curses don't die easy."

"Neither do Foxgloves," Briar forced out even as the wind tried to steal her breath and the petals tried to choke her and her blood dripped on the cold stones.

The roses had reached the tower, and now they were at the windows, snaking through the arched doorway. Seeking, claiming, strangling. Another witch globe popped, showering them with glass dust. A lantern toppled, candlelight extinguished.

Briar tried to ignore it all. There was only the amulet in her hand, the fire in the center of the tower, sparks glowing with the power of the Iron Witches. The taste of salt and fennel seeds and blood. The drag of her shoes on the stones as she fought for purchase.

The bite of vines snapping around her, quick as a snakebite.

Briar did fall that time, taken off balance and unable to steady herself. Her wrist and shoulder took the brunt, and her hip. The force of it jarred into her teeth. Thorns bound her ankles, biting. Merciless. She had no magic to fight them.

Ethan hacked at the roses with an iron dagger to get to her, and covered her with his body to shield her. He pressed over her, grim-faced and determined. She squinted into the petal-choked wind. The fire flared. She was close enough.

Maybe.

The sea churned out of sight, a constant thundering. The iron collar was made of ice and thorns. More blood dripped down her collarbones.

Gasping with pain, Briar tossed the amulet at the fire.

The wind roared and caught it.

Her eyelids felt too heavy even as desperation and frustration coursed through her. Her fingers shook. She coughed on a rose petal. The curse had come for her.

And then the wind changed.

Just a little.

Just enough.

Because Ethan had also come for her. As he lay over her, bearing the brunt of the attack, he continued to pull water into the tower until he filled the air with rain, sending every drop like bolts. Weighing down the wind, tearing through the roses. The sea lapped at the doorway.

The wind stuttered.

The amulet fell into the fire.

It rolled down a rowan log, perilously close to rolling clear out of the embers. The ashes turned silver. Briar could not breathe, not until the amulet teetered, but was eventually swallowed by the flames. The pearls melted. It took longer for the moonstone to crack, but when it did, the vines around Briar's ankles loosened.

Her eyelids did not weigh as much as a castle.

The rose petals froze in the air for a moment and then dropped, all at once, all of a sudden. The silence was nearly painful, swelling in the ears. Her heart beat too hard. She felt it inside every cut and pinprick.

She lowered her head with a thump, exhausted and exhilarated. Ethan's breath was ragged on the back of her neck.

The rain receded. The moonlight did not find her inside the tower.

The roses became roses once more.

Briar rolled over onto her back and Ethan pressed up on his hands, still looming over her, soaked through, sleeve torn, jaw hard. His gaze roamed, cataloguing her wounds, narrowing over the collar. But before he could say anything, the Iron Witch rose to her feet. She sliced a cut over her witch knot and then slapped her palm to the wall, over the triple spiral of Lyonesse carved deep into one of the damp stones.

The shields, invisible but palpable all the same, lifted.

It was the sound of a rusty iron portcullis being raised. Creaking, groaning, and then, finally, opened.

Briar sat up, hardly daring to believe it was over.

The island shields were lifted; the roses had stopped growing. Her sister was safe.

Ethan reached out to touch her cheek, pulling free the hair stuck there. "Briar, your hair."

She followed his gaze. A streak of her brown hair had turned white—white as salt, white as bone.

White as the moon.

He searched her expression. She shrugged. But when she spoke, her voice was smaller than she would have liked. Would this be the last evidence of her magic? That she had witchcraft in her blood once? That flowers knew her name? "Do you think the Keepers will take this collar off now that the shields have been mended?"

The empty space where her green magic should be was even more exhausting than the battles and the curse breaking. There should be a hundred little conversations to take for granted, a whisper from the rowan-twig crown, the dried mint in her apron, the roses everywhere. The seaweed just outside the door, the soft green moss, the sacred rowan trees on the cliff.

But there was nothing. Not just silence, which could be gentle. This was raw and jagged and *wrong*.

"Bah, Keepers," the Iron Witch said with disdain while Briar fought back tears. Petal was safe. Sorcha and Ethan and the witches of Lyonesse were safe. It should be enough.

It would have to be enough, if the Order chose to punish her by leaving the iron to trap her swan. Was Snapdragon scared? Or asleep? She had no way of knowing.

Her nails cut little half-moons into her palm.

"I'll make them take it off," Ethan swore, low and rough. "Or I'll find a warlock who will."

The Iron Witch snorted. "All of that will take too long. The Order does like to make a fuss. Come here, girl."

Briar crossed the uneven stones littered with roses and rowanberries and broken glass. The Iron Witch clicked her tongue at the collar, drawing her fingertips over the patterns hammered into it. "You are a beast, aren't you?" she murmured, as if it had spoken to her. Perhaps it had. Iron Witch magic was a bit of a mystery to everyone else.

The collar silvered with frost when she touched the clasp, as if fighting back.

"That's enough of that," the Iron Witch snapped, her eyes flaring. "You may be Order-bound, but I am Iron-bound."

The clasp opened and the collar dropped to the stones with a clang.

The rush of power was like a dry riverbed flooding after a drought. It prickled painfully, perfectly. Briar tasted mint and tea and lavender. Snapdragon burst from her chest with a cry of relief and, it had to be said, vengeance. Swans were not pretty, gentle creatures.

And neither was she.

This time it was a relief to think it.

The Iron Witch studied the irate swan, the rose leaves fluttering even though the air was still. "You'd make a decent Iron Witch," she said.

"I'm not banished from Holdfast?" Briar asked, leaning back into the comfort of Ethan's chest because she wanted to and did not know how many chances were left to her. She had expected the Holdfast witches to hold a grudge. She had messed with their shields, after all.

But the Iron Witch only shrugged. "It's not our mistakes, usually, but what we do with them. But I'm keeping the collar."

And that was that. Iron Witches were a pragmatic lot, it seemed.

She strode out of the tower into the graying pre-morning light. Briar gathered rose petals and rowanberries and tucked them into one of her apron pockets before following. Just in case. A green witch was a green witch, after all. And the whispers were a balm, little stories of roots and branches and blossoms.

They stepped out of the tower, the sea tossing whitecaps around them. There was a tiny glint of fire in the distance. The dawn bonfire at the stone circle at the old hillfort. It was solstice morning.

Briar made a face. "I don't relish having to ride another kelpie."

The Iron Witch raised her eyebrows. "You rode a kelpie?"

"Isn't that how you cross?"

She snorted and pointed around the back of the island where a rowboat was tied to the rocks.

"We take the boat. Only a lunatic would ride a bloody kelpie."

# Chapter Twenty-Nine

THE CROSSING BACK to the main island was a far simpler affair.

There were still kelpies, but they were mostly waiting for Ethan to toss them chicken bones. Even the Iron Witch shook her head at that.

The keel dragged on the rocks as several villagers rushed forward to bring them the rest of the way in. They steadied the boat, helping the Iron Witch to her feet, then Briar, but Ethan was already knee-deep in the waves, lifting her out.

Holdfast was full of roses but did not look otherwise the worse for wear. No one had choked on petals or been strangled to death by thorny vines. Briar let out a breath of relief. Someone had lit a fire in the center of the small square and it popped cheerfully, sending sparks into the sky. There would be bonfires all over the island this morning.

Oliver and Ambrose were where they had been left, tied up with rope, mostly being ignored by the villagers. Sorcha was nearby, tossing a large branch into the field behind the road. "Is she playing fetch with a Black Shuck?" Ethan asked.

Briar smiled fondly at her friend. "Yes, of course she is."

"Of course. Stupid of me to ask, really."

Sorcha spotted them and darted over to throw her arms around Briar. "You did it! Your hair! Your throat! Is that blood? Are you hurt?"

Briar shook her head. She was beyond tired, had passed to that glittering, liminal pace beyond it. Her hip ached like the devil. She wanted a pot of tea and a tower of Matthias's madeleines. An entire chicken pie. A raspberry cake. Cheese. Three days of sleep.

But she was surprisingly…well.

"Happy Midsummer," she said instead, because it was a less complicated answer and a soft pink touched the horizon, barely there.

"Happy Midsummer!" Sorcha returned, eyes sharp as she glanced at Ethan, then back at Briar. Briar had no answers. The Black Shuck barreled toward them, the half of a toppled tree he had traded the branch for in his giant jaw. "Happy Midsummer, Shadow," Sorcha added. "Give me that, you absolute monster. Don't you dare drool on me. I'll stink for a month."

"You named him Shadow?" Briar groaned, the moment of ordinary such a balm it made her eyes sting. "You are the worst at naming things."

"What? How can you say that? He's dark, a bit scary. Shadow is perfect. I am *very* good at this," she informed Ethan haughtily.

"You called your familiar Shiny Murder Bird until you were twelve," Briar reminded her.

"And he *is* a shiny murder bird. I fail to see the problem. And then he wanted to be addressed as Sir Elderberry."

Elderberry, the murder bird in question, was busy flying low circles over Shadow with a taunting cry.

"What about these two?" Ethan asked, looking rather like a shiny murder bird himself. Oliver squirmed to get out of reach. Sorcha had stuffed a piece of cloth in his mouth.

"He wouldn't stop complaining," she said, rolling her eyes. "'My arm hurts, I'm a Keeper,' demanding this, demanding that. So it was this or let Shadow eat his face." She sniffed. "All options are still on the table."

Ethan didn't say a word, but he took a step closer, shirt bloodied, hair tangled and crusted with salt water. Oliver paled. Ambrose yelped.

Briar sighed. "Technically he was within his rights to make

me wear the iron collar," she pointed out.

"Like hell!" both Ethan and Sorcha bellowed together. Shadow growled once. Ethan's dragon dove low, fire streaming from his nostrils.

It was rather nice.

"I'm not saying I'm going to bake him a cake," Briar assured them. "But we can let Bear deal with him."

Ethan studied her silently, iron dagger at the ready.

"I know you're not staying on Lyonesse," she said softly. "But if you murder a Keeper, you won't ever be able to come back."

Would he want to come back? Was she being presumptuous? Her cheeks warmed.

"Not that… I mean…"

*Very articulate, Briar.*

It had been a trying night. Allowances ought to be made.

Ethan's expression was hard to read, but a muscle twitched in his jaw. He nodded once, eyes dark as the sea behind them. Then he crouched to whisper something in Oliver's ear. Briar could not hear what he said. She exchanged a glance with Sorcha.

When Ethan straightened, Oliver was even paler and had broken out into a cold sweat. Ethan looked grimly satisfied.

"What do we do with them now?" Sorcha wondered aloud. "Do we just let them go?"

"I am sure the Order is on their way already," Briar said.

Sorcha turned hastily to the Black Shuck. "Time to go! Don't let them see you!"

Shadow panted at them, his breath eye-watering, before dashing into the fields. Swallows and starlings burst out of the grass, squawking as he passed.

"You can't just let a Black Shuck—"

"Shut up, Ambrose," Sorcha snapped. "You tried to stab me. You do not get an opinion."

"Best not tarry," said the Iron Witch from the tower—who, they had discovered, was also the daughter of a selkie from the Orkneys and a sailor from Samoa. Her name was Scathach. "The

Order is bad enough when they *don't* feel the need to posture on top of everything. Today they will be unbearable."

"Thank you," Briar said. They had been more understanding than she could have ever expected.

Scathach waved that away. "Go on with you. But come back and talk to our rowan trees soon, would you? We don't have a green witch here anymore, and between the stone and the iron, they do have a time of it."

"I will," Briar promised. It would be a pleasure. She had never worked with a grove of sacred trees before. And Holdfast was lovely in its own way: harsh, wind-worn, unassuming.

"What about Petal? And the others?" Briar asked as she and Ethan and Sorcha followed the Black Shuck's example and chose the fields over the road. "We need to make sure they weren't hurt or captured."

"They're fine," Ethan said.

"How can you know that?"

He nodded to the shimmering albatross flying toward them. "That's my boatswain's familiar. Three flicks of his tail feathers mean everyone is accounted for."

"Even Petal?"

He grunted. "Do you think my crew would leave her out now? You saw them."

Relief felt strange after everything. It made her lightheaded. She swallowed a giggle. Too much had happened, was still happening. Her swan flew in the dragon's fiery wake but did not stray far, for which she was glad. They had only been separated by the iron collar for a short time, but the shock of it lingered under her skin. It was like having a limb removed. An organ.

The sky turned to a lighter gray with swirls of pink and a thin, thin line of orange on the eastern horizon. There was the flicker of firelight from several small bonfires. The main solstice fire would be at the Crown, the circle of standing stone at the top of the highest hill overlooking the hillfort remains.

"Is that Goliath?" Sorcha asked, spotting the horse picking

through the grass for dandelions. "What's he doing out here?"

"Ethan stole him," Briar said.

"Later you'll tell me how we all ended up in Holdfast. And about the roses. You know I hate roses." She waggled her brows at Briar, angling away so Ethan would not see her face. "I'll get Goliath home and meet you at the Crown?"

Briar nodded, feeling oddly nervous. She had fought off Iron Crows, a grimsong, a truth spell, an iron collar. She could have this conversation.

"I know you are leaving as soon as may be," she said to Ethan, watching her friend charge through the fields singing a song to the puzzled horse. She couldn't quite look at him. "But it's tradition to light the main bonfire at dawn for the solstice."

"Like swimming at midnight and counting fireflies."

She nodded. He paused. She heard the shift when he stepped closer. He tipped her face up toward his, smiling faintly.

"I suppose I had better. Whenever you go off for a bit of good luck, you come up against kelpies and Keepers."

She smiled back shyly. "That's true."

"But I do have to leave, little thorn."

Her smile did not waver. "I know."


HAVEN MIGHT BE the social jewel of Lyonesse, all propriety and luxury, but even they bent the rules for summer festival days. There was a wildness and a rawness to the celebrations, white dresses stained with strawberry wine, folks wearing daisies with their pearls, bare toes in the grass. Music swelled as the fire burned higher, drums and flutes and fiddles reaching to the rising sun. Familiars glowed everywhere: toads and cats, badgers, hedgehogs and hawks. A giant whale made of sparkling light swam through the sky as if it were the sea. A Pegasus's hooves flashed gold as it landed down in the valley.

"Miss Foxglove!" The wheelwright's son stumbled to a stop when he recognized Briar. He was flushed with wine. "Is your sister here?"

She shook her head, smiling. "I'm afraid not."

He looked devastated. "Do you know that she is prettier than the sun?"

Ethan grunted. Briar nodded. "I do know that." If the villagers were asking after her sister in that lovesick manner, it was better than demanding she be brought to the Order to pay for her crimes. The shields had lifted; solstice was here. They would forgive her everything. Maybe not the Order, but most of Lyonesse would.

Three more villagers stopped to inquire about Petal. They all wore crowns of white roses. Trust Haven to turn a threat into a new fashion. Briar had picked dandelions and buttercups and pink mallows and woven them into a circlet instead. The smell of the roses made her nose itch.

Ethan was clearly bristling, standing big and mean behind her. The hatmaker opened his mouth to ask Briar a question, no doubt about Petal, and then changed his mind. The sun rose higher and higher in a bed of pinks and oranges. The chain of dancers around the giant bonfire went faster, and faster. Magic sparkled, sweetening the air.

The sun finally rose completely, beams piercing between two of the standing stones. A cheer erupted. More strawberry wine was poured, baskets of blackcurrant cakes passed from hand to hand. There would be lazy walks back down to the village, breakfasts taken on the beach.

And Ethan sailing away.

The thought of it pulsed like a bruise, one Briar could not stop pressing.

He would leave. And she would stay.

She slipped her hand into his. She would keep him for a little while longer.

And then she would let him go.


IF ONE MORE person glanced at Briar vaguely before immediately inquiring about her sister, Ethan might flood the moors. Hilltop to valley. Let them all swim home. Or drown. It was beyond intolerable that he had agreed not to kill Oliver. Not because of logic or what was morally right, but only because Briar asked him not to. That Keeper had hurt her. The man deserved nothing less than annihilation.

Instead Ethan was watching villagers dance. It was flower crowns and firelight and songs being sung to the sun. It was lovely, in its own way.

But not nearly good enough for Briar. It was an ill-fitting dress. One of those damned driftwood canes that were not the right size or shape for her. And it infuriated him.

Rain pattered suddenly, sizzling when it hit the flames. Briar nudged him. "Stop that."

"Not me."

"Ha."

It ate at him, the way their eyes drifted over her. Worse, when two Keepers, ones he did not recognize, paused. Lingered. "Had enough of this?" he murmured, not taking his sharp gaze from them. The sun was bright on their iron-nail pendants.

Briar's nod was all he needed.

He gave in to the need to claim her, impossible as it might be. She deserved better. But her giggle when he scooped her over his shoulder made him feel like a king, even if it was of a kingdom he could not claim. It might be Midsummer, but this was still Haven, still Lyonesse. The scandal of the Dragon carting away the flower witch from the pink cottage whispered through the crowd.

"What are you doing?" Briar asked, still trying not to giggle. He had been listening to sirens singing since he was a lad, and nothing, *nothing* compared to her surprised little laugh.

"You said you'd had enough," he replied.

"Not of *walking*," she corrected him. Her hair swung, smelling of roses and mint. The soft roundedness of her arse under his palm was a threat to his sanity. It made him want to bare his teeth.

The murmurs continued, the sidelong glances.

Let them remember him. Perhaps he would not always be here, but he could come back at any time, the Iron Crow with blood on his hands. His reputation could protect her, even as it demolished hers.

Someone clapped. He'd bet his ship it was Sorcha. The flash of a crow familiar confirmed it. He kept walking. He wasn't sure where he was taking Briar, as long as it was away.

Someone stepped out of the crowd, familiar, proper all the way down to his museum shoes, even now. Ethan sighed, annoyed at the interruption.

"Lord Coventry," Briar greeted him pleasantly, propping herself up on Ethan's shoulder.

"Miss Foxglove."

At least Aidan had always shown her respect. Ethan might not eviscerate him after all. As long as he got out of the bloody way. He did not have long with Briar, and like hell was he going to spend any of it making conversation with an earl.

"You got the amulet to Holdfast. Well done."

"We did, thank you," she said.

"Did you leave it with the Iron Witches?"

Briar winced. "I'm sorry, but there's nothing left of it."

Aidan closed his eyes briefly. "I was afraid of that."

"It's not Petal's fault."

"Pardon me, but it is."

At least on that, he and Ethan agreed.

"Will you arrest her?" Briar's sweet, throaty voice went hard. And then Ethan went hard. Immediately.

Aidan ran a hand over his face. "I do not command the Order, despite what Swansea here might think. I work for the museum. No artifact, no need for me to follow."

"Oh, good." Briar beamed at him. Ethan could feel it. "Then I won't have to poison you."

Aidan blinked.

This was interminable.

"Coventry?" Ethan snapped.

"Yes?"

"Bit busy," he said. "Sod off."

Aidan stepped back, lips twitching as he fully realized he had been conversing with an upside-down Briar. A curator's focus could not be faulted, if nothing else.

As Ethan stalked away, Briar still over his shoulder, he heard Sorcha. "Are you smiling, Lord Coventry? Careful, you might hurt your pretty face. And I believe that's my job."

# Chapter Thirty

B RIAR SHOULD PROBABLY not enjoy being hauled about quite so much. She was sure it said something unsavory about her character. But as she had almost accidentally murdered all of the witches of Lyonesse with roses, her character was clearly already beyond salvation.

She may as well enjoy it.

Ethan stalked through the edge of the crowd, past the tables laden with the remnants of feasting, past empty bottles of honey mead, past couples being handfasted by the stones, past all of it as if it meant nothing. As if all that mattered was Briar pinned to his shoulder, his palm pressing against her backside, thumb tracing the spot at the bottom of her spine. She'd had no idea that very spot could make her shiver, could make heat crawl into her belly.

He crossed the fields to a thick grove of oak trees, green leaves deepening at their approach. The shadows were cool, dappled with light. Ethan set her down on her feet, and before the blood had rushed back through her body, he had pressed her against a tree, pinning her there. Keeping her there.

There was silence between them, and craving, and power. His eyes were dark, searching. His sleeve was torn and stained with blood. She was covered in the pinprick marks of thorns, on her arms, her fingers, her ankles. She must look as wild and unkempt as she felt. And she did not mind it so much. There was already something untamed flaring between them, the pull of their bodies, the need to get closer. *Closer.*

Ethan lifted his hand, silver rings flashing, and curled it around her throat. Gentle but inexorable. As if he could erase the memory of the iron collar and the welts it had left behind.

She found he could, if only for that moment.

They still had not spoken, had not looked away from each other. Her breath came in gasps, every part of her electrified. When she sucked her bottom lip into her mouth, his eyes flared. It was the spark of a wick catching fire. That snap of light. Hunger.

His hold tightened slightly, and he tilted her head back. The bark was rough against her neck, her shoulders. A welcome bite when she might otherwise float away. She was no longer convinced that she was in charge of her own body. Everything was Ethan. The parts of her that were not touching him felt cold, while also tingling with anticipation. When her eyes drifted shut at the waves of want and need crashing through her, he clicked his tongue in displeasure, fingers tightening again. He caught her gaze, snared it.

And then he smiled.

Slowly, darkly.

Something sharper than anticipation hummed through her.

His kiss was devastating. Deep, thorough. Deliberate. He demanded every bit of her attention, tongue stroking into her mouth, pulling her bottom lip into his mouth with a nip. Another stroke of his tongue against hers, their breaths tangling, ragged and desperate. He dragged those same kisses along her jaw, bit her ear, her collarbone, sucking at her skin along the top of her breasts, to her nipple. As if he were desperate to leave his mark on her.

As though he hadn't already.

When she whimpered, he smiled against her pinkened flesh. "I've got you, little thorn. It's not enough, is it?" When she shook her head frantically, he agreed, almost sounding angry, "It's never enough."

He lifted her higher against the tree, pushing her skirts up, parting her legs to step between them. The press of his cock against her mound made her whimper again, even through the layers of fabric. The ferns at their feet grew tender pale-green fronds, primrose flowers glowing in between.

She was so wet that when he finally touched her, he slipped between her folds with ease, sliding up toward her bud, back down again, his other hand still around her throat. He groaned, sounding broken in a way he had not sounded even when the arrow struck him. "So wet for me. So perfect."

She wanted to eat his delicious, filthy words like frosted cakes. She wanted more of everything. She clamped her thighs around his hips, demanding.

He groaned again. "Perfect little thorn."

She rubbed against him. "Please, Ethan."

"Please what, sweetheart?"

She growled. She actually *growled*. Then she turned her head, whispering in his ear, "Take me against this tree, Ethan. *Now.*"

He pulled at the buttons of his trousers, finally freeing himself. She wanted to touch him, stroke him until he groaned again, but she couldn't reach him at this angle. He dragged the crown of his cock through her wetness, a teasing pressure between her folds. She pushed up, trying to take him deeper. And then finally, finally, he thrust into her and she fluttered, stretched around him. The slide against her intimate muscles made her gasp.

"Never enough," he repeated, low voice tickling gooseflesh up her nape. He thrust deeper, angling, not rushing, until she wasn't sure if she wanted to scream or whimper. Or bite him.

He let go of her throat to cradle the back of her head, cushioning her as they rocked together in a frenzy, chasing every lick of fire, every shudder of desire. He gripped her bad hip with his other hand, steadying her, taking the weight. Taking everything. Giving everything.

There were no thoughts left, only heat and a sweet ache that threatened to tear her apart. He plunged into her again and again and she met him thrust for thrust, not just chasing pleasure but hunting it. Trapping it. It spiraled through her, stiffening her muscles, curling her toes, stealing the last gasp from her mouth. He followed with a hoarse grunt, pulling her closer to him, impossibly close until she wrapped her arms around his neck, and they stayed that way until the sweat dried on their skin.

When he finally set her back down, her legs wobbled. There was already the sting of strained muscles. She hoped she would feel it for days. A reminder. A secret that was just hers alone. Her Iron Crow. At least for a little while.

She smiled when she found him watching her, those dark eyes steady and intense. She did not know if he expected histrionics. Begging. Tears. But this was what was going to happen all along. He had told her he was leaving. It was practically the first thing he had said to her, before she convinced him to abduct her. And he needn't have warned her.

People left.

Especially Lyonesse. For most, the island was a vacation, a moment outside of their real lives and the tearoom just another stop along the way. A cup of tea, a frosted cake. A sachet of dried leaves as a souvenir. And then back to London or Cardiff or Dublin. Back to the seas.


THE WALK ACROSS the hills back to Haven was filled with birdsong and the wind in the thistles. The sun was warm on her hair and her shoulders and the tip of her nose. She snuck Ethan glances, drinking in his lazy, confident strides, the tattoo peeking out of his open collar, his silver rings flashing.

It swelled inside her ribcage—sorrow, wishes best left unsaid, the prickle of unshed tears behind her eyelids. The way she already missed him when he was still right there beside her.

*Love.*

She loved him.

There was no sense denying it to herself. It wouldn't make it any less true. Or any less painful. She loved his ruthlessness, his secret gentleness. His unwavering, uncomplaining strength. The way he'd fixed her door without being asked. The cane of roses. He *saw* her. And she knew how precious that was.

She loved *him*. Iron Crow. Dragon. Captain.

And so she let him go.

It was the only gift she could offer, the green witch spinster in the cottage that would be seized for unpaid debt within the week.

They had reached the cliff's edge. The ship, the glittering light of his dragon, the white roses. She did not blink, even when her eyes watered. She didn't want to miss a single moment. Ethan kissed her again, chasing the little sounds she made, holding firm but fingers gentle on her jaw. He pressed his brow to hers. "Little thorn."

"Dragon."

"Aster won't be a problem," he said. "I'll see to it."

What did that mean? She wasn't entirely sure she should ask. "You can't murder him."

"You keep saying that." He exhaled. "You have a lot of rules."

"Just the one, really. But if someone out there is trying to murder *you*, you can murder them right back."

"So the rules change."

She shrugged. "Usually no one's trying to murder *me*." She slanted him a look through her lashes. "You, on the other hand..."

He chuckled, but there was no humor to it. It was layered with too many threads for her to unpick. Wryness? Regret? Agreement? "Don't let his mother bully you. And don't let any Keepers through your front door, woman."

She ran her palms down his thick arms, memorizing the warmth of him, the sinewy strength. She did not mention that she might not have a tearoom for much longer.

"And don't use those driftwood canes anymore."

"I know."

"Have someone move a comfortable bed into your downstairs parlor. No more sleeping on the bloody stones."

Warmth filled her at his hard, stern tone. "I'll be fine, Ethan. I promise."

"I know. But I want you to be better than fine. And I want Haven to tremble at your feet."

"I don't need that."

He grunted, unconvinced. "I have to go."

"I know."

He pulled away, and she let him. He descended the stone steps, wind tugging at his dark hair. Briar stayed on the cliff, thinking of bees at window panes, spiders trapped in flower garlands, thistles that needed the field instead of the garden. The sparrow trapped in the roses.

"Don't forget me, Ethan Swansea," she whispered, too softly for him to hear. The scent of roses was strong.

He stopped but did not turn around. The line of his spine was like a sword. Sunlight flashed on the sea. He whispered back as though she was not meant to hear him either.

"I'd sooner forget how to breathe."

# Chapter Thirty-One

WHEN ETHAN LEFT Lyonesse, he took Petal with him.
She could no longer feasibly hide herself away on the island, not so long as the Order was still calling for her arrest for questioning. Aidan had withdrawn any interest in her whereabouts on behalf of the museum, but the Order persisted. The islanders might have hidden Petal, but she and Bramble preferred to take their chances between the moors of Yorkshire and the forests of Nottingham, where no one traveled across the country for a glimpse of the most beautiful witch in Britain.

Petal packed only her dresses, her shawl, and the coins Briar pressed into her hand. "You need these," Petal objected. "For Mother's debt."

Briar sighed. "They won't make much of a difference now, but they'll make a difference to you."

"I'm sorry I caused you so much trouble." Petal hugged her sister. "But when I go, I'll take the trouble with me."

"Be careful."

"Better than that, I'm going to be invisible."

As if he had been waiting for his cue, Basil was suddenly on the walkway, stars in his eyes and holding a posy of daisies. Daisies made Petal sneeze. "Miss Petal! Miss Petal, is that you?"

Bramble, who had been waiting in the lilac bushes, threw a shoe at him. It was only partially successful as a discouragement.

"I don't even know how he spotted me," Petal muttered. "Three Keepers walked right past me last night without noticing me, and they were bloody well *hunting* me."

"Miss Petal?" Basil sounded confused, blinking furiously. Bramble's rabbit magic had drawn veils of shadows across the cottage.

"She's not home," Briar called out before shutting the door and locking it.

"I should hurry," Petal said. "And I'll be careful, if *you* promise me you'll be a little bit reckless."

Briar snorted. "I grow flowers."

"You grow poisons too, you don't fool me, Briar Foxglove. And I know it's not been all roses—"

"Except when it was."

"Except when it was," Petal amended. "But I've never seen you more yourself. You seduced an Iron Crow."

"Hardly!"

"Ha." She softened. "This tearoom is not everything."

"I know."

"You are more important," she added fiercely. "Will you come visit me?"

Briar nodded, her eyes stinging. It had been her and her sister for as long as she could remember. Even when their mother was alive. "If I can find you."

"You can always find me." Petal hurried outside. The Sea Dragons would not wait much longer. "Are you coming to the ship?"

Briar shook her head. "We've said our goodbyes."

Petal looked dubious. "If you say so." She hugged Briar one last time, holding tight. "I like him, Briar. He doesn't care for me at all."

"You are *so* odd."

Petal's laugh trailed behind her as she darted into the long grasses with her rabbit wife.

She was not the only one eager to leave.

The lines of witches keen to get through the portal and back home wound all the way up the hill to the tearoom. Oliver and

Ambrose were among the first to leave. Whatever Ethan had said to him had made him too scared to even look in Briar's direction. Sorcha treated it as her own personal form of entertainment.

But no one else was keen to stay, even with the proof and promise that the shields had been mended. The smell of smoke lingered in the square from the charred remains of the Order's headquarters. Salves for the marks left by rose thorns were cleaned right off the shelves of every shop. Briar made several batches and left them in the square.

Matthias stayed behind, still enamored with Briar's kitchen. Briar knew Ethan had put them together so that Matthias could help protect her. And so she could give him an excuse to give up sailing. Which he did not miss a bit.

Charles, as promised, had been dealt with.

He was, in fact, nowhere to be found.

Aidan stayed for another three days, growing more pinched around the eyes with every passing hour. Even Briar's sleep tea did not appear to be helping much, judging by the shadows under his eyes. On the fourth day, he left for the museums and universities of Hallow.

"Good riddance," Sorcha muttered, but she was frowning when she said it.

On the fifth day, Mr. Crane came to the tearoom. He bore a letter, and an expression of extreme discomfort. "I'm sorry," he said. "Your mother signed her name on the debt vowel. There's really nothing to be done. Even without my assistance, the spell would change ownership to Mrs. Aster."

Briar nodded, expecting to feel angry, betrayed, scared. Mostly, she felt resignation. Which was not nearly violent enough for Sorcha's liking. She helped Briar cut every flower, harvest every cherry and gooseberry from the cottage garden. Every mint leaf, every cabbage, every stalk of celery that Briar had only planted because Petal asked her. She hated celery.

The blooming, vibrant garden was shorn to its roots. The orchards were picked clean.

And then the rabbits descended.

And they never left.

Mrs. Aster and her horrible son had wanted Briar's green witch magic and her garden. They were entitled to her garden by the letter of the law and her mother's agreement.

But they were not entitled to her magic.

When Sorcha saw the army of rabbits and Mrs. Aster's furiously pursed lips three mornings in a row, she smirked so hard she pulled a muscle in her cheek.

Sorcha had insisted Briar move in with her while she pondered her options. Living in the manor house was not a hardship, even if Briar knew it was not a permanent solution. It was nice to be near her friend, to drink wine in the evenings and watch the swallows fly through the hole in the roof of the ruins. It was peaceful, even if it was difficult not to think of Ethan and her sister and miss them fiercely. That would have been impossible no matter where she was. Snapdragon enjoyed marching around the overgrown pond and disturbing the insects.

Matthias tried to join them, but it was a three-hour walk from Haven and Briar would not have it.

"The captain will murder me if I don't stay near," Matthias said.

She kissed his cheek. "And I will murder you if you give up your dreams to lurk around the moors. You won't even have a kitchen. Sorcha will stab you with a fork the first time you try to use her oven." And he shone too brightly for that, already a favorite in the village. A fistfight had broken out over the last of his leek tarts two mornings in a row.

"Promise you'll send for me if there's trouble."

"I promise," she said. "But what kind of trouble could a spinster green witch possibly get into?"

Matthias snorted. "You're not a spinster."

She snorted back. She was the very definition of a spinster. No one in Haven would court her now—they could barely look her way without suspicion. And even if they got over it, none of them were Ethan.

She did not bring him up in conversations, not even late at night when Sorcha gave her chocolate buns and too much strawberry wine. But she could see the standing stone circle from the roof, and the dark oak grove where Ethan had last touched her. She had climbed down to the grove once, but only once.

She listened for rumors of the Sea Dragons, of the Order chasing down Iron Crows. Of pirates, kelpies, sirens. Anything that hinted at Ethan, of where he might be and what he might be doing. She missed him so much her bones hurt. She kept her cane of roses nearby, after Sorcha found it still strapped to Goliath's saddle that morning outside of Holdfast.

Briar found herself visiting Holdfast more and more, and there she whispered to the rowan trees, gathered lemon balm and peppermint for tea for a fisherman's widow, thyme and a key wrapped in chamomile for an Iron Witch with nightmares. She found shells and ropes of kelp that had started to speak to her. She sang to the rowan trees.

If the weather turned, she slept in the cottage next to the grove, listening to the wind and the silver chimes in the branches. She whispered to the leeks and the carrots and the onions in the kitchen gardens until they flourished. Peas crawled up stone walls around the rowan groves, and the village children liked to challenge the gulls to see who could eat the most.

Briar began to sleep in that cottage more and more often. She swept out the cobwebs, encouraged the nightshade to release its grip on the single wind-twisted lilac tree. She planted rosemary and mint and lavender.

And then she painted it pink.

She was still herself, still the witch who lived in the pink house even as the storms howled in from the sea and the hail pockmarked the roof. Holdfast suited her. There were no white houses, no glamours expected when you had a spot on your chin or a tear in your hem. No assembly rooms, just the main room in the tavern with scuffed floors and stone walls that held the heat from the hearth. There were gulls and fish and seals and dozens of cats who waited for the fishermen's boats. Kelpies, mermaids in the cove. The gilded bones of dead witches. The tower and the heavy weight of witchery rippling from it.

Briar loved it.

So she stayed when Scathach asked her to care for the rowan groves, which powered so many of the spells in Holdfast and on Lyonesse. Spells ran on rowanberries all throughout Britain.

It might not be exactly the life she had thought she would have, but in so many ways it was better.

She even received a letter, unsigned, with a sketch of a hare. Petal was thriving, utterly anonymous and unnoticed in the wild as she and her wife pushed further and further north. She sent seeds with the letter: bilberries, eyebright, along with pine needles and heather.

And then, two months after the solstice, the full moon found Briar standing on the beach, both lonely and content.

As did Ethan.

She was throwing chicken bones to a hungry kelpie, her apron filled with rowanberries and dandelions and seashells. The light glittered on the waves and the snap of white teeth. After the tracking spell, moonlight made her feel a little odd, exposed somehow, even though it did not seek her out any more than it sought out the rocks or the white tower. The curse was well and truly broken. Even the white roses did not grow in Holdfast anymore.

And so she attributed the frisson of awareness only to that.

Until the kelpie shrieked and Briar turned to glance behind her.

Ethan stood silently on the edge of the stone wall, silhouetted against the lanterns of Holdfast swinging in the wind like fireflies.

Briar froze. She stopped breathing altogether.

Had she missed him so much that she was imagining him now?

He wore the customary leather cross-belt across his chest,

crow claw and hagstone around his neck. But there was a new scar on the side of his throat, angry and red. And a tattoo of a rose tangled with thorns on the back of his left hand.

"Did you forget me already, sweetheart?" he asked, that Irish accent, that deep, smooth voice, curling around every bruise inside her ribcage, every spot that ached with the memory of him.

"Are you really here?" she asked as he closed the distance between them. Her pulse ricocheted all over her body.

"I'm really here." He wiped a tear from her cheekbone before she'd realized it was there. "You little liar. You were so brave and so stoic when I left."

"So were you." She clutched his arms, needing to feel him. Wanting to kiss him. Punch him. "What are you doing here?"

She could not let herself hope. Iron Crows had dozens of reasons to be in Lyonesse. He could be here for the Iron Witches, for all she knew. A tendril of hope did not want to think so, but she did not whisper it to grow. She couldn't. Ethan would leave her again and she would be right back where she started. She had to be smart. Practical. She had seen her mother work too many love spells, and the results were never quite what you expected. Love never was.

"The real question is, what are *you* doing here?" Ethan asked. "In Holdfast?"

"I like it here."

"And they like you. I had to run the gauntlet of Iron Witches, three fishermen with cudgels, and a feral child who threatened to turn me into fish stew before anyone would tell me where to find you."

Briar smiled. "That was Simon. He's afraid I'll stop growing peas for him to steal."

"I wouldn't want to cross him."

"No."

"Your pink cottage in Haven has been painted white, and the gardens are…not the same." His hands tightened on her. His eyes were a little wild. "I thought something happened to you."

"Just Mrs. Aster," she said wryly. "And my mother. Some debts can't be paid."

"Why the hell didn't you tell me?"

She lifted her chin. "It would have made no difference. And you were already helping Petal. That's what really mattered."

"You are infuriating, woman."

She blinked. "As are you, Dragon."

He grunted. "Aye."

"Ethan?"

"Yes, sweetheart?"

"What are *you* doing here?" she blurted out, not the least bit romantic or coy. "Are you selling spells to the Iron Witches?" They always needed ingredients, some unavailable on the island. Some unsavory.

Ethan looked at her for a long moment. "I'm here for you."

That tendril of hope strengthened without her permission, clinging like ivy.

"I took Petal to the mainland, as you asked. And I also dropped Aster somewhere in the Outer Hebrides. I hope he can swim."

"What? You know he can't."

"Pity for him, then." Ethan shrugged one shoulder. "You didn't want me to kill him. I had to get creative. After that, I had one last job I was hired to finish, the kind that would bring pain on the people around me if I didn't follow through," he explained. "And then there were the three bounties on my head I had to deal with. It all took longer than it bloody well should have."

Briar swallowed, her throat dry, her nose stinging.

"Nothing to say?" he pressed, sounding fond and demanding and…uncertain?

Could the infamous Ethan Swansea be nervous? About *her*?

"You didn't think I'd come back to you with that kind of danger at my back?" His jaw clenched, reading her expression. "You didn't think I'd come back for you at all." He shook his head. "Of course you didn't. You're always setting things free, aren't you? Bees in your kitchen, weeds, sparrows. But I don't want you to let me go, little thorn. I never did. Because I'm sure as hell not letting *you* go."

"But…you hate Lyonesse," she said even as elation made her voice tremble.

"I may hate Haven, but I love *you*."

The words bloomed inside her body. She was made of dandelion wishes and strawberries and red, red roses.

"And Holdfast is already growing on me," he continued. "I like them for threatening me on your behalf. It's a comfort." It would be, for him. "And I'd bloody well live in Mayfair if you wanted me to. Because I love you, Briar Foxglove."

"I love you too," she whispered.

He tilted her chin up, focusing on her with the stillness of a predator. "Say it again."

"I love you."

He kissed her so fiercely, so deeply, that it left no room for doubts, no room for anything but the magic between them.

"But you're a captain," she pointed out when they paused to catch their breath. Why was she pulling at the threads like an idiot? Why wasn't she still kissing him? Breathing was overrated. "And an Iron Crow."

"I can be that with you."

"Living in a pink house on Lyonesse? Even if it's in Holdfast?" she asked, doubtfully. "No sailor has ever chosen anything but the sea."

"The sea is right here," he said, not even bothering to look at it. He was too busy looking at her. "And as it happens, the coast needs patrolling. The war with the French isn't likely to end quickly."

"Oh." Could this work? Was he really here, choosing *her*?

"And I'm not a sailor or a captain or an Iron Crow, Briar. I am just *yours*."

He was.

He was hers.

And she was his.

It was glorious. Perfect.

One small detail remained.

"The next time you make all of these big plans and decisions?" She poked him hard in the chest. "Let *me* know about it first, you cabbagehead."

He caught her fingers in his, keeping them pressed to him. "You're right. I'm sorry."

She was not entirely mollified, mostly because she enjoyed the fire in his eyes, the determination in the set of his shoulders. The way his gaze drifted down to her mouth, and the way her body instantly responded. She swayed toward him like a peony grown too full for its stalk. Like a sunflower, a vine of morning glories, seeking, seeking. But she did not let herself fully close the inches between them.

"Still not convinced?" Ethan's smile was devious and not the least bit charming.

He was every bit the dragon and never the knight in shining armor.

"Then it will be my pleasure to convince you, little thorn."

# About the Author

Alyxandra Harvey lives in an old stone house with her husband, multiple dogs, and a few resident ghosts who are allowed to stay as long as they keep company manners. She likes chai lattes, tattoos, and books. Sometimes fueled by literary rage.

Author of The Drake Chronicles, The Witches of London, Haunting Violet, Red, Love Me Love Me Not.

Twitter: AlyxandraH
Instagram: alyxandraharveyauthor